DEATH

OF AN ARTIST

ALSO BY KATE WILHELM

DEATH

OF AN ARTIST

KATE WILHELM

ST. MARTIN'S MINOTAUR ☙ NEW YORK

DEATH OF AN ARTIST. Copyright © 2012 by Kate Wilhelm. All rights reserved. Printed in the United States of America. For information address St. Martin's Press, 175 Fifth Avenue, New York, N.Y. 10010.

www.minotaurbooks.com

Design by Anna Gorovoy

Library of Congress Cataloging-in-Publication Data

Wilhelm, Kate.
    Death of an artist : a mystery / Kate Wilhelm.
       p. cm.
    ISBN 978-0-312-65861-8 (hardback)
    ISBN 978-1-4299-4223-2 (e-book)
   1. Artists—Crimes against—Fiction.   2. Oregon—Fiction.
3. Domestic fiction.   I. Title.
    PS3573.I434D38 2012
    813'.54—dc23

                                        2011041007

            10 9 8 7 6 5 4 3 2 1

DEATH

OF AN ARTIST

1

MARNIE MARKOV STILL had a flush of cold on her cheeks that March afternoon when Tony walked into her gift shop. Few outsiders showed up in the middle of the day before the weekend at this time of year. She sized this one up quickly. He was not a serious shopper. His cursory glance at the merchandise was not the searching look of anyone seeking a particular gift or memento. The shop held the usual assortment of shells from around the world, the lovely floats sometimes found on the local beaches, rarer now than they had been in the past, kites, souvenir sweatshirts, gift mugs decorated with whales or fir trees . . . Marnie knew that much of the merchandise could be found in any other shop up and down the Oregon coast, but a lot of it was unique to her shop. Handblown glass items from Bepe LaRoche; handcrafted pottery by local artisans; jewelry made by locals. None of these held the attention of the tall man approaching.

While Tony's glance had appeared cursory, he had taken in and would remember the merchandise, where it was, even the posted prices. His swift look at Marnie was also exhaustive. A gray-haired, pink-cheeked woman, blue eyes, sixty to seventy years old, weight within a pound or two of 135, five feet three. She had a mole on her cheek.

He was a big man, not only tall, at least six-one or -two, but big in every dimension without appearing overweight. He walked with a limp, not bad, but noticeable.

As he moved toward her, Marnie suddenly had a vivid memory of seeing Ed approaching another counter, a long time ago. He had walked with a swaying motion unlike any she had seen before. Then, she had stood behind a Macy's counter in New York City, not quite nineteen years old, one year out of high school in Indiana, and filled with an unaccountable dread and even fear of big, tall men.

The memory was so sharp, so immediate, Marnie caught the edge of the counter and gripped it hard, relieved when the stranger came to a halt, abruptly turned, and headed toward the alcove, which was what made her shop unique along the coast.

Now, for the first time, Tipper, her wirehaired terrier, raised his head to watch the man. He was used to customers and paid little attention to them, but his job was to help guard the alcove, and he was reliable. Marnie motioned to him, and he didn't move from the floor at the end of the counter, but he was watching.

The alcove was set off with a velvet rope. Beyond the rope a pale-violet silk scarf edged with exquisite lace was draped over a low table. A small placard read CREATED BY JUSTINE LINCOLN. The table was satin-smooth cherrywood, with curved legs, and a gently scalloped edge. It had its own placard: FURNITURE HANDCRAFTED BY DAVE MCADAMS. A handblown-glass wall lamp, translucent pale green, hung above it, Bepe's work. Behind it all on the wall was a painting signed by Stef. That was what seemed to hold the tall man's attention. As well it should, Marnie thought, leaving her counter to cross the shop and stand near the man.

"These are all the work of local artists," she said, motioning toward the arrangement.

"That's a beautiful painting," he said. "He's a very fine artist."

"She," Marnie said with a smile. "She's a woman."

His surprise did not change his expression of interest as he turned his attention back to the painting. He wasn't surprised that a woman had done it, but that she had chosen such an unlikely name for herself. "Stef," he said, "captured a rare mood."

It was one of her better pieces. An impressionistic view of Newport Bay, caught when the setting sun was revealed by soft, muted peach tones on small swells in the water, on the wings of gulls in flight, in sails. All the colors were muted by dusk. Pale yellow shone from suggestions of lights in windows onshore and in the lights of fishing boats. As he had said, the painting generated a mood. To Marnie's mind it was a feeling of peace, the quietude found at the close of a day.

He turned toward her then. "Actually, I came in to get directions to Dave McAdams's shop. I wasn't expecting to find a miniature art gallery."

"I showcase our local artists. Drop in again if you're around. I change everything about once a month. There are business cards that tell where the items can be purchased." She pointed to another table on the near side of the rope. He did not take one.

He didn't look like a salesman, Marnie decided, or a

thief, either. He was dressed in a lined Windbreaker, jeans, hiking shoes, and he was too tall not to be picked out of a crowd. His hair was curly, black, with a sprinkling of white that looked almost like a salon adornment; his eyes were dark, black or close to it. His gaze held hers steadily, not the gaze of an ax murderer. But she would call Dave, she also decided. She gave him directions.

"North to Fourth Street, turn right, and he's on the right side in the middle of the second block. His shop looks like a shed, set back quite a bit from the street."

The man nodded. "Thanks." After another glance at the painting, he left.

She watched him walk out, returned to her counter, and put in a call to her old friend Dave McAdams. After alerting him that she had sent a visitor his way, she looked again at Stef's painting. She had tried again and again to understand how Stef managed to get that particular feeling of peace in her work now and then. Stef had never had a peaceful moment in her life. Restless, constantly in motion, never satisfied with her work, with anyone around her, the world in general—peace was as alien to her as confession to an atheist.

Stef had been a colicky baby, a poor student, too restless and impatient to sit still in class, to pay attention to anything that didn't feature her at its center. As an adult, nothing had changed. Stef was Marnie's only child, nearing her fiftieth birthday, as unsettled now as she had been as a hormone-driven adolescent. Yet she managed to express through painting what eluded her in life.

DAVE MCADAMS WORKED alone, had worked alone for years after trying out two assistants decades earlier, and accustomed to solitude, he did not relish uninvited visitors. Wiry, seventy-one years old, he had sparse white hair, which was seldom seen, since his icon appeared to be an old baseball cap that had long since lost any distinguishable color or marking. What Dave liked best in life was working with beautiful wood, fruit woods, mahogany, teak, all the hardwoods, and he hummed tunelessly as he turned the planks and blocks into one beautiful and useful piece after another, each one meant to be appreciated for itself. Satiny finishes, oil patiently rubbed in over and over until he had the perfect surface that would hold up under daily use and grow lovelier with age. That day he was at his bench when the visitor knocked at his door and entered when Dave grudgingly said, "Come on in. Door's not locked."

Marnie had told him the guy was big, but still it was a bit of a surprise to see how big. Probably 220, 240, and not fat. He was carrying a bulky duffel bag.

Tony stood by the door, transfixed momentarily by a strong feeling of déjà vu. The shop was so like his father's own shop had been, it was like walking through the door into the past, expecting to see his father look up, grin, and wave toward some unfinished piece of Tony's, as if to say, *Get to work, son*. The moment passed.

Everything in the workroom was neat and clean, no piles of scraps anywhere, tools aligned on a bench or hung on a rack where they belonged. The lathe was clean. Oils, sanding papers, lacquers, varnishes, stains, all lined up, stacked up. A bench with a table saw, other saws hanging from a Peg-Board . . . His searching look came to rest on Dave, who was holding a spindle for a chair. He didn't put it down or make any other gesture to indicate that he didn't intend to go back to smoothing out a rough spot as soon as the visitor stated his business and left.

5

"I came to apply for a job," Tony said.

"Don't recall putting an ad in the paper, or hanging a help-wanted sign out."

"I talked to Willoughby in his store in Portland. He said he could sell twice as much as you can produce, that there's a constant call for more of your furniture."

Dave snorted. "Not hiring. You're wasting your time."

"My name's Anthony Mauricio," Tony said, as if he had not heard a word. "Retired. I'll just leave this and come by to collect it in a day or two." He was opening his duffel bag. He pulled out an object wrapped in cloth, uncovered it to reveal a box.

From across the room it looked like cherry, or something with a cherry stain, with painting on the sides and top. Not like anything that Dave did or wanted to do. "Not my kind of thing," he said, dismissing it.

"I'll be driving around the coast a couple of days and come back on Friday," Tony said, again as if oblivious to Dave's rejection. He looked around the shop, then set the box on the bench with the table saw. "I'll leave my card, too, and a couple of pictures. A reference you can call if you want." He put them by the box, strode to the door, and walked out.

Dave cursed under his breath. "Damn fool!" he muttered, and turned his attention back to the spindle, but after a moment he put it down and crossed the room to examine the fancy box. It wasn't stained, nor was it painted. It was cherry. The design was inlay, a pale rosewood inlay of a leaf motif that wrapped around the box and to the top, where it opened to a fleur-de-lis. Dave picked up the box to look at it more closely. Dovetailed joints, tiny brass hinges, an oiled patina finish, top and bottom. Inside, it was just as beautifully finished. He set it down carefully and regarded it again as an object in itself. Jewelry box? A lot of jewelry. It was twelve by fourteen, four inches deep. Love letters? What would it be used for? The fleur-de-lis pattern invited touching, as did the delicate stems winding up the sides. He knew the kind of work that went into inlay like that and the reason it was seldom seen. His fingers could not discern any seam.

After another minute or two of handling the box, as if testing it, he picked up the card. There was his name, ANTHONY MAURICIO, under it a single line, RET. NYC POLICE DEPARTMENT, and under that another single line, REF. CAPTAIN MARK ROSINI, followed by a phone number.

There were three snapshots of furniture: a small table with the same fleur-de-lis pattern, a chair, boudoir chair probably, and a coffee table inlaid with pale wood scrolling. Fancier than anything that Dave produced, but usable pieces, meant to be used, or possibly to be acquired as art. He sighed and, taking the card with him, went to his desk and dialed Williard Comley, the chief of police of Silver Bay.

Silver Bay had a population of 922 citizens, and Will was its police force in its entirety. In the summer with the influx of tourists Will had a deputy, although neither man was called into action to do much more than write parking tickets. But Dave knew that Will could get some background dope on Anthony Mauricio, whom, he had come to realize, he intended to hire, if he could afford him and if he hadn't left New York City under a cloud.

USUALLY, WHEN THE days lengthened enough, Marnie walked to the shop and back home. Never in the darkest of the winter, she was too cautious for that, especially on Ridge Road, which was without any streetlamps. She and Molly Barnett split the day, Molly from nine until one, and Marnie from one until she closed at five or six, depending on customers.

When business picked up, Molly came back at six and stayed until nine. On Thursday that week Marnie hung her CLOSED sign at five. A storm was blowing in with driving rain and a stiff wind, not too cold, but not good walking weather either. She had taken her car that day, and she had called Dave to tell him she'd be by to give him a lift. His house was next to hers up on the ridge, and he had no business walking in such weather, although left to his own devices he would have done so. At his shop, she motioned to Tipper to come along, and they hurried to the door and entered without knocking.

"If you're not ready, I'll wait," she said, taking off a rain hat and shaking it inside the door.

"Just a couple of minutes," Dave said, wiping a bench top with an oiled cloth that lifted fine sawdust and held it. "Have a look at what your big guy left here." He waved toward his desk, where he had put the box, and continued on to the sink to rinse his cloth and wash his hands.

"Oh, my," Marnie said, examining the box. "Did he make this? It's beautiful."

"Guess he did. Least he gave that impression." Dave joined her at the desk. "The guy wants a job. Guess I'll take him on."

Marnie looked at Dave in surprise. "Just off the street like that? Who is he? Where'd he come from?"

"Name's Anthony Mauricio, used to be a New York detective, homicide, retired with a disability. I had Will get the lowdown on him. His captain gave him a high recommendation."

"Disability? What's wrong with him?" She was thinking of the limp.

"Shot up. A couple of operations, and that's all I know about that. He doesn't seem to be a talker, so that's all right."

She nodded. Dave couldn't abide empty chatter, and he had so little small talk it was almost as if he were retarded, or even mute at times. She would ask Will for more information. Will loved to talk so much it was hard to get him to shut up most of the time. And he wouldn't have been satisfied with such bare bones.

THAT LATE AFTERNOON, and on into night until it got dark, Tony stood at the window of a motel several blocks from Dave's shop and watched the storm. He had driven up the coast to Lincoln City and had spent a long time in Newport, where he had eaten in a restaurant overlooking the bay. Trying to see what it was that the artist Stef had seen out there had proved futile. The water was choppy, the sky gray, and blowing rain was pelting down slantwise. And now he was back in Silver Bay. He had to smile at the name of the town. There was no silver, and there was no bay, just a scooped-out bit of shore with sand on it. Even he, never having lived on a seacoast in his life, could see the marks made by high tides, the long, ragged-looking strands of seaweed halfway up the beach. He suspected that a storm like the one that had arrived that day would claim even more of the beach.

Then, lying on the bed, he thought about the zigzag trail he had cut across the country after leaving New York City. Up to see his sister in Albany, down to Phoenix, Arizona, to visit his mother, who had moved there from upstate New York following the death of Tony's father. On to Las Vegas, on again, driving a few hours every day from place to place with no destination in mind, just driving with the thought that he would know it when he saw it. He had arrived in Portland, Oregon, with that vague thought still in his head and a bit of regret that he had not yet found it, a place where he wanted to stay and stop the insane driving.

In Portland, he had decided to head north, see what Seattle had to offer, and if it wasn't there, head south. Maybe near San Francisco, along there somewhere. Then, walking in downtown Portland, window-shopping, he had thought derisively, he had stopped at the showroom window of Willoughby's Furniture store, where he had seen Dave McAdams's furniture on display, two chairs with SOLD notices on them.

And now here he was in Silver Bay, Oregon, and he intended to stay here, and he intended to work in Dave's meticulous shop. Tony's father had been a fine craftsman, a cabinetmaker, and he had taught Tony how to use the tools, how to make things that were beautiful and could be used.

That day in Portland, gazing at the two chairs in the window of the furniture store had brought the first moment of clarity that he had experienced in a long time, he reflected, lying on a motel bed on the Oregon coast in a place he had never heard of less than a week before. He had gone to school, gone to law school, joined the police force, had used up most of his life unaware that what he really wanted to do, what he was meant to do, was to work with wood, to make things, to work with his hands, and not only during a stolen hour or two now and then, with the guilt that had always followed.

A moment of clarity, he repeated to himself. An epiphany of sorts. He smiled, listening to the wind, the sound of crashing waves distant and constant, and he knew this was it. He had found the place.

2

ON FRIDAY MORNING Tony explored his new place. It didn't take long. Coming in from the south the coast road descended a mountain in a precipitous plunge that was one long curve, straightened out to cross a bridge over Silver Creek, and continued on through town as Main Street. Fronting the creek, with an ocean view, was the Sand Dollar Inn and Restaurant, and a street that led to three other motels overlooking the ocean. Beach access was at the edge of the inn's parking area, steps fashioned from sea-delivered logs. The town was high above the water; it was a long staircase. On Main Street was a grocery store with not many choices available, but necessities for those who ran out of supplies, with regular shopping probably done up the coast in Newport. A general-merchandise store next to the market sold kitchenware, clothing, some camping supplies—again not many selections. Two gas stations, a small library that shared a building with the police department. Tony gave it a mocking salute as he passed by. Marnie's gift shop was across the street from the market, next to the Silver Dollar Café, and in the next block was Tom's Fine Foods and a real estate office. He suspected that their specialty was rentals. A city hall and historical museum shared a building on Second Street, and a seafood store was across the street. An elementary school and playground were on Third Street. A lot of houses had BED-AND-BREAKFAST signs, or APARTMENT FOR RENT signs. Many houses looked empty—weekend retreats or summer homes. A pottery shop was at the north edge of town, where on one side of the highway a neat sign indicated lodging, a motel access road. On the other side was another road, Ridge Road, which wound up the side of the mountain that was a backdrop to the town. There was little else to see. No matter, he thought, driving up Ridge Road, Newport was a dozen miles north, and Portland two hours away. Cities enough.

Ridge Road was fairly steep, and like all mountain roads, curvy. No doubt this was prime real estate with a magnificent ocean view from every house. He drove until he came to the end of the road, where there was space to turn around. A gate was across a narrower road posted PRIVATE PROPERTY leading up the mountain. After making his turn, he stopped to look out over the town with the flashing, sparkling creek one boundary, the ocean another, and deep forest behind and ahead. The town was not destined to grow. From where he was, he could see the white foam and sprays from ocean waves breaking over black formations offshore, stacks and columns that told a story of a mountain losing a battle with the sea, a battle that had lasted eons and was still ongoing. He drew in a long breath and could feel something coiled tight within him loosen a little.

It was time to pay a call on Dave McAdams, he decided, and he followed Ridge Road back down to Fourth and Dave's shop.

That morning Dave was working on the third of five spindles he had turned on the lathe in short order. Smoothing them down and finishing them was slow work, which he didn't mind at all. Just part of what he did. He put the spindle down this time when Tony entered the shop.

"How much you asking for?" Dave asked without preamble.

"Whatever you think I'm worth," Tony said. "Try me out a week or two, then decide."

Dave's expression was dubious, even suspicious. Not an answer he had been expecting, he realized, regathering his thoughts. "You'd have to do things my way, do what I want done," he said almost truculently.

"Sure. One request. I'd like to work in here after hours, weekends, on my own time."

Dave's gaze turned to the box on his desk, back to Tony. "Means I'd have to give you a key," he said slowly.

"I could post a security bond," Tony said. "And you can keep the box as hostage. I won't leave home without it."

Dave didn't miss the amusement that flickered momentarily in Tony's dark eyes. He'd take the damned box home and keep it there for a time, he decided. He didn't believe the fellow would leave without it any more than he would if it were his.

"You can't use my wood," Dave said, "and electricity's expensive."

"I'll keep an hour log and you can take my share out of my pay. I picked up a few pieces of wood in Portland after I talked to Willoughby."

It wasn't going to work, Dave thought. This guy was too

13

cocksure of himself, too . . . maybe too superior in a funny way, as if he had figured Dave out and knew how to game him. Again he glanced at the box, then he shrugged. "Okay. We'll give it a try."

For the next hour they talked about the work. Dave showed Tony his own supply of wood in the storage shed behind the shop, and when Tony left, Dave knew little more about his new employee than he had known when he'd first walked in. Tony knew wood, and he knew the tools and how to use them, and those were the big ones. On the other hand, he had been so sure he would get the job, he had come prepared with some wood of his own. It was infuriating, yet it was also reassuring. Dave put a lot of stock in self-confidence. Instantly the contradictory thought followed: too self-confident? Tony wasn't much of a talker, and that was a big plus that tended to outweigh most of the lingering doubts Dave had about hiring anyone.

MARNIE HAD TIMED her visit to Chief Williard Comley to the minute. First a stop at the library to check out two books to read to her great-grandson that weekend, and two for him to read to her. Josh, in kindergarten, had learned to read that year. She chatted a few minutes with Beverly, the librarian, who always asked about Josh's mother, Van, and never asked a question about Stef. Few people in town did.

"They'll be down for the weekend," Marnie told her. "Van will bring an armload of books, of course, and spend most of her time studying. This last year has been a hard one."

"And then off to an internship," Beverly said in awe.

Van was a medical student in her final year, a fact that awed Marnie as much as it did most folks in town. Their own doctor. She was determined to return home to practice, at least to Newport, on getting her license. Marnie was enormously proud of her granddaughter.

After leaving the library with her books, she stopped by the chief's office next door. It was twelve-thirty, and she had a perfect excuse to leave a little before one in order to relieve Molly at the shop. She knew Will's habits probably better than he did. At one he would stroll home, have lunch with his wife, take a nap, and at three, uniformed in mufti, strut around town a little. Weekenders were coming and he would be on the job.

"Marnie! Good to see you," Will said jovially. He was always happy to have anyone drop in. "Been tidying up a little, getting ready for the weekend. Let me give you a cup of coffee."

His coffee was terrible, but she smiled and accepted it, murmuring her thanks. A good caricature of Will, done by Stef, depicted a balloon with stubby legs and a smiley face, Huckleberry hair that always fell over his forehead, from a cowlick that wouldn't be tamed, and a cup of coffee in his hand. Marnie knew he had tidied up the single holding cell, probably hoping to use it over the weekend, just to have someone to talk to.

His office held a desk with a few papers and a computer, a filing cabinet, three chairs, and a coatrack. He seated himself behind his desk and she sat opposite it, nursing the mug of coffee.

"Dave tells me he's hiring a man to help out in the shop," she said, then sipped a little coffee. "I never thought the day would come when he would do that, he's so picky."

"Well, he found himself a good one," Will said, leaning forward. "Let me tell you."

He told her in great detail, and even discounting some of it as his own embellishments, it was impressive, she thought as she listened. SUNY Buffalo, three years at Columbia Law School, dropped it, and joined the police force, where he had made lieutenant. "His captain said he was top-notch, not a mark against him in twenty years.

"He's fifty," Will said. "Divorced about five years ago. That's always sad. And two years ago he got it in a shooting. Seems a kid went crazy, waving a gun around, and Mauricio was trying to talk him down when shooting started. Mauricio got it in the leg and hip. The kid was riddled, seventeen shots, and the family is suing the department. Middle-class family, good neighborhood, only the dad made a practice of beating up on his wife and kid on the weekend, and that tore it. Mauricio was in the clear. His weapon never left his holster."

There was more, but that was the gist of it, Marnie decided at ten minutes before one. Will was saying, "His captain said they tried to get him to stay on the force, with a desk job, one of the best detectives they had, they didn't want to lose him. He turned it down. If he came here looking to take my job, I'd be looking into retirement."

Marnie glanced at her watch and set the coffee mug down on his desk. It was still nearly full. "Oh my. I have to get to the shop. Molly will think I abandoned her. You and Susan come by sometime, Will. Thanks for the coffee."

He glanced at a wall clock and nodded. "Me, too. Lunchtime. Drop in anytime, Marnie. Always good to see you, chat a little."

He was still talking when she opened the door, waved to him, and left. *Well,* she thought as she headed downtown to the shop. *Well, well.* An interesting man had come to join their small community.

———

MARNIE'S HOUSE HAD been built by a man named Huddleston and was one of the first houses in Silver Bay. When the Huddlestons outgrew the original house, not wanting to give up such a choice location, they had built what he called an addition. In reality he had built a second house on the property, keeping a small footprint by going up two stories, conforming to the drop in the land, with most of the new structure behind the garage, in order not to obstruct the stunning view from the original building. There was an overlap, just enough space for a passage from the front house to the rear. From Marnie's back door, a few steps down led to the passageway and the entrance of the upper floor of the addition. They called them the front house, where Marnie lived, and the rear house, where Stef lived with her current husband. The rear house had a frequently changing population.

When Van and Josh came for a visit, theoretically they stayed in the rear house where Van and Stef both had grown up, but usually Josh stayed with Marnie. The arrangement gave Van a little time without the responsibility of being a single mom.

When Van pulled into the driveway at the rear house that day, she was tired down to her toenails. All she wanted to do was go to bed the minute Josh did and sleep for ten or eleven hours. She unbuckled her seat belt as Josh was climbing out of his car seat, and shouldering their two backpacks, they entered the rear house. Stef met them at the door.

"I thought you'd never get here," she cried, embracing Van, then stooping to catch Josh up in a hug that he endured without struggling this time. Sometimes he wriggled out of it.

"Well, come on in and tell me what's new, what's exciting in Portland. Dale's here already. Dinner's in half an hour," Stef said gaily. "Just leave those packs anywhere. You can take them up later."

She was a thin woman, sharp faced with prominent bones. That year her hair was hot pink, straight and down to her shoulders, and she wore no makeup except for her eyes. Cleopatra eyes, heavily mascaraed with heavy eyeliner. Her eyes looked unnaturally blue against the paleness of her face and the black eye makeup. She was wearing a bulky black sweatshirt and baggy red pants. Van thought she looked like a clown.

Van and Josh left the backpacks by the stairs and followed her into the living room, taking off their jackets as they went. After nodding to Dale, who nodded back just as coolly without leaving the deep chair he was in, Van went straight to the windows that made up most of the ocean side of the room and drew in a long breath. It was getting dark, but she could see the froth breaking over the stacks out there, and already she was feeling a bit looser, the way she always did when she came to the coast, as if one knot after another were untying itself. She turned back to the room again.

"How's the boy?" Dale was saying to Josh, who did not respond. Van suspected that Dale had forgotten his name.

At the same time Stef said, "Van, darling, you look absolutely exhausted. You're doing too much. I keep telling you, you don't have to do it all at once. Slow down a little and take your time. We're having a martini. Can I fix you one? Or a little wine?"

"Nothing for me," Van said. "I'm fine."

"Gramma," Josh said. "Can I paint a fence pink if I want to?"

"Of course you can! Or green or striped or anything else. Why do you ask?"

"Miss Blakey said farmers don't paint their fences pink."

At the window Van felt the knot tie itself again. She hadn't realized it had bothered him for his teacher to say that in front of the parents who had attended the open house that week. She should have known, she thought. She should have understood.

"Darling," Stef said, "is Miss Blakey an artist?"

"She's my teacher," he said.

"Am I an artist?"

He nodded.

"Well, I'm the boss about art. And I say you can paint the damn fence any way you feel like. Tomorrow, tell you what we'll do. We'll go to town and buy you an easel and your own paints, and you can paint anything you want to, any color you want to. How does that sound?"

She meant well, Van thought distantly, hating the promise that would more than likely have been forgotten by the next day. How many times had she heard that same phrase while growing up? Stef meant well. Van had come to accept the truth of it. Stef really did. Her impulses were well-intentioned—and seldom carried out. If she didn't get the easel and paints, Van knew she would do it herself. Kids didn't forget. Josh was nodding and looked excited by the promise.

Scowling, Stef said to Van, "Yank him out of that art class."

"It isn't a separate class, just something they do in the course of the day."

"Then take him out of such a school. That teacher shouldn't be allowed near children."

"Stef—" Van let it go. Don't get Stef started about schools, she thought, especially not in front of Josh. "We'd better get our stuff upstairs and wash our hands," Van said. "We'll pop in to say hello to Marnie and be back in a few minutes." Stef's forecast of dinner in half an hour could mean anything, Van well knew. She had given Josh a peanut-butter-and-jelly sandwich to eat in the car on the drive over.

Upstairs, two bedrooms were separated by a hall that continued to a door at the end that was to Stef's studio, which made up half of the upper floor. After washing their hands, they went down the hall to the studio and through it to the outside door to the passage to the front house. Marnie's door wasn't locked, and after tapping lightly, Van opened it and they went inside.

Marnie welcomed them with her arms outspread. Josh never ducked her embrace. He hugged back fiercely. Tipper circled them excitedly, and Josh released Marnie and dropped to his knees to take the squirming dog in his arms. "Can we take Tipper to the beach tomorrow? I brought a new ball for him to play with."

Boy and dog rolled over with Tipper licking Josh's face. Marnie didn't tell Van how tired she looked. Van knew well how fatigued she was. She was not beautiful in any sense of the word, but she was striking with long black hair, fine high cheekbones, straight, heavy eyebrows, and deep-set, dark-blue eyes that seemed to be looking at the world with a question mark.

Marnie smiled at Josh and nodded, then said, "Molly's niece is coming in tomorrow. That girl is always looking for a way to make a few dollars, and I was happy to let her take my place. I want a day off to play ball on the beach with Josh and Tipper."

Van laughed and felt another of the knots untying itself. "We can't stay now, but we'll drop in again after dinner. Okay?"

"You know it is. Is Dale already here?"

"Yes, and he looks pretty sour."

"Stef says business at the gallery is down. I suppose he's worried."

"I think he sucks lemons," Van said. "Come on, Josh. We'll go eat dinner and come back later."

"Can I wait here?"

"Nope. Your gramma invited you to dinner. Marnie will be here when we come back."

After they left, Marnie ate her own dinner and thought about Dale. Husband number four, a few years younger than Stef, and gloomy. That would end it fairly soon, she decided. Stef could not abide gloom and doom. Dale was handsome, with a fair complexion and platinum-blond hair, and was an impeccable dresser, usually in a handsome business suit and tie, and now and then in designer jeans and whatever boots were in style and a cashmere sweater. Van called him Stef's pretty boy, her Ken doll. He was a partner in a Portland gallery that had Stef's art on permanent display. He handled the business end of the gallery, while the other partner, Winifred, Freddi, managed it. Dale lived in Portland and was no more than a visitor when at the coast, and both Marnie and Van had an almost visceral dislike of him. Opportunist, Marnie had thought at their first meeting, and nothing since had changed her mind about her first impression.

She had not been invited to dinner that night and would have said no if she had been. Early on she had said to Stef, "You two have so little time together, a third wheel would just get in the way." Stef got the message and rarely asked Marnie to join them.

Van had no choice about it. After all, Stef was her mother, and Silver Bay had been her home and would be again after she got her license. She wanted Josh to have family around. So she returned for visits when she could make it—holidays, spring break, and over the summers. She ignored Dale as much as possible and spent a lot of time with Marnie, who had been her mother more than Stef had ever been.

Van and Josh were back with Marnie before eight that night, and he was carrying his little backpack. "Can I sleep here tonight?" he asked Marnie.

"If you'll share the bed with Tipper," she said.

He whooped and raced to the second bedroom with Tipper at his heels. When he came back, he was carrying two plastic boats. "They were on my bed," he told Van, holding them up for her to see. "They're racing boats."

"Now, who on earth would come in here and leave boats?" Marnie said. "Let's have a look." She examined one, then exclaimed, "Windup boats. See? You wind this up, and if you push this, it must move the boat or something. I guess they need water to work."

"Can I take a bath now?"

Going with him to the bathroom, Marnie showed him how to turn the rudder to make the boats go straight or in circles, how to release the catch to let a rubber band spin a propeller, and in a few minutes she was back in the living room with Van, who had accepted a glass of wine.

"Marnie, there's something I wanted to talk about with you," Van said slowly. "Did you know that Stef's work is for sale? She never mentioned it to me."

"What work? I know she said some things could go, some of the charcoal sketches, at least."

"Not just them. Freddi called me and mentioned it and I stopped by on Wednesday. Everything has a price posted, all of it."

Marnie was taken by surprise. Stef had always been adamant about her work not being for sale, except for the few things she no longer liked or felt represented her real art.

"I don't know if I should bring it up, ask her outright, or just leave it alone," Van said. "Are they hurting for money?"

"No more than usual, I guess. Don't bring it up. Relax this weekend. Put it out of mind. I'll talk to her on Monday."

Relieved, Van sipped her wine and closed her eyes briefly. "I really have to go or I'll fall asleep on your couch," she said apologetically.

That night after Josh was in bed asleep, with Tipper on the bed with him, Marnie thought again about what Van had said. All of the work in the gallery? She didn't believe it. One of the pieces was titled *Feathers and Ferns,* and she thought it was the finest picture Stef had ever done. She didn't believe Stef had agreed to sell it. She couldn't believe that. Stef was possessive of her work and didn't really want to sell any of it, but especially that one. Marnie was afraid that a major storm was brewing. *Monday,* she told herself firmly, after Van and Josh were out of it, after Dale was back in Portland.

But what if he got a buyer before then? Then what? She didn't believe he could sell it without Stef's consent. She had to agree on a price and sign a form of some sort. The storm could wait a few days. *Monday,* Marnie repeated to herself.

She thought of her earlier assessment. If Dale was being gloomy, and now this, it could well mean that the end was even closer than she had suspected.

3

ON MONDAY MORNING Marnie went through the passage between the houses to the studio, where she expected to find Stef. Stef always was up early, and if she painted, it was before noon; later it was impossible to even guess where she might be. Some days she drove up to Lincoln City to shop in the brand-name outlets—Gucci, Jones New York, Givenchy . . . Later she might come home with a shopping bag stuffed full, or empty-handed. Often she would thrust an overflowing bag at Marnie, saying, "It's for you." A few days later Marnie would return it all and have Stef's card credited. Stef was just as likely to head over to the valley, to Salem or Eugene, and prowl through thrift shops for hours and return with outlandish items, things she never looked at again. Or she might spend a day on the beach somewhere. But at ten in the morning, she was most likely to be in the studio.

She was working on a painting she called *Ladies in Waiting*. Four women were strolling in the picture, one wearing a wide-brimmed straw hat, one carrying a sun umbrella, all with long-sleeve blouses, fashionably arranged hair, the essence of turn-of-the-century primness and propriety from the waist up. Their skirts were diaphanous, transparent, revealing pregnancies in advanced stages. The bulging bellies were shocking in the setting of a genteel garden party. Two of the women were barefoot, their feet swollen and red, angry looking, their ankles like sausages. The other two wore misshapen sneakers without laces.

Marnie hated the picture. It was a cruel mockery, a travesty. That morning she kept her gaze on her daughter, who was wearing a man's oversize shirt, the one she always wore when she was working. It was badly stained and to all appearances had never been laundered. Stef didn't glance Marnie's way when she entered the studio.

"I won't keep you," Marnie said. "I just wanted to ask when you decided to put your pictures up for sale, and if you intend to include *Feathers and Ferns*."

Stef stopped a brushstroke in midair and, without turning toward Marnie, asked, "What pictures for sale? What are you talking about?"

"Van said she dropped in at the gallery last week and they're all for sale. She was surprised. And so am I."

Stef looked at her then for a moment without speaking. "Not just the charcoals?"

"All of them," Marnie said.

Stef's face flamed red and her mouth tightened to a thin line. Savagely she flung her paintbrush across the studio and threw her palette to the floor. "That fucking asshole! That fuck of a dickhead!"

Marnie had long since ceased being shocked by Stef's

cursing and her temper fits, but she still flinched in the face of it. She held up her hand, spoke, and was ignored. Cursing, Stef yanked off her shirt and flung it down with the palette. She wore nothing under it, and bare-breasted, she dashed from the studio, down the hall with Marnie following.

The torrent of curses continued as Stef raced downstairs, through the house to the bedroom, where she grabbed a sweatshirt and pulled it on. "I'll show that motherfucker who owns that work! He thinks he can go behind my back like that, I'll kill him. He's dead meat!"

"Stef, for God's sake, stop acting like a maniac! Calm down. Where are you going?"

Stef had snatched up her purse and was pawing through it. She pulled out her car keys, and when Marnie tried to block her at the door, she pushed past her. "I'm going to get my paintings!" she cried.

A minute later her car tires screamed as she roared out of the driveway. Marnie sank down into a chair and drew in a long, shuddering breath. After a few minutes she pulled herself upright and called Freddi Wordling at the For Arts Sake gallery.

"Oh, dear God," Freddi said softly.

"Amen," Marnie said in total understanding. "Is Dale there?"

"No, and with any luck he won't come in until after she's been here and gone. Thanks, Marnie." Freddi hung up and closed her eyes, praying that this would be one of the days that Dale chose to drive in late, stay a few minutes, and leave.

Stef was icily calm when she entered through the back door. "Why didn't you tell me?" she demanded when Freddi stepped out from her office.

"He said you knew."

"And you believed him? Give me the key to the van. I'm taking everything home with me."

Without a word Freddi handed Stef the key. Her prayer was almost answered, she was thinking, when Stef came from the showroom with a few charcoal studies, the last of the lot, but at that moment Dale entered.

"Stef, what a surprise!" He smiled and extended his arms as if to embrace her or possibly to prevent her leaving.

"Get out of the way, asshole! Get out of my life, you low, lying piece of shit! Sell my art? Go behind my back? You're done, finished, you fuck of a dickhead!" Her voice rose with each word, and her face flared red as she yelled.

"Stef, let me explain—"

"Just shut your fucking mouth! Get out of my way! And don't come back with your sniveling explanation! Tell it to that cute little twenty-year-old you have tucked away. I don't want to hear it. I never want to see you again, you bastard!"

She pushed past him and out the door, then kicked it shut. Seconds later the van tires squealed as she pulled out of the parking space.

Freddi slipped back into her office and closed the door softly. There was a door slam, and she assumed Dale had gone into his own office. In a minute, she thought, she would go to the showroom and hope for the best, that no customer had been there during the past few minutes.

She was still at her desk when she heard the back door open and close, and cautiously she went out into the hall to see if Stef had returned. Dale's office door was open and he was gone. She breathed a sigh of relief, squared her shoulders, and went to the door of the showroom.

———

DALE DROVE TO an apartment complex on Eighteenth. Jasmine would be home that time of day, and he needed a drink, which she could provide, and a little sympathy and comforting, too, which she could also provide. She was not a twenty-year-old, but thirtysomething, and it didn't make a bit of difference.

She was tall and beautiful, the most beautiful woman he had ever been comforted by. When they danced in the club where she worked, people stopped what they were doing to watch because they looked so great together. She was the singer in the group that called themselves the N.O. Jazzmen, a successful group that had been in Portland for the last six months. That day when she opened her door, she was wearing an expensive silk apricot-colored kimono. He knew how expensive it was because he had given it to her. Her skin was velvety, the color of café au lait, her eyes as melting as milk chocolate, and her hair dark auburn with deep waves. The kimono was exactly the right color for her. His taste in clothes was impeccable, his own and hers as well.

"Jasmine, sweetheart, the scarecrow bitch came and took out all of her stuff," he said, entering the apartment.

Jasmine shrugged. "Tough, but I'm pretty busy right now, and I'm expecting someone."

"Who is he?"

She walked ahead of him into the bedroom, where a partly packed suitcase was on the bed. "She, it's a girl. She's going to sublease the apartment for the next few months, apartment-sit, something like that."

"You're going somewhere? Where?"

"Austin first, then Shreveport, and finally New Orleans. Didn't I tell you? I thought I did."

"You know damn well you didn't," he said angrily. "Just

like that, you were going to hightail it out without a word? What about us?"

"Dale, baby, there is no us. You know that and you've always known it. You're a married man, remember? And I'm with a group that hits the road now and then. It's now time, baby. Back to our roots for a while."

"Jesus God! First Stef, now you. Both running out on me."

Jasmine took a blouse from her closet, folded it, and added it to the suitcase. "Honey," she drawled, "maybe the scarecrow doesn't like being pushed around. And I sure as hell don't. Now, why don't you run along and let me get on with my packing."

He took a step toward her, his fists balled, and she laughed. "Baby, don't even think about it. I have insurance, honey. Four big, strong guys who'd slice and dice you into so many little pieces they'd never reassemble the package."

He wanted to strangle her, but he knew the guys. Growing up in Newark, he had seen enough guys like that to know what they would do to a blond white man who messed up their woman. He had even worked with guys like that when it suited his purposes and theirs. He well knew what they would do, and she was their woman, their singer. Then he thought, Insurance! That was it, insurance.

He turned toward the door, where he paused and said, "Jasmine, sweetheart, have you noticed the lines at your eyes? Botox time, sweetheart. And your tits are hanging a little low, don't you think? See you around." He smiled maliciously as she stopped moving.

It was a torturous afternoon, one that stretched minute by laborious minute. At five-thirty Marnie closed the shop. She went to the market and bought two thick steaks, a nice bottle of wine, and lettuce. She knew that Stef would have eaten nothing and would, in all likelihood, be home drinking with no thought of food for the rest of the night.

To her surprise, when Marnie entered the driveway at home, she saw the gallery van parked near the entrance of the rear house. She went straight to the house and let herself in without knocking. Just inside the door on both sides of the entryway the paintings were leaning against the walls along with the charcoal studies and sketches. Stef had cleaned out the gallery of all her work. She was sitting near the window, her back to the room. She didn't move or speak when Marnie said hello. On the counter separating the dining area from the kitchen was a bottle of Jack Daniel's. Marnie set her grocery bag down on the counter and took off her jacket, then joined Stef at the window.

"Are you all right?"

"Sure. Got them. Safe and sound where they belong."

Stef held a glass of bourbon and water, too dark to have much water in it. Marnie could tell from her voice that it was not her first such drink.

"I made Freddi give me the key. I would have killed her with my bare hands if she'd tried to stop me."

Talking about the van, Marnie guessed, and nodded. "In a few minutes I'll make us some dinner. Have you eaten anything today?"

Stef shrugged. "Why didn't Van tell me herself? Why you?"

"I suppose she thought you knew about it."

Stef shook her head. "Why does Josh always stay at your place when they come home?"

"Well, you know how crazy he is about Tipper," Marnie said, suppressing a groan. Stef was going to get maudlin, go into her self-pity mode.

"They hate me," Stef said in a low voice. "Dale, Van, Josh,

you. No one in town will even speak to me. They all look somewhere else when they see me coming. I don't blame them. Or Van either. Poor little Josh, even poor little Josh." She looked at Marnie then, her eyes red rimmed. "I'm his grandmother, not you. You always do that, take my place, elbow me out."

"Stef, don't torment yourself this way. You know we all love you. You're my child, I've always loved you and always will. I'll fix dinner and you'll feel better with some food in your stomach. Wait and see." Marnie stood and took a step toward the kitchen, but at that moment Dale came into the room.

"Hello, Dale," Marnie said, more in warning to Stef than in greeting. At the sound of his name Stef twisted around in her chair, instantly aflame again.

"You! Get out of my house! Get out of here! I never want to see your face again, you fucking asshole!"

"I won't stay," he said in a grating voice. "I just came to tell you something you need to hear."

Marnie took another step, prepared to leave, and he said, "You need to hear it, too. And pass it on to Van. Both of you treat me like the Boston Strangler, and I'm fed up with it. Yes, I put price tags on those paintings. I had to, to get insurance. How much is a van Gogh worth, five million, six? Who sets that price? A buyer, that's who. I tried to get the work appraised and it can't be done without someone setting a price first. How much is a willing buyer prepared to spend? That's the test, and without it, they're worth the canvas they're painted on. You know damn well I can't sell any of them without your consent, but I have to get some insurance. That work in that damn gift shop is there for the taking. What will you do if someone breaks in and lifts one? Call Humpty Dumpty to climb off his wall and waddle over?"

32

He raked Marnie with a cold, mean look. "Try to talk some sense into her, if you can. I came to get the van. We need it at the gallery. I brought her car back. Call me sometime," he said to Stef, still sitting in a twist glaring at him. He stalked out.

For a moment or two neither Stef nor Marnie moved or spoke. Then Marnie said, "I'll go make dinner now." Stef had turned back to face the window, the sky dimly reflecting a lowering sun through clouds.

In the kitchen, with Tipper at her feet, Marnie scrubbed potatoes and started to dice them. She had thought to have baked potatoes, but changed her mind. Something faster than that, she had decided, hash browns with onions, something Stef was fond of, something quick. Soon she stopped cutting the potatoes, rehearing Dale's words, seeing his stance, everything about that scene. It wasn't right, she thought, thinking about his words *Boston Strangler*. She had involuntarily glanced at his hands when he uttered those words, and they had not been clenched in anger. Nothing about him had suggested real anger except the words and the harsh way he had uttered them. It had been as if he had rehearsed those lines, refined them for effect without a thought about body language. She began to dice the potatoes again, and she felt certain that Dale's performance had been exactly that, a performance.

When she collected Stef to come to dinner, her glass was empty again, and she was unsteady on her feet. She picked at her food and ignored the bit of wine Marnie had poured for her. Marnie searched for something to talk about, nothing to do with Josh and his prowess at reading, nothing to do with Van or Dale, or anything else that might set off the laments Stef had been voicing earlier.

"There's a fascinating new man in town," Marnie said, and told what she had learned from Will. "Can you believe

Dave actually hired him? Incredible. I stopped by to say hello to Harriet, and there it is, a beautiful box being held as a security bond or something. You should drop in and have a look. Harriet said it's working out very well at the shop. Dave's quite pleased with his new helper."

Stef made no response to indicate that she had heard any of it, and Marnie began to talk brightly about a new glass bowl Bepe had left at the shop. Stef picked at her steak, then abruptly put down her fork.

"I have to pee and I want to go to bed," she said, getting up unsteadily.

Marnie went with her, holding her arm, and when Stef went into the bathroom, Marnie turned down the bed and got a nightshirt from a drawer. She helped Stef undress, slipped the nightshirt over her head, and pulled a blanket up over her when Stef collapsed onto the bed. Marnie made sure the night-light was on in the bathroom before she left. At the door, she stopped moving when Stef said in a plaintive voice, "Frankie should have stayed. I keep screwing up because he left. I loved him, Marnie. I loved him so much. He shouldn't have left me."

Marnie returned to the bed, sat on the side of it, and gently stroked Stef's hair. It was coarse, hard from years of bleaching and coloring.

"Hush, darling," Marnie murmured. "That was a long time ago. It's all right. Don't brood about it. Close your eyes and rest now. It's all right."

Stef sighed deeply and rolled over to her side and said no more, and in a few minutes Marnie rose and left her. She knew she would not return to her own house for a long time, not until Stef was sound asleep, and that never happened quickly.

In the kitchen she covered Stef's uneaten dinner with plastic wrap and put it in the refrigerator. Then, after cutting the meat from the bone, and giving it to Tipper, letting him out with it, she wrapped her own plate. Tomorrow's dinner. She took her glass of wine to sit by the window in the living room. Nothing could be seen at sea, and the town lights seemed a long distance away. She was thinking about Frankie. *A long time ago,* she repeated to herself.

Immediately after high school, which had allowed Stef to graduate only through the kindness or the relief of her teachers, Stef had insisted on going to Paris to study art, the one thing that held her attention. Marnie and Ed had given in and permitted her to do so. A year later she had returned, pregnant, and with Frankie in tow. He had been her age, nineteen, and frightened by the enormity of what they had done, just beginning to comprehend what it really meant. Stef had been ecstatic.

Marnie had not been able to fault her. She had done the same thing at that age. The tall man with the strange walk who had approached her counter that day in Macy's had come to a dead standstill when he heard her talking to her customer. As soon as the customer departed with her purchase, he had rushed to the counter.

"Indiana!" he had said. "Me, too. A farm near Indianapolis. Where was your home?"

"Near Muncie," she had said, taken aback by his evident happiness, his wide smile, his eagerness.

"What time do you get off? I'll wait for you. Just talk. I want to talk to someone from Indiana."

He was there that day, and every day for the next nine, and on the tenth day she left New York with him to go make a new life on the West Coast, a distant place that she had only the vaguest idea about. They were married in Las Vegas, and eight months later Stef was born.

During those ten days she'd learned that Ed had been in the navy for twenty years. He still had his sea legs, he told her. His folks had died while he was at sea, and his uncle Oscar had begged him to come to Oregon to help out with his fishing business. Oscar owned three fishing boats, he was getting on, and he wanted Ed, a sailor, to take over the business one day.

Marnie sipped wine with a soft smile on her face. She had not dared tell her mother a thing for a long time, not that Ed was nearly twenty years older than she was, that he had been a sailor, that she got pregnant before a wedding, none of it. Ed had treated her like a delicate, rare china doll from day one until he died twenty-two years later. She never told her mother that, either, but said merely that he was good to her.

But Stef had brought home her young lover, and that had made a difference. Marnie and Ed had felt great sympathy for the boy, so out of his depth, so bewildered and frightened, but she knew it would not have changed Stef if he had stayed. Her daughter was what she was, beyond the power of young love to change. Frankie, Frank now, had become the head of the design department in a big ad agency in Los Angeles, and he had supported Van through the years, was still helping with her medical education. After she went to college in Portland, he had visited her often, but he had never returned to Silver Bay. Van was fond of him.

Marnie and Ed had worried about Stef from the time she was an infant. Counselors and doctors had diagnosed everything from manic-depressive to a sociopathic personality. Now they had new tag words, Marnie thought: hyperactive, bipolar, attention deficit, narcissistic, egotistical . . .

36

They had tried tranquilizers, which Stef had refused to take after one or two times. She had not been able to paint, she had complained. Talk therapy had been fine with her, she liked having attention focused that way, but it had not changed anything. Stef was what she was. And that was that.

The thought was followed quickly by another that was more disquieting. Stef would call Dale. After her boy lover left her, no man had been allowed to set the agenda again. Stef decided when he would go, whether just a live-in lover or a spouse. Stef made that decision. This was not over yet.

Marnie hated that Stef believed that Marnie had deliberately usurped her place with both Van and Josh, but she could do little about it. Marnie had filled a vacuum. The first time Van had come over to spend the night, she had been carrying a small Barbie overnight bag and asked, exactly the way Josh had asked, if she could sleep there. When Van found herself pregnant, she had come to Marnie to weep and tell her about it. Stef still didn't know who the father was, although Van had confessed to Marnie that he was married, a doctor, and her instructor, and that she had loved him. She had broken it off, although he had wanted to keep her in a separate apartment, his second family, she had said, weeping. He had set up a trust for Josh. She promised to tell Josh when he was mature. He would need to know his genetic heritage, she had said, weeping in Marnie's arms.

Marnie sighed deeply, drained her wineglass, and rose to go check on Stef. Her bedding was a jumble almost past straightening out, and she had not yet slipped into the deep sleep that would finally overtake her. Marnie sat in a chair near the bed for a long time wondering about the glitch in Stef's brain that refused to be quieted all day and for much of the night. Nothing had ever been found in tests, but something refused to yield until utter exhaustion set in.

It was late when Marnie finally left the rear house to enter her own house. Tipper had long since buried his bone and was more than ready to leap onto her bed and settle down. And so was she, Marnie thought tiredly. So was she.

4

ON FRIDAY AFTERNOON Tony and Dave stood back from the two chairs they had finished that week. The chairs glowed with a soft shine and were smooth as satin to the touch. Tony nodded approval and said, "They're good."

Dave grunted. Tony had given up trying to interpret Dave's grunts, which could mean anything from deep disapproval to equally deep satisfaction.

That time it seemed to mean satisfaction. The chairs had been finished weeks earlier than Dave had expected, and no outsider could have told where his work left off and Tony's started, although he knew, and he suspected that Tony did, too. Dave went to the back storeroom and returned with two old blankets.

"We'll wrap them and stow them in the truck," he said. "In the morning I'll take them in to Willoughby."

After they secured the chairs in the truck and they were once again in the shop, Dave glanced around and started to move toward his bench.

"I'll straighten up," Tony said, and Dave grunted again.

He went to the door, paused there, and said, "You do good work, Tony. See you Monday."

It was the first time Dave had acknowledged that, Tony reflected, and said, "Thanks."

One of their longer conversations, he thought when Dave had left and he was alone in the shop. Their talk about the work didn't qualify as conversation, and there was absolutely no small talk, no gossip, nothing else. He had quickly become used to Dave's tuneless hum, white noise, and again and again Tony had been so concentrated on the work itself that conversation would have been a nuisance, no matter how little real attention it demanded.

Now and then he strolled through town after he closed up the shop, and people nodded, and gradually the nods had been accompanied by a word or two. Several times he had gone down to the Sand Dollar Inn for a beer and chatted with the bartender Bill, meaningless chatter that people did with a bartender. And once Chief Will Comley had come in and sat next to him at the bar. In the next hour Tony had listened to nonstop talk and had come away knowing a brief history of the town and many of its residents. He had learned that Bill was married to Molly Barnett, who worked for Marnie in the gift shop, that Molly's sister had five daughters who helped out there from time to time. Beverly the librarian played piano at a nonsectarian church in Newport and read a book a day, or so she claimed. Will talked about coast storms and landslides, the city council that didn't do squat, how Silver Bay was safe from clear-cutting up the mountain because all that property up on the ridge past Marnie's house was a retreat for Catholic priests. They never appeared in town, but now and then a dark minibus went to Portland, likely to take someone to the airport or bring a new priest to the retreat. They went to Newport for supplies, and only one of them ever talked. A vow of silence or something, Will had said with a shake of his head. But they kept that land safe from the loggers and landslides up there. "God's ways," he said, "are mysterious."

Will looked like a cherub, Tony thought, with round, smooth cheeks, double chins, even dimpled fingers, but Tony suspected Chief Will was shrewder than he appeared. He looked over strangers who entered the restaurant or bar almost exactly the same way Tony did. He assumed that Will had looked into Tony's past, his record, had called his captain to check out this particular stranger who had come to be hired by his friend Dave.

Will had suggested that much during that one-hour course in history and biography. "Must seem awfully tame around here after working so long in New York," he had said, nursing a stein of beer.

"Relaxing," Tony had said.

"I guess you need some relaxing, what you've been through and all."

Tony laughed and did not respond.

Will got around to mentioning Stef. "She's a wild one. Her hair color changes the way some people change their shirts. Red, blue, green . . ." He shook his head. "How a good woman like Marnie ended up with such a daughter is one of those mysteries, I guess. Marnie's a fine woman, and Ed was a good man, dead twenty-five years now. We all thought Marnie would find another husband. She was a real good-looking woman, still is, but I guess trying to keep the lid on Stef was enough of a job for her, that and running the shop.

Then it looked like Stef's daughter would be like her mother. Vanessa, but she goes by Van. Van and Stef, what kind of names are they for women? She came back with a little baby and no man, but she straightened herself out and is fixing to be a doctor. Stef's never without a man, if you know what I mean. One at a time, you've got to give her that much, but she doesn't stay alone very long. Soon as she boots out that Portland dude, probably she'll come after you. New man, unattached, right age. You'll see. Folks say she's a real good artist. Me, I don't know about art, so I couldn't say one way or other."

The monologue would have continued into the second hour, Tony suspected, if he hadn't said he had to be going. He left Will talking to the bartender, who was paying little or no attention. On the way to his apartment Tony regretted that he had not picked up one of the cards with the name and address of the gallery where Stef's art was on display. Her painting of Newport Bay had impressed him, and he wanted to see more of her work.

That Friday after Dave left, Tony cleaned the shop and stood for a moment considering whether he would return after he had some dinner. With all of Saturday and Sunday at his disposal, there was little point in working that night, he decided. Back to the apartment, maybe watch a movie on TV, read, relax. For the first time in his adult life, he had time to make such decisions and feel good about them. That was a gift he had never expected to receive, and he was grateful for it. He was sleeping well, a deep, restful sleep, with no traffic noise, no airplanes overhead, no middle-of-the-night emergencies, no difficult investigation eating away at him day and night. His hip still ached, but not constantly and not with the intensity as months before. His knee seldom was a problem. This place was turning out to be exactly the right place, as if all his life it had been here waiting for him, possibly calling him, and he had been deaf and blind.

He was ready to leave the shop when the door opened and Stef walked in. He knew who she was the minute he saw her, before she said, "Hello, Tony. I'm Stef."

"If you're looking for Dave, he already left."

"I know. I saw him drive home. I'm looking for you. I want to show your box in Marnie's shop. Dave said it's up to you."

"Where your painting is? In that display?"

She nodded. "I'll change it Monday, hang something else, show something else. I want your box in the group. I like it."

"Thanks."

She looked garish with pink hair, her lips exactly the same hot pink, too much eye makeup. Every fingernail was a different color, the full spectrum of color. She was wearing slim jeans that accentuated her thinness, and a bulky, black sweatshirt that somehow seemed to emphasize it. Her wrists were nearly skeletal, as were her hands. He watched her silently as she moved about the shop touching the tools, the lathe, and stopped in front of his bench, where he had covered a piece he was working on with a beach towel. She pulled it aside, glanced at him, and said, "That's yours, isn't it?"

He nodded. It was a tabletop with a tulip inlay pattern. Parts of the slender inlaid stem bulged slightly.

She touched it. "What's wrong with it? It's too big or something."

"Drying. It will shrink and I'll smooth it down the rest of the way."

She replaced the towel and looked at him. "How can you make wood bend like that? Why doesn't it break?"

"I soak it until it gets pliable."

"I wondered how you did the box. It's beautiful. How much is it?"

"Not for sale."

She nodded. "Good. Art isn't a commodity, a product priced by the pound."

"I was very impressed by *Newport Bay*. That's a beautiful painting. Where is your work on display?"

"It isn't." She was moving toward the door. "You didn't answer my question. Can I include the box at the shop?"

"Yes."

"I'll change things on Monday morning. Get ready for spring break, a lot of visitors. Drop in and have a look later." She opened the door, then turned again to face him. "Come by the house tomorrow after you get through here. I'll give you a private showing."

"Okay," he said after a moment.

"The rear house, not the other one. That's Marnie's. I'll have her over, too. Time for you to start socializing or something." She left as swiftly as she had come, and he leaned against the bench and laughed softly. Stef, the wild one, he thought, didn't beat around the bush.

HE LOCKED UP and walked toward his apartment a few blocks away, but then veered off to take a side street another block to the motel access road. Across it he had found a way down to the shoreline, basalt rocks that were almost like deliberate stairs, and he descended it that sunny afternoon. Here was a little beach, no more than ten feet from the cliffs to the water when the tide was out, and gone when it was in.

But he didn't intend to go down all the way, only to a point where he had found basalt ledges, perfect for sitting in sunshine, protected from the wind, which seemed almost as constant as the incessant waves. The ledge was sun warmed, welcoming, and he sank down to contemplate waves breaking against a twenty-foot-high cliff, no more than thirty feet away, the southern barrier to the minuscule beach. Sea and cliff were engaged in a battle the cliff was destined to lose in time.

Winners and losers, he thought, always winners and losers. He was thinking of the box that was not for sale and would never be for sale. He had made it five years ago, working on it in stolen minutes at a time in a closetlike space that was barely big enough to hold him, his workbench, and his tools, many of them inherited from his father.

On Evelyn's birthday he had presented the box to her, a peace offering as well as birthday gift. In a marriage that had started turning sour several years earlier and was deteriorating faster month by month, it had seemed right at the time.

She had eyed it eagerly, opened it, and said in a disbelieving voice, "It's empty! You gave me an empty box?" She snapped it shut and put it down hard on a table. "You gave me an empty box! Your idea of a joke? It's not funny."

She left to go to her sister's condo, where a birthday party was being given, and he stayed home and got drunk. The next day she flashed a bracelet studded with diamonds.

"Where did that come from?" he demanded.

"I bought it!" she said defiantly. "Leonard gave Judith a twenty-thousand-dollar necklace for her birthday. I deserve a little something."

"Your sister's married to a millionaire broker. You married a cop. We can't afford that."

"I didn't! I married a man less than a year away from being a lawyer! By now you'd have the corner office and we'd live the way Judith lives. But you couldn't stand the idea of having a desk job," she said scornfully. "You wanted to play cops and robbers."

He had gone to the telephone, taken out his wallet, and extracted four credit cards, two of them maxed out, a third one probably also maxed with that bracelet. He jerked open the telephone book, then jabbed in the number he found and reported a lost credit card. After the woman on the other end got the necessary information, she said they would send a replacement. He had said, "No, don't send a new one yet. We're moving and I don't have the new address yet."

From across the room Evelyn stared at him, white-faced and shaking. "You can't do that to me," she said harshly. "How dare you pull a filthy trick like that!"

He found a second number and was punching it in when she ran from the room.

The following day he dismantled his shop and started selling the tools, and Evelyn went to stay with her sister. Two months later they sold the condominium, which they had bought when the price was affordable, and it brought a handsome profit with the skyrocketing prices that had since set in. His attorney and hers had agreed that the mortgage and all debts had to be paid before the proceeds could be divided. It didn't leave much. He hadn't cared. For the first time in years he was debt-free, and he had thought mockingly she might even have to go back to work. She had left a good job, buyer for a hotel consortium, because it hadn't left her enough free time to go places with her sister. He hadn't seen her since the day of the divorce.

He closed his eyes and leaned back against warm basalt,

while in his mind's eye he was seeing the condo bedroom the day she moved out. She had taken the tables and chair he had made, probably to sell, but the empty box was in the middle of the bed.

5

TONY DROVE TO Stef's house that Saturday. He had found that walking uphill was to be avoided, although he had no trouble on flat ground and little on stairs. The weather had turned gray and rather cold with a steady wind and the smell of rain or fog in the air. Stef opened the door promptly at the doorbell. She was in baggy black pants with a loose, bright-red, long-sleeved shirt that clashed with her pink hair.

"Hi. Come on in."

She didn't offer to take his Windbreaker, and he kept it on as he followed her past stairs through a hall to where the house opened to a large room that took up the rear half of the house, with a kitchen at one end, a counter separating it from a dining area, and the living room. The view from the back of the room was panoramic, unobstructed through oversize windows and a sliding door to a deck beyond. Ocean and sky were almost the same gray color, broken by white spray and breaking waves, merging in the distance.

Opposite the window wall a low fire was burning in a fireplace, with a grouping of chairs and a sofa in front of it. The furniture in the comfortable room was in shades of dark green, gold, and russet, with russet and deep-red throw rugs, and pillows on the sofa.

Marnie set a glass of wine on a low table, then rose from a chair before the windows. She nodded to him. "It's warm in here. Let me take your jacket. I'm Marnie Markov, by the way. We almost met before."

"Just toss it anywhere," Stef said. "I'm having bourbon and water. Bloody Mary, rum, beer, name it, it's probably available."

"Beer would be fine." He went to Marnie, held out his hand. "Tony Mauricio. Glad to meet you more formally." Her hand was soft and warm, her handshake firm.

He nodded toward the window. "That's spectacular. Do people get used to it, stop seeing it?"

"I haven't yet. And I've been here for forty-five years."

Stef brought a bottle of beer and a glass and her own glass and sat in one of the chairs, pointed to another one, and said, "He's making a table now. He doesn't sell his art, either."

"What do you do with furniture after a certain point is reached?" Marnie asked curiously. "Finite space being what it is."

Tony grinned. "Just the box. Anything else will be up to Dave. He'll decide and handle it."

"Oh," Stef said. "You do sell things, then?"

She had an ever-changing expression, Tony thought. Seconds earlier an approving one, now a distant, colder look, not entirely disdainful, but almost.

"It's never been an issue," he said. "I never had anything

to sell before. But I guess I'm less interested in the object than in the process of making it."

"Process," Stef said. "The act of creation. For me it's what I end up with that counts. Getting there is . . ." She took a long drink and turned to face the window. "It's hard to know when it's finished or if it ever is. There's always a little more that can be done, a final touch that needs doing. I don't think I ever finish anything. How can you part with something that isn't finished?"

"You do what you can," Marnie said, "and then you let it go. Or you drive yourself crazy."

"And it's off to the attic with you and a padlock on the door," Stef said gaily. She set her glass down and jumped to her feet. "Come on, have a look at my stuff."

He followed her upstairs, through another hall with two open doors opposite each other, revealing bedrooms, two closed doors, and on to the studio, which took up the whole end of that floor. Windows were on three walls, the north and east windows high, and wide, sash windows facing south. An outside door was near the corner of the east wall. He had seen a passageway up there, with stairs down to the sidewalk below.

Paintings leaned against every inch of available wall, hung on every available inch of wall space. A long table held portfolios, a stack of sketches, and a counter with a utility sink took up several feet of another side. The sink and counter were badly stained, daubed with paint that entirely covered the original surface. Five easels held more paintings, one with a cover over a work.

He was surprised to see so many styles, impressionist, abstracts, realistic . . . and it appeared that she had switched mediums often. Acrylics and oils, side by side with watercolors and charcoals. He asked if she had settled on any of them and she said she was sticking to watercolors. For now.

Gazing at a landscape in oils, with glaring yellow and orange, dead black slashes, forest green, he said, "I don't know the language of art, how to express a reaction in technical terms. But I think that's great, shocking and great."

She was watching him closely. "Why?"

"I think it's honest," he said after a moment. "And I don't know what I mean by that. It's stark, cruel in a way, and honest. Hard-edged." The painting had nothing of the serenity she had captured in her *Newport Bay,* nothing of the pastoral gentleness of some conventional paintings that any fine painter might have produced. This one screamed Stef. It depicted a dynamic landscape that could kill you if you weren't on guard.

Two paintings were turned to the wall and she didn't offer to turn them around. He didn't comment as they passed by them to continue the tour. It was a tour, he felt, through the mind and sensibilities of this woman with her chameleon changes and what she was willing or perhaps compelled to reveal of herself.

Finally she led him to the covered painting on an easel and threw back the cover to reveal *Ladies in Waiting.* He took a step back and gazed at it silently for a long time before he turned to study her face. She was watching him intently again. "It belongs in a museum," he said.

"Not in a private house, adorning the space above a family sofa?" Her tone was mocking as if she was aware of what she had done, what it meant.

"You know not that. Who would be willing to live with it, face its truth every day? A world of hypocrisy, deceit, reality hiding behind a facade of gentility, animality in skirts, the roles women play . . . A museum."

For a moment longer her gaze held his, then abruptly she covered the painting again and gestured. "Let's go down. I have some pizzas in the freezer. We'll have pizza."

Marnie felt only a mild surprise that Stef had asked him to share a pizza. Marnie made a salad and they ate pizza and salad. Stef said little during the scant meal, and Marnie talked about the early days of Silver Bay, how few people had discovered the livability of the coast back then, how deserted it had been.

"We had an apartment in Newport," she said. "Then Ed found out that the builders of this house were leaving and he wanted it. Stef was three when we came here, and at that time ours was the only house on the ridge, except for the retreat up above us. Land here was cheap, a cottage could be had for twenty-five thousand, and now a postage-stamp-sized lot goes for sixty-five thousand or more. Progress, I think they call it."

Something had changed, Marnie thought as they ate and chatted. Her own flow of conversation was light and easy, requiring little thought. She told him about Van, studying to be a doctor, with her internship coming in the fall. As she spoke, she became aware of the difference in the air. A wariness between Stef and Tony had vanished, and Stef was no longer eyeing him speculatively. Marnie hadn't known the thought had been in her head until it was no longer there, and its absence made her conscious of the change. She was surprised with a second thought: a mutual respect had replaced wariness, Stef's former speculative interest had been replaced by respect, a far deeper and more meaningful emotion. And, before, Tony had regarded Stef as he might have regarded a puzzle, with an almost analytical attitude. Marnie imagined that was how he looked at those he interviewed in his investigations, as if asking, *Who are you and where do you fit in?* That was gone also, replaced by a respectful regard that was still questioning, but different. She wished she had gone to the studio with them, heard what they had said there.

Stef had not mentioned Dale since that last ugly scene, and Marnie had asked nothing. She had stopped asking her daughter questions long ago after accepting that she would not get a satisfactory answer. But Stef had never appeared respectful of Dale, or any other man in her life.

Tony didn't stay long that evening. When he pulled on his jacket to leave, Marnie said, "Next week, Sunday, please come to a real dinner. Van and her little boy will be here. I'd like you to meet her." Smiling, she added, "She'll be here through spring break and she'll sleep for the first two days, but by Sunday evening she'll be conscious."

"Thanks," Tony said. "I'd like to meet her. And thank you, Stef, for letting me see your art. I regard that as a privilege."

"I'm glad you saw it," she said.

The response was not sarcastic or self-deprecating in any way, Marnie realized, but trusting. Respect and trust, she mused that night, two qualities she had thought never to see in her daughter.

TONY DIDN'T GET to the gift shop to see the new display until Thursday. It seemed that the days slipped away before he had a chance to realize one had come and gone and another was already upon him.

When he entered the gift shop, Marnie was helping several young people wearing green-and-yellow sweatshirts with UO letters. They were examining the kites, and he continued past them after waving to her. His glance at his own box was quick. It was open, a lace glove draped over a side, a mirror positioned in such a way that the top was clearly visible. He nodded approvingly and turned his attention to the new painting by Stef.

At first, from across the shop, he had thought it was an abstract, or impressionist, something that had beautifully combined blues in all shades and tones, from a cold iciness, to a warm, larger expanse, to muted blue-green. . . . As he drew nearer, a pattern emerged. There were fern leaves in pale green, a grouping of white feathers, what had to be a contrail, a wake from a swimming bird, a bigger wake made by a ship possibly, clouds. . . . The shapes were as alike as snowflakes, and all completely different from one another, each one exquisitely rendered, each shaft precise, each branching form unmistakably itself. The frost patterns brought memories of a car windshield in upstate New York. The longer he gazed at the painting, the more shapes became clear, overlapping, one merging into the next, each one perfect, the same general form again and again expressed in plants, in water, ice. He didn't know how long he had been trying to discern where one shape morphed into another until he became aware that Marnie had come to stand near him.

"It's beautiful, isn't it?" she said. "I think it's the best thing she ever did."

"It's beautiful." That seemed inadequate, but he didn't add to it. When he finally turned away from the painting, he said, "She should be recognized, have her work shown to the world."

Marnie shook her head. "She says she isn't ready."

The three earlier shoppers had left, Tony saw, and now two different boys, high school boys from the look of them, entered the shop. "I should get back to work," he said. After one more lingering look at the painting, he turned and walked out.

MARNIE'S GLOWING ACCOUNT of her granddaughter, Van, had set him up to like her, Tony thought that Sunday when he was admitted inside the front house on the ridge, Marnie's house. And he did like her almost instantly. Her level gaze, strong, straight eyebrows, long black hair in a low ponytail, tiny gold studs in her ears, and no makeup. She was inches taller than Marnie and her mother both, slender, dressed in jeans, sneakers, and a gray sweatshirt that looked much laundered, a bit faded. Her handshake was as no-nonsense as her appearance, and there couldn't have been a bigger contrast between her and Stef if she had labored to achieve one. Where Stef was all clashing colors, nervous energy, her hands never quiet, Van was composed, and her movements were purposeful or absent.

"And this is Josh," Marnie said, completing the introductions.

A pretty child, he had the same kind of eyebrows as Van, and hair that was as straight and black. He shook hands with Tony soberly, then asked, "Are you a policeman?"

"No. I used to be one."

Josh looked disappointed and turned a reproachful face toward Stef. "You said."

"I said he was once."

"Can I go out and play with Tipper now?" he asked Van.

Her response was reflexive. "*May* I."

"Yeah," he said with a grin. "You can come, too."

Tony suppressed a smile and Van said, "Get lost, brat. Out with you."

Josh ran out with Tipper, and as the others entered the

living room, they could see the pair race across a fenced deck and vanish around the side. There was no backyard here, as the ground fell off steeply, leaving a small level area on the side of the house.

This was another good house, Tony thought as Marnie excused herself to finish up dinner. Like the rear house, the back of the living room here was mostly glass, with the same stunning vista. That day the sea was the deep blue of picture postcards, and high clouds moved along briskly. A dark-leather-covered sofa and chairs flanked the windows, a coffee table within reach. Other chairs were arranged before a television on the opposite side of the room. Among them was a half-size chair, a Josh chair. A dog bed was near it. Many books were on end tables, and a bookshelf was overfilled with more books. Not one book had been visible in Stef's house. An array of potted plants on a stepped bench was at one end of the windows.

No one explained two paintings on a wall, but they had obviously not been done by Stef. One was a battleship, and the other a destroyer, navy ships. They were amateurish, but carefully executed. Near them hung a map rack, with maps that could be pulled down to be displayed or rolled up like window shades. One was open for inspection, a map not readily recognizable to him. Another time, he thought turning from them, he would have a closer look.

Stef was talking. "I like a little something before dinner. How about you guys?"

"Maybe wine," Van said. "Tony?" He said wine, and she started to move toward the kitchen.

Stef waved her back. "I'll get it."

"And I'll let her," Van said, smiling. "It's been a tough year and all I want to do is absolutely nothing. Except sleep, that is." She looked thoughtful. "What we need to develop is a sleep bank. A human sleep bank. You know, the way bears gorge, storing fat for hibernation."

Stef brought a tray with wine and her own mixed drink, and after the brief interruption Van continued, "I'd be willing to sleep twelve, fifteen hours a day and store the excess in preparation for the future."

"For her internship," Stef said. "It seems they work the slaves eighty hours or longer week after week."

"Do you know where it will be?" Tony asked.

"Chicago," Van said with a shrug. "I had hoped for the West Coast, but it's going to be Chicago for the first year, then Newport General for year two. Rural areas, small communities like ours, are begging for more help and it gives me a real break."

"Can you imagine what it's going to be like for her?" Stef said sharply. "After living out here, bang, Chicago."

"I've lived in Portland for quite a few years," Van pointed out.

"A small town with delusions of grandeur and traffic," Stef said.

From across the room where she was putting something on the table, Marnie said, "You adapt. People do. I got used to New York City, and you, Stef, learned to live in Paris, not just a strange big city but a foreign one with a foreign language. Van will do just fine in Chicago."

"The hardest part will be leaving Josh here," Van said. "I won't be able to take care of him while doing an internship."

"You know that kids' book the nuts raised hell about, somebody has two mommies?" Stef said. "Lucky Josh, he has three." She added to Tony, "He'll stay with Marnie and me, and I intend to spoil him shitless."

"It's time to bring him in," Marnie said, going back around the counter to the kitchen. "Dinner in five."

Van paused on her way to the sliding door. "I keep thinking of all those young mothers and fathers going off to Iraq, leaving little kids. At least I won't be going into a war zone, and I'll have an end date. Count my blessings."

Chicago, Tony thought but did not voice, might prove to be more of a war zone than she realized, especially when she did a stint in the ER.

THE DINNER WAS wonderful, Tony said later quite sincerely, the best he'd had in years. Pork loin with a crust of spices and garlic, tiny new potatoes, asparagus. Van waved her hand over the table and said, "She always makes my favorite meals when I come home. I love it! Talk about being spoiled."

"Will you specialize?" Tony asked Van when Marnie began to clear the table.

"No. Too many specialists. Internal medicine, family practice, general practice, that's for me. And right here in my own territory." Van rose to help Marnie.

"What do you want to be when you get big?" Tony asked Josh when it appeared that Stef was going to remain speechless for the time being.

"A painter like Gramma," Josh said. "I got an easel and paints but they're in my other house."

For a second Stef's mobile expression registered displeasure perhaps, or something else that Tony couldn't interpret, and at the same moment he was aware that Van, putting a bowl on the counter, had stopped.

Then Stef said brightly, "I intend to set him up in the studio this week. A fellow artist."

Van put the bowl down a bit too hard, and a few seconds later she and Marnie were back with strawberries and cream.

"California berries," Marnie said. "Nothing like the ones we'll get from the valley later on, but not bad."

Josh had kept his bread dish and was playing with a piece of bread, ignoring the berries. When Marnie asked if he didn't like them, he shook his head. "Too sour."

"The kid has taste," Stef said to Tony, and poured herself more wine.

At that moment there was a knock on the back door, and a draft of cool air flowed through the room. Marnie rose to see who was there, but she stopped abruptly when Dale appeared at the kitchen door to the back hall. She sank back into her chair.

"Stef, have I got some great news for you!" He glanced at the others and nodded toward them.

Stef had turned partway in her chair and said icily, "Dale, have you noticed that we're having dinner? And that Marnie has a guest."

"Oh. Sorry. Excited, I guess."

But Dale had noticed, Tony knew. A suspicious darting glance had taken him in, flashed to Stef, to him again. Tony had started to rise, but when the newcomer stopped at the door, he remained seated, watching. The man looked like a male model, a walking ad for an upscale male fashion magazine. Raw-silk jacket in dove gray, dazzlingly white silk shirt, open at the throat, fine worsted trousers. A thousand-dollar casual outfit, Tony estimated.

Stef turned her back on Dale and deliberately picked up a strawberry, swirled it in cream, and popped it into her mouth. A look of satisfaction crossed her face, vanished. At the same time Van became aware that Josh was rolling little, discolored bread balls. "Josh, stop playing with your food. If you're done eating, let's go wash your hands." Josh jumped up without hesitation, she murmured, "Excuse us," and they left the room.

"I won't stay," Dale said. "Stef, come over as soon as you can. I can't wait to tell you." He waved generally at the room, revealing a Rolex watch, and went out the way he had come in.

"My husband," Stef said, and drank her wine.

"Tony, do you drink coffee?" Marnie asked in the silence that followed.

"Yes. Probably too much. Can I help?"

"No. It's ready to pour." She went to the counter and brought back a tray with three cups and a carafe. "One thing we can get all over this state is decent coffee," she said, pouring. "I'm afraid I'm rather addicted, and it seems that Van is, too. I think it goes with the territory for students."

Van and Josh returned. He was holding a box. "It's a puzzle," he said. "I found it on my bed."

Smiling, Marnie said, "Whoever keeps coming in here and leaving things knows what you like, I guess."

"Yeah, thanks." Josh went to the coffee table to open the box and spread out jigsaw-puzzle pieces.

"His newest favorite thing," Van said, taking her seat again.

Abruptly Stef rose. "I'd better go."

Marnie watched her walk out, then started to reminisce about her year in New York City. "I was eighteen, and terrified at first . . ."

LATER, AFTER TONY had left and Josh was in bed, Marnie and Van sat talking quietly. "I like him," Marnie said, speaking of Tony. "And I know that Stef does. She respects him, too."

"Did you notice that he didn't say a single revealing word about himself? And I bet he didn't miss a thing going on here. I'd put money on it that he knows what color socks Dale was wearing."

"Not a bet I'd go against. Maybe that's one of the reasons I like him. He notices things and he's not full of himself. On the other hand, he was pretty much surrounded by three women who didn't give him many openings."

Van made a rude noise. "The men I've known never waited for an opening. They jumped right in and ran with the ball."

Marnie smiled. "You've known too many instructors and doctors."

"Damn right." Van yawned. "I'll go over and see how stormy it is. Maybe I'll be back. Okay with you?"

"You know it is. The door will be unlocked."

Marnie suspected that Van would be back soon, and then she pondered the quick look of satisfaction she had seen on Stef's face when Dale appeared. Stef had known he would be back, Marnie thought, and Stef had not called him. She had expected him to return, and before long she would be the one to slam the door in his face. No man could be allowed to make that decision, it was hers alone. And it would be soon now, Marnie believed.

As soon as Van entered the upper hall in the rear house, she could hear Stef yelling.

"I don't give a shit about your millionaire fuck! It's not for sale! And I don't want to hear another goddamn word about a fucking patron!"

Van closed her bedroom door, but it didn't help. Stef's voice was still there.

"I told you to haul ass out of my life! I meant it, you bastard!"

There was the sound of something breaking, a glass, cup, something. Hoping it wasn't a window, Van gathered up a few things she would want ovenight, but with her hand on the doorknob, she paused, listening. Stef was coming upstairs. Sighing, Van backed away from the door and sat on the side of her bed to wait.

"What part of *no* don't you understand, you bloody idiot? How many times do I have to say it? No! N-O." Stef ran into the studio and slammed the door.

Van could hear every word as Dale said in an anguished voice, "Stef, please don't do this. I'm begging you. I'm sorry I didn't talk it over with you first. God, I'm sorry. I wasn't even thinking of selling anything, just to get legitimate offers, so we could go on from there. That's what this is, a legitimate offer by someone who recognizes your genius. I know I can't sell anything without your approval. I wouldn't even consider doing such a thing."

He paused, and when there was no response, he said, "Stef, listen a second. I have a duty to protect your work, to protect you. It's a sacred duty to me. To take a valuable painting like that from a secure place and put it in the shop is too dangerous. There could be a fire, or a maniac could mutilate it. It could be stolen. You'd be devastated if anything happened to it. Or to any of them."

He sounded as if he were choking on tears then as he said, "Stef, I can't stand this. It's tearing me up. I can't sleep or eat. God, if only I could take it back, undo it. Please, Stef, please. Give me three minutes, and then if you say get out, that's it. Please."

Stef came out of the studio. "You fool! You said he would be my patron. Now you're saying it's not about a sale. You

63

can't keep your story straight for five minutes. There's nothing to talk about!"

Her voice rose as she neared Van's door, then began to grow fainter as she went down the stairs, calling him names, yelling at him all the way.

After a few seconds, Van opened her door a crack and peered out. They were both downstairs, Stef still yelling. Van slipped out of her room and fled down the hall to the studio door and out, to return to Marnie's house.

Downstairs, Stef raced through the living room to the kitchen, back, without a pause in her tirade, and Dale sank into a chair and covered his face.

"Just listen a minute," he pleaded. "Please calm down and listen a minute. Then I'll leave if you want me to. Stef, I'd cut off my arm if you wanted me to."

She was at the window and turned to face him, but for the moment she became silent.

His body was shaking as if he were weeping. "It's been agony thinking you were leaving. I thought you'd be pleased to find out that a multimillionaire had seen your art and thinks it's the work of a genius. It could be important to have someone like him promoting your art. I know it's not for sale and I didn't tell him it was, but he made the offer."

"You put price tags on everything in the gallery! Behind my back!"

"I explained, Stef. For insurance, that's all. You need insurance, darling. For such work to be unprotected is unthinkable. Please sit down and let's talk about all this. I beg you. At least we can talk about it."

She perched on the edge of a chair across the coffee table from him. "So talk."

"I'll have our attorney draw up a contract, a real business contract, between you and me, that will give you an iron-clad guarantee that I'll never sell or offer your art for sale without your express approval."

"What's the point? You went behind my back, and now you come up with a billionaire dickhead of a patron, acting like I'm a starving medieval peasant grateful for crumbs off his table."

"I'm a businessman. If I break a contract, you sue and I go to jail, or lose my socks, lose everything I own. And I'm totally ruined. No sale I made would be legitimate, you could reclaim anything I sold. But that's not going to happen. Never." He looked down at his hands and said in a low voice, "I've lost your trust and I want to get it back. If a contract will reassure you, that's how we should do it. As soon as possible, we should do it."

"What if I want out of it?"

"It's standard to have a clause that says plainly that if you decide to terminate the contract, you can do it. I guarantee that such a clause will be there. But I hope that neither one of us will ever even think of it again."

Stef jerked up to her feet. "I want a drink."

He continued to sit and watch her at the counter with her back to him. A few more weeks, he thought at that garish, skinny back. He could endure anything for a few weeks. But, God, he added to himself, he wanted a woman he could take into a fine restaurant or club, one who looked as good as he did, someone like Jasmine. She knew how to dress, what clothes to wear and how to wear them, how to walk and sit. She had been his perfect accessory, one that he dared not show off where anyone he knew might see them. Angrily he pushed aside the thought of Jasmine. Other Jasmines were out there, just waiting until he was free.

He stood and went to the counter, where he put his arm around Stef's shoulders. She did not push him away.

When Van entered Marnie's house she paused in the living room long enough to say, "Gale-force winds, storming up and down stairs. I'm going to bed. I think he wants to sell *Feathers and Ferns*. Good night, Marnie."

It was the painting Stef had hung at the shop that week, and Marnie knew beyond doubt that Stef would not sell it.

6

NO VACANCY SIGNS began appearing on the coast during the middle of the weeks, apartments that had been dark most of the winter began showing lights in windows, empty driveways were being used. The summer people were arriving.

Marnie and Molly Barnett had agreed to let Molly's two teenaged nieces work in the shop all summer, giving Marnie time to spend with Van and Josh. The girls were eager for the jobs since they were saving for college, and Marnie had little desire to be closeted most of the day when she knew how little she would be seeing of Van during the coming year.

Barney Stokely brought Marnie a large piece of halibut one day and would take nothing in return. He had bought the fishing business after Ed's sudden death from pneumonia, and she had permitted him to retain the name, Markov's Fisheries, which had built up a good clientele over a seventy-year history and had an excellent reputation. Barney frequently showed up with a such a gift.

It was too much not to freeze most of it, Marnie knew, and the texture changed with freezing. She wanted to serve at least some of it while it was still freshly caught, in its prime. Van was back in Portland, and for the past several days Stef had been in Portland also. Marnie cut off a big piece of fish and took it to Harriet McAdams for her and Dave, then, after cutting off two steaks and freezing the rest with a sigh of regret, she called Tony and invited him to dinner.

When he arrived, he brought a book as well as a bottle of nicely chilled pinot grigio.

"It's a history of maps," he said. "I've had it a long time and thought you might like it. I noticed the maps on the wall the last time I was here."

"They were Ed's maps. My husband was in the navy for years, and at ports he prowled in book stalls and began collecting maps he came across. He didn't keep most of the books, not enough storage room, but he kept the maps."

They went to look at them and she said, "I tried comparing one of them to other maps and got hopelessly confused. Some of them are so wrong. Ed said they were egocentric. I liked that, egocentric, geocentric. You put the important thing in the center and never apologize." She pointed to a map of Japan after drawing it down. "See? The emperor's palace, dead center, instead of off in the province where it actually was."

"Did he paint the navy ships?" Tony asked when they moved away from the maps. He indicated the two naval ships hanging near the maps.

"Yes. Stef said they were baroque, done in that style, before they got the hang of perspective." Marnie had a flash of memory of the night Ed had come home to find them hanging. She'd had them framed for a surprise. How husky his voice had become, how his eyes had softened . . .

Briskly she turned away and said, "Come keep me company while I toss the salad. I didn't want to broil that nice fish until we were ready to eat. It won't take more than ten minutes, and you can have a glass of wine. Are you finding it hard to get service in restaurants yet? Our little town is starting to fill up again."

"Do the locals hate the summer people?" he asked, sitting at the dining table while she finished cooking.

"Can't live with them, can't survive without them. Isn't that the way with most tourist towns? The traffic on 101 gets impossible, and speeders don't see the stop signs. The usual complaints, I guess."

How easy it was to talk to him, she thought later that night. He asked few questions, but somehow she had kept finding herself telling him things that surprised her. Such as her early life with Ed, how it worried her if he was out on one of the boats and a storm was coming in, how colicky Stef had been.

At least, she thought then, she had not mentioned that her mother had come to meet her new granddaughter when Stef was two months old. She had said Stef's constant crying was just punishment, that babies conceived in sin were never happy. She had not liked the coast. The mountain roads were dangerous, the mountains might erupt or something, and all those dark trees had been forbidding. Also, she had felt threatened by the ocean. It was too rough, too violent. She had never come back, and Marnie had never taken Stef to Indiana. Marnie had not been willing to expose her to the kind of criticism she knew her mother would heap on Stef for not doing as ordered, things she was incapable of doing. Sit still. Stop racing around. Go to bed and stay there.

Keep out of those cabinets. Clean your plate. A visit to her old home, her mother's house, would have been a nightmare, and she had never gone to the Indiana farm again.

Also, she thought, reflecting on what she had not talked about to Tony, she had not said why she and Ed had bought a house obviously too big for them. Stef was three, and Marnie had been pregnant again, with twins. They would need a big house, Ed had said. The twins came prematurely and one died two days later, the other one a week after that. There was never another pregnancy, and the big upper room had remained empty until Stef claimed it as her studio when she was thirteen. When Stef married the first time, Marnie and Ed had moved into the front house, leaving the rear house to the new family. That family history remained locked within her.

Having coffee after dinner that night, Marnie told Tony about Stef's name. "Ed filled out the birth certificate and he spelled her name *Stefany*. I said I'd never seen it spelled like that, and he said there had been a distant relative in his family who spelled it that way, and besides, she was unique, no one else on earth like her, and she deserved a unique name. What could I do?"

Marnie laughed softly. "Stef liked it and insisted on keeping the spelling. God alone knows how many times she had to defend it during her school years."

And she had talked about Ed's last days, Marnie thought with a sense of wonder. "We took turns staying with him," she had said that night. "I had gone home to shower and put on clean clothes, and when I returned, at the door, I could hear her talking to him. She was reminding him of the good times, a hike up Mount Rainier, picnics, the time he took her out on one of the fishing boats. She was holding his hand, just talking, and he was dying. She called him Daddy. When I went inside the room, he was smiling."

How had that come into the conversation? she wondered after Tony had left and she sat at her windows and watched lights at sea vanish as darkness fell. She had no answer to her question.

Then she was thinking only of Stef. She was playing with Dale, Marnie knew. He was her fish and she was playing him, pretending to accept his apology for not telling her about insurance and why he had put prices on her work. Marnie didn't know if Stef believed that excuse, and she didn't know the rules of the game Stef was playing, but she knew the signs, and they were there in abundance. She had seen the same pattern more than once over the years. It varied little from man to man. Big fights, a lot of yelling back and forth, contrition, a loving relationship restored, then the exit line and the door slam. Over. They had reached the reconciliation stage. There was no way of knowing when the next act would begin, but begin it would. Dale had betrayed her and he could not be forgiven. Period.

It was cruel, merciless, and Marnie could do nothing about it beyond hope that Dale would go quietly. Sometimes they did, sometimes not.

Only the town lights were visible when she left the window, sat in her favorite chair across the room, and started to read the book Tony had brought.

THURSDAY, VAN WAS graduating that week. *Dr. Vanessa Markov.* Marnie mouthed the words silently and basked in the glow they afforded her. Marnie planned to drive to Portland on Saturday, attend the graduation ceremony, and return that night. She hoped it would not be as tedious as Van's undergraduate ceremony had been, with an endless line of students marching onstage, the handshake, receiving the diploma, off, like a lot of windup robots, Marnie had thought, at least until it was Van who was marching up. It wouldn't be like that, she reminded herself, if only because there were far fewer students.

As she finished up in the kitchen before going to the gift shop, she kept hearing Stef going in and out from the studio, and finally Marnie opened her back door, descended the few steps to the passage, and went to the studio to see what was going on. The studio door was open with Stef inside still in her oversize nightshirt.

"I decided to take the charcoals in," she said. "Might as well sell them, for all I care. Marnie, why don't you come in with us? You could come back with Van on Sunday."

Marnie shook her head. "Van doesn't need a houseguest right now. Probably the apartment is unlivable anyway, all packed up, ready for her to leave. She's already shipped a lot of her things."

"Stay in our apartment."

Marnie would get a hotel room, sleep under a bridge, or walk home in the middle of the night before she would stay in Dale's apartment. She shook her head. "I'll be there early Saturday, that's time enough."

"Maybe I'll take a couple of the landscapes," Stef said, turning away from her. "They're just about bad enough to appeal to someone."

Marnie nodded, aware that Stef was talking about some of her conventional landscapes that she claimed to despise. "I'll see you on Saturday," she said, leaving. Below, Marnie saw the gallery van in the driveway with the side door open. Apparently they had already taken the charcoals down.

IN THE SHOP a few minutes after one, Marnie heard sirens and paid little attention. The highway invited accidents, with impatient motorists irritated past reason by slow-moving camping trailers, house trailers, strangers on the road taking chances on passing, inviting disaster. The police car or rescue unit, whatever it was, did not pass the shop.

Minutes later the phone rang, and Harriet, her voice high-pitched and frightened, said, "Marnie, something's happened at your house! The emergency truck is there and Will just drove in."

Marnie ran from the shop without a word to Molly's niece and drove home as fast as she could. Will hurried to meet her in the driveway, where the fire truck and other cars blocked her way. Will put his arm around her shoulders. "Don't go back there, Marnie. There's been an accident. It looks like Stef fell down those stairs. Let's go in your place, Marnie. There's nothing you can do."

Marnie jerked away from him, and he caught her arm and held her back.

"She's dead, Marnie."

7

MARNIE IS DREAMING. Frozen in sleep paralysis, she is watching Stef race from tide pool to tide pool, oblivious of incoming waves that are growing higher, encroaching farther and farther upon the scant beach. Stef's hair is wild, wind-tangled, the way it always is. Seconds after being brushed, her hair, pale and baby-fine, is in a tangle. She is wet from wading in the shallow pools. She is laughing. Marnie knows the outcome, knows how the dream ends, knows the beach will be swept clean and there is nothing she can do. Voiceless, immobilized, her despair mounting, she can only watch in horror. Her screams are stilled in her throat as she watches a new wave crest and break, and then the beach is empty, the tide pools underwater, and water, foaming and hissing, withdraws before another thrust.

"Stef!" she cries. "Stef!"

"Hush, Marnie," Ed says. "Shh."

"Ed?"

"I'm here, Marnie."

She feels his presence behind her on the bed and sighs deeply. "I couldn't help her," she whispers. "She's gone. Our daughter is dead."

"I know, Marnie. You did all you could."

"I knew what was happening. I saw it happening and I didn't do anything. Now she's dead."

"You couldn't save her, Marnie. No one could."

"He killed her. It wasn't an accident. He did it."

"What are you going to do about it?"

"I don't know." In her sleep she is weeping. "I don't know."

"Decide, Marnie. Decide." His voice is growing fainter, receding into a distance.

"I want to kill him," Marnie said, and with the words spoken aloud, she came wide-awake, bolted upright in bed, shaking.

"I want to kill him," she repeated. She waited for her heart to stop pounding, then threw back the blanket and got up. Pale predawn light seeped through the blinds on her windows, but she knew she was done with sleep for now.

Across the hall Van slipped into the room she was sharing with Josh. She closed the door silently and stood leaning against it. She had heard Marnie mumbling incoherently in her sleep, but the spoken words had been clear and distinct. Marnie thought so, too, then, Van realized with a shudder. For two weeks Van had been struggling with the belief that her mother, that Stef, had not simply fallen down the stairs, that somehow Dale had managed to kill her without raising a suspicion. But Marnie thought so, too. Did that make a difference? Van didn't know.

She lay down on her bed and stared at the ceiling, barely discernible, like an insubstantial fog, but growing more and more solid as the minutes passed. When she smelled coffee, she got up, put on her robe, and went to the kitchen, where Marnie was already sipping coffee.

"I'm sorry," Marnie said. "I must have made more noise than I thought. Or was it the smell of coffee? It's awfully early."

"The kind of hours I'm pretty much used to. Nothing you did." Van poured coffee and sat opposite Marnie at the table. "If I get you some sleeping pills, will you take them?"

"No, of course not. I don't need anything."

"You do, though. You're not sleeping worth a damn. You need to get some rest."

"This has been a hard time to get through," Marnie said, gazing at her coffee cup. "It will pass. Things do, after all."

"I want to get Eva Granger over to help gather Stef's clothes to give to Beverly. She said she'd take them to her church whenever we're ready. Is that all right with you?"

Marnie nodded. "It's time, I guess." She felt strangely distant from Van, from her own kitchen, from everything. In her mind the question kept repeating, *What are you going to do about it?* Nothing else seemed to mean a great deal as she pondered the question and her answer to it. It was true, she thought. She wanted to kill Dale Oliver.

Van sipped her coffee, unable to broach the bigger problem. If they both believed Dale had been responsible for Stef's fall, her death, what could be done about it? There had been an investigation of sorts, she knew, but Dale said he had been at the front window, on the phone with Freddi, when they both heard Stef scream, and then Freddi had heard Dale's hoarse voice crying out Stef's name, heard the phone bang when he dropped it, and hadn't been able to get a response from Dale again. She had called 911 in Portland, and the dispatcher had transferred her to the Newport sheriff's office. Dale had not been able to find his cell phone and used the landline phone to put in his own frantic call to 911 from the house. The sheriff had found the cell phone later outside the door to the house. The battery had run down by then.

Van had not believed his story then and didn't believe it two weeks later. She had asked Will Comley about opening a real investigation, and he had in effect said, "There, there. Nothing to it." He had added a twist of the knife by saying one of Josh's toy trucks had been under Stef's body, that apparently she had stepped on it on the stairs, and it was just enough to throw her off-balance.

Sipping coffee that morning, Van decided this was not the time to talk about it. Josh would be up any minute and be underfoot until eleven, when she took him to the day-care play school for the afternoon.

It would keep until that evening, after Josh was in bed, and a whole night stretched before them without interruption. But she was worried about Marnie. Her eyes were deeply shadowed and she looked haggard and tired. Van had thought it was simply grief that was wearing her down, but if Marnie believed Dale was responsible, that made it different. And if she really meant it when she said she wanted to kill him, that made it significantly different.

By two-thirty Eva Granger had come and gone again with boxes of Stef's clothes in her van. She and Van had played together as children, had gone through high school together, and stayed close since. She had married a fisherman, ran a bed-and-breakfast, and was efficient and businesslike in dismantling an entire life in a few hours. Van was grateful for her friend's matter-of-fact attitude about getting rid of things that would have posed a dilemma for her alone. They had stripped the bed, and the bedding was in the clothes dryer. Eva had taken Stef's special tiger-print comforter with her, to go into a large washer at a Laundromat, on to Beverly. Now the room looked bleak and barren. A few of Dale's things remained. He never actually lived in the house, but used it as a weekend retreat from time to time and rarely stayed more than a few days. Van resisted the temptation to toss everything of his into the trash.

She made coffee, and while waiting for it, she wandered through the house, which felt emptier than she had thought possible. Although the furniture had been left there by Marnie and Ed when they moved into the front house, this one still felt like Stef's house. Van couldn't account for that, except that Stef had seemed to fill any space she occupied if for no reason other than her constant motion. She was always all over it, here, there, back, always moving.

Van heard the door opening and closing and, expecting Marnie, was startled when she met Dale near the stairs. He was carrying a manila envelope.

He nodded. "I came to get a few things," he said coolly. "And to give you and Marnie a copy of a contract signed by Stef."

"What contract?"

"An agent's contract with me. Is Marnie around?"

"I'll call her," Van said, but there was no need. Marnie had entered.

Dale's nod to her was as cool as his toward Van. Marnie barely acknowledged it.

"I'll get my things," he said. "And leave you a copy of my contract. Next week I'll bring someone to help with picking up some of the paintings. I'll pick up *Feathers and Ferns* at the same time at the shop. We'll do a retrospective memorial showing of Stef's work early next month."

"You will not," Marnie said.

"I have legal authority to show her things, to sell them if I can. She signed a contract to that effect. The paintings can stay in your possession, and officially you'll still be the executor of her art estate, but I have the right to make all decisions concerning shows and sales. I advise you to read the contract, show it to your attorney if you're so inclined, and to accept that it is a valid contract."

He withdrew two paper-clipped sets of papers, thrust one at Van and the other at Marnie. "Now I'll get my things."

He strode past them, on the way to the bedroom. Marnie pulled the paper clip off and skimmed the contract without comprehending much of it. Then she looked at Van, who had not yet moved.

"Look at it," Marnie said in a low voice. "Skip the first two pages. Look at the last one."

Van turned to the last page, and after a moment she gasped. "Her signature!" she whispered.

"Or someone's." Marnie went to the counter and put the contract down on it, then poured herself a cup of coffee. A few minutes later Dale returned with a suitcase.

"Next Monday," Dale said. "I plan to get here by eleven."

"Don't bother," Marnie said. "That contract is a joke. And the joke's on you. She was laughing at you."

His eyes narrowed and his mouth tightened. "No point in trying to bluff about this, Marnie. Eleven, next Monday."

"Look at that signature, you fool." She opened the contract to the final page. "Just look at it. *Stephanie Markoff.* Then look at her signature on her driver's license, her marriage license, any other official document. She spelled her name *S-t-e-f-a-n-y* and her last name *M-a-r-k-o-v*. That paper doesn't mean a thing. Just her little joke." Marnie drew herself up straighter. "Now get out of my house and don't come back. If you ever enter this house again uninvited, I'll charge you with trespassing."

"We'll see about that," he said in a grating, mean voice. "My attorney will be in touch with you."

Van went to the door with him and slammed it shut as soon as he had left, before he had reached his car. When she returned, she went to the phone book on a small table in the kitchen. "I'm calling a locksmith. I want every lock changed on both houses, today if possible."

Marnie picked up the contract, sank into a chair at the dining table, and drew in a deep breath. "I need to see Ted Gladstone in the morning," she said faintly. He was her attorney in Newport. "I hope I'm right in that signature making the contract invalid." She began to read it as Van made her call to the locksmith. She had missed another clause, she realized. Her permission was needed, after all. It was followed by another clause: such permission shall not be unreasonably withheld. What did that mean legally? Ted Gladstone would know. What would be considered unreasonable if the rest of the contract was determined to be valid? Her head was beginning to ache and she leaned back in her chair, closed her eyes.

"Nine in the morning," Van said after talking to a locksmith. She sat down and picked up the contract and began to read it, her fury and frustration mounting with every paragraph. Done, she flung it onto the table and jumped up. "If it holds, he controls everything," she said angrily. "You'll be no more than a custodian."

"It won't hold," Marnie said faintly, her voice carrying no conviction.

Van leaned on the table, bracing herself with both hands.

"He killed her, Marnie. It may sound irrational, and Freddi will confirm that he was on the phone with her when . . . I don't care about that. I don't know how he managed it, but I know he did. And this is the reason. His motive."

After a moment Marnie nodded, as if reluctant to admit to anyone that she believed her daughter had been murdered. Or, she thought then, reluctant to admit that was her belief and she had done nothing about it.

Van jerked away from the table and crossed the room to the wide windows overlooking the spectacular vista of a deep-blue sea at rest that afternoon. Facing Marnie again, she said, "I'm moving back over here. Josh and I will move back into our rooms upstairs. I'll get some rods to secure the sliding doors and put chairs under the outside doors. We'll install a security system. . . ." She was thinking out loud, she realized, and became silent again.

"We'll all come back," Marnie said. "But he won't do anything until he talks to a lawyer. I'll call Ted and get an appointment for first thing in the morning."

"Will's hopeless," Van said. "He doesn't want any trouble and wouldn't know how to handle it if it bit him in the ass. Do you know that sheriff who looked into it?"

"No."

"Why would either of us?" Van said with a shrug. She paced the living room a moment, thinking. There was something else, not just immediate control of the art, she decided, something she had not read thoroughly, something about heirs and assigns. She returned to the table to read the whole contract more carefully. This time when she finished, she avoided Marnie's gaze. Did she know? Had that brief paragraph registered with her? They both had been so fixated on the immediate threat to the artwork, Marnie might have passed over that bit exactly as Van had done on her first reading.

If she had read it properly this time, she thought clearly, what it meant was that in the event of Marnie's death or incapacitation, Dale would automatically become the executor of all the work without having to consult anyone about its dispensation. He would in effect own it.

Van recalled an early meeting with him for lunch, to get acquainted, he had said when he called to invite her. He had been charming, flattering almost to the point of embarrassing her, before broaching the matter of Stef's art.

"She's like so many artists," he had said with a condescending smile. "No business sense whatsoever. I've seen it many times in very talented artists. Such artistic genius leaves little or no room for a practical side to develop, it seems, and even less for a business understanding to grow. Yet there is great commercial value in fine art. Leonardo's *David* can be had as a print, a poster, even a refrigerator magnet. It has real commercial value, you see, and that's not at all to demean the genius of the artist who produced it. Mozart's music, Picasso's art, Georgia O'Keeffe's, it all has commercial value. And so does Stef's. But she can't accept that for some reason."

"Wallpaper, greeting cards, wrapping paper," Van murmured.

"Exac—" He stopped and his face flushed. He sipped his wine, then said coolly, "A bit of advice, Van. Don't mock commercial enterprises. By the time you finish medical school and your internship, you'll have such a mountain of debt that you'll be paying it off for the next twenty years. Stef is making pennies with her art, and she could be making a fortune. She could be of enormous help to you, and eventually it will happen, maybe not in her lifetime, but her art will be appreciated and money will be exchanged. Why not while she's still young? While you're still in school? What's she waiting for?"

Van looked at her watch. "I have to go. Afternoon lab. Observing an autopsy. Thanks for lunch. It's been interesting." She left him at the table and felt his cold gaze on her all the way to the restaurant entrance.

The phrase *maybe not in her lifetime* repeated now in her mind. No! She looked across the table at Marnie, whose eyes were closed as she wrestled with her own thoughts.

"Marnie, do you trust Tony Mauricio? I know you said that Stef did. How about you?"

Marnie opened her eyes, looked surprised. "Yes. Of course, none of us really knows him, but yes. I do."

"I'm going to ask him for help. He knows about murder investigations. He'll know what we can do and how to do it. We can't let Dale get away with this! We won't!"

8

TONY AND DAVE McAdams both stopped working that after-noon when Van tapped on the door and entered at Dave's call that it wasn't locked. She took a step or two away from the door and said, "I'm sorry to interrupt you. I won't take more than a minute. Mr. McAdams, we—Marnie, Josh, and I—are moving back into the rear house, and we won-der if you have some scrap wood or something that would be suitable to put in the runners of those sliding doors and windows. You know, to keep them from opening."

Dave crossed the workroom to embrace her warmly. "Van, my dear, it's no problem at all. Sure I do. I'll go back and round up some dowels. Would you like a cup of coffee while you wait?"

"No, thank you. I really can't wait. I'm on my way to pick up Josh. There's something else, though." She looked at Tony. "We also wonder if it would be possible for you to come around tonight. There's something we'd like to discuss with you, if you have the time."

"Plenty of time," Tony said. "I'll be glad to come. I can bring the dowels with me, if you'd like."

She nodded. "That would be fine. Around eight-thirty? Josh will be in bed by then."

"Eight-thirty," Tony said.

"Thank you both," Van said. "I'll be on my way. See you later, Tony." She left it with that.

For a moment neither man moved. Then Dave said slowly, "I've known Marnie for more than forty years, and she doesn't scare easy. Now they need to secure doors and windows. I'll go rustle up those dowels." He was frowning as he headed for the storeroom. At the back door he hesitated, then turned to face Tony. "If Marnie needed me to close shop and come to do something, anything, this place would close down in a flash." Dave's frown deepened to a scowl. "I hope you get my meaning."

"Loud and clear." Tony understood that his job description, such as it was, had just changed.

VAN ADMITTED HIM that night. He was carrying an armload of dowels. "Come in," she said. "Marnie's up giving Josh a good-night kiss. She'll be here in a second. Let's leave all those here in the hall for now. Thanks for bringing them. We'll distribute them later."

After he put the dowels in a basket on the floor, she led the way to the living room and the furniture at the broad windows. A coffee carafe and cups were on the table there along with a manila folder.

The sun, low in the western sky, was hidden by fog at sea,

causing the fog to glow with an amber light, tinging the room with the same touch of pale gold.

"Nice," Tony said, nodding toward the windows.

Van nodded. "Sometimes, not often, but now and then I realize just how magical it can be. Too often we take it for granted. Let me take your jacket."

"This is okay," he said, draping his light Windbreaker over the back of a chair.

"At least let me pour you a cup of coffee," she said, smiling. "I'm supposed to play hostess for a few minutes. House rules or something."

She looked too tense and tired to attempt a smile, but it was a nice smile in spite of that. As she busied herself with the coffee, he thought the prod was for her to have something to do with her hands while they waited for Marnie rather than to fulfill her role as hostess.

"I didn't get a chance to express my sympathy at the memorial service," he said. "You have my deepest sympathy for your loss."

She nodded. "Thanks. I saw you there, of course. We appreciated your coming."

Since it had appeared that half the county had been there, he doubted that many individuals had registered with her at the time. Both she and Marnie had appeared to be shell-shocked, stunned by Stef's death.

Marnie joined them in the brief silence that followed Van's words. She accepted Tony's condolences with a silent nod, then thanked him for coming as she settled into a chair. "We have a problem that we hope you will help with," she said.

Van looked tired, but Marnie looked devastated, haggard even. She had lost some weight and had, to all appearances, given up sleep. Her hands were shaking.

She leaned forward and said quietly, "We both are convinced that Dale Oliver killed my daughter, Van's mother. He murdered her."

Tony felt himself tighten in an old familiar way that he did not welcome. "Tell me what you're thinking." Even he heard the difference in his voice, which had become more distant, colder, as if another persona had flowed into his body, ousting the friendly neighbor and local craftsman.

"From the day he first came here and saw how much art she had produced, how very fine it is, he'd been pressuring her to sell more, the recent things especially, and she wouldn't do it. He said as much the first day he came to the house with Freddi, just to meet her. That day I had the impression that he had been annoyed that Freddi was keeping some of her work on display when it wasn't for sale. I saw the change come over him when he saw how much work she had done, how good it was. I really thought that day that he had come to tell her the free ride was over, either price the work or remove it. I still think that's why he came out here. After he saw the paintings, the way he looked at her, his manner, something changed. I saw it happen. Then he said that she was sitting on a fortune. They were married less than a month later, and the pressure to sell was constant."

Tony held up his hand. "Wait a minute. Let's do this a different way. Why precisely do you think it was murder, not the accident the investigators decided it was?"

"For all her problems and faults, balance was never one of them," Marnie said fiercely. "She was up and down those stairs all her life. I don't believe she fell accidentally. And that oil painting they said she was taking down was not for sale. There were a lot of them that she was not willing to sell, and that was one of them. I don't know how he managed it, but he did it. I know he did."

"They said that Josh left a toy truck on the stairs, and he didn't," Van said just as fiercely. "He was never allowed to play on the stairs, or in the passageway between the houses. He hadn't even been here for a couple of weeks before that day."

"The news account said that Dale was at the other side of the house, at the windows here, on the telephone, when he and the person he was talking to heard her cry out. The officers must have looked into that, accepted it," Tony said slowly. He felt that both Marnie and Van were missing the point, that their dislike of Dale and his attempts to sell art, which was his business after all, was not reason enough to accuse him of murder. An intuitive belief reinforced one by the other that was contradicted by all other accounts was irrational.

"I can't explain that," Marnie said. "I only know that he did it. I don't know how he did." She lifted her coffee and took a sip, then set it down again. Her hands were no longer shaking, and she looked harder. "This started, this final act started, back in the spring. Dale put a price tag on all of her art in the gallery, including the pieces she refused to sell, and she was furious with him. She brought everything home and they had a fight over it. The marriage ended that day when he walked out, but she wasn't satisfied. She wanted revenge, to make him pay a price for what she considered betrayal." Marnie glanced at Van, who was as still as an ice carving, and as pale as one. "I'm sorry, Van, but this has to be said."

Van nodded. "I know. I saw what was going on."

"Yes. Stef let him come back. You were here that day when he came back. They fought that night and made up the next day. She pretended things were good between them for a time. He must have thought he had won, and he gave her a contract to sign. This contract." Marnie opened the folder on the table and brought out the contract, handed it to Tony. "Read it." She leaned back in her chair.

Tony read it carefully, then looked at Marnie, who was watching him. "Did she ever sign her name that way?"

"No. She was laughing at him, mocking him. When he tried to exercise that contract, she was going to pull the rug out from under him, make a fool of him, and then kick him out." Marnie drew in a breath. "It was cruel, and she could be cruel, but it was her way."

"You're speculating," Tony said. "That's conjectural, not conclusive. Did she say as much to you, admit that was her intention?"

"No. Tony, she was my daughter and I loved her more than I can say, but I'm not blind. I knew what she was doing. She had done similar things in the past. An eye for an eye. Payback for betrayal. I knew what she was doing, and that signature is all the proof I need to know beyond any doubt that I'm right."

Tony knew just as undeniably that it wasn't enough to justify calling it a murder and Dale a murderer. He turned to Van. "Why do you dislike him so much?"

"It probably boils down to the same basic reason. He has dollar signs instead of pupils in his eyes. A month or two after they were married, he asked me to lunch to get acquainted better." Van told Tony about it, adding, "He said that Leonardo's *David* had great commercial significance, something to that effect—"

Marnie interrupted, "He said *Leonardo*?"

"Yes. He said there were posters, prints, even refrigerator magnets. That's when I decided I had to get back to class. We were to observe an autopsy, and it seemed more appealing than continuing our conversation." Van directed her level gaze at Tony. "He doesn't know a thing about art, the difference between Leonardo and Michelangelo. All he sees is a product to exploit. His interest in me, charm, flattery, all an act, gone in an instant. He was as cold as a snake when he realized I had no intention of becoming his ally."

Still not enough, Tony knew, but he didn't press that issue yet. "Who was it on the phone with him that day? The news accounts simply listed her as his associate at the gallery."

"Freddi Wordling," Marnie said. "She's part owner of the art gallery, has been for more than twenty years, I guess, and Dale joined the company about four years ago when her former partner retired."

"Anything between her and Dale Oliver?"

Marnie and Van both shook their heads emphatically. "She was a good friend to Stef," Marnie said. "She understands artists and likes them, and she does know art. For the past twenty years she's carried Stef's art, most of it not for sale, and that was all right with her. No pressure to let go, nothing like that. She said when Stef was ready was time enough."

"The gallery makes something on the art it does sell, obviously," Tony said. "Do you know what that arrangement was?"

"Thirty-five percent," Marnie said. "That's pretty standard. I don't think Freddi makes much profit, and she isn't in it just for the money or she wouldn't show so much of Stef's work knowing it isn't for sale."

Van said, "Freddi called me when Dale put prices on everything of Stef's in the spring. She felt certain that no one here knew about that, and she was right. I told Marnie, and she told Stef."

"The beginning of the end," Marnie said bitterly. She

touched her coffee cup to her lips, put it down, and rose from her chair. "We've all let the coffee get cold. I'll dump it and put on a fresh pot."

Van stood to help her, and Tony rose also and went to the windows. It had grown dark as they talked, and the town lights were so obscured by fog that had moved inland that they looked like pastel smears of color against a solid-gray background. With his hands thrust into his pockets, standing slightly hunched, his thoughts were bleak. He knew what they wanted of him, and he suspected he could not provide it. Accusations, assertions, suspicions, two women who openly hated the man, a dead woman with the death labeled accidental already, and not a bare-bones bit of evidence. The contract was not enough, no matter what Marnie and Van thought. Stef had signed it. If Marnie's reasoning was correct, that Stef was making a mockery of it, laughing at Dale, prepared to renounce the contract later, it no longer mattered. Stef's little joke had seriously backfired.

Still at the window, he turned to ask, "Do you have an attorney you can confide in?"

Marnie let Van make the coffee and returned to stand near the chair she had vacated. "I already called him. I have an appointment in the morning." She drew in a long breath. "Tony, you've already guessed why we asked you to come tonight. We want you to look into this, find whatever the sheriff overlooked, help us prove that Dale killed my daughter."

Her gaze was steady as she waited for his response. He wanted to turn away, to leave now, to forget he had ever met her or Stef, forget that he'd had a mini-tour of Stef's work, that he had come to look on her as a likely genius, her work as brilliant. Reluctantly, he nodded.

Marnie bowed her head for a moment. "Thank you," she

said quietly, and returned to the kitchen to rinse the coffee cups.

"Did you receive an autopsy?" He kept his tone almost impersonal, a businesslike tone, dealing with a business matter.

"Just a summary," she said, bringing the cups to the table. She sat in the chair she had left, folded her hands in her lap, and watched him.

"Ask your attorney to get one. He'll know how to do it. That contract might require a bit of research to determine its validity. It could get tricky, and I don't know enough about it to make a guess as to how it will come down. Is there still some of Stef's art at the gallery?"

Marnie nodded.

"You should pull it as soon as you can, tomorrow if possible. The attorney might advise getting a court to issue a restraining order, something of that sort, freezing all the art until the contract business is settled, but you should have it all together in any event."

"I'll go tomorrow," Van said from the kitchen. "I'll take off in the morning as soon as the locksmith finishes here." She added to Tony, "We're changing the locks on both houses. He still has his key."

"Good," Tony said. "Will Freddi Wordling talk to me? One of you might have to put in a word with her first." He rubbed his eyes. "Ms. Markov, Van, listen for a second. I'm not licensed as a private investigator. I don't have access to the databases to do any kind of real checking on anyone's background. What I will be able to dig up will be superficial, available to anyone with a computer. And no one has to talk to me who doesn't want to, and if they do talk to me, they don't have to answer any questions or even tell me the truth.

Of course, Dale Oliver isn't going to cooperate with an investigation in any way, and he could file a complaint that there is harassment, invasion of privacy, or something else. I may be able to find out a little, but this wouldn't be like it was with a whole department and its resources backing me. Also, there may not be anything to find beyond what you've already told me. It could end exactly where it is right now with both of you convinced that he's a murderer, and no way on earth to prove it. People suffer from fatal falls daily, and absent an eyewitness, there's no way to disprove that it was accidental."

"You don't believe it was murder, do you?" Van returned with the fresh coffee and filled the three cups that Marnie had emptied and rinsed.

"I don't know enough to believe or not believe that it was murder," Tony said deliberately. "If that contract holds up, he'll get twenty-five percent of any sale. It's not a fortune. Not a multimillion-dollar windfall for anyone. Worth killing for? No prosecutor would accept it as sufficient motive for murder, I'm afraid. There's not enough to take to a grand jury."

"Twenty-five percent for him, thirty-five for the gallery— part of that would be his as a partner, and if we're talking about big sales, it could start adding up." Van glanced at Marnie, then continued, "That night when he came back, you heard him say that there was an exciting offer, something to that effect. When I came over here that night, he was going on about a sale of *Feathers and Ferns*. A dot-com millionaire from Seattle had seen it and wanted it and was willing to go high. Dale was calling it her breakout sale, one that would launch a lot of others. She would be the new hot item, a must-have artist, and so on. They were yelling back and forth and I left. But he had a significant sale in mind, a breakout sale, and she was saying no. I imagine he knew what he was talking about, that others would follow suit and want her work. Isn't that how it often works?"

It wasn't a real question and Van didn't wait for an answer as she said, "I know you saw the work in the studio, but she didn't show you what's in the other downstairs bedroom, did she? It's full of her work, too. Thirty years' worth of art waiting to be sold. He could be looking at an income stream for many years to come, with the prices increasing steadily."

Tony sat down again and picked up his coffee. It was good, he realized. He had pretty much ignored it before and appreciated it this time. "I assume she didn't rely on selling her art for an income."

"After Ed died and I sold the fishing business, I set up a trust for her," Marnie said without hesitation. "Stef never did care about money or regard it as a goal. She really couldn't have been trusted to manage money. She would have been as likely to give it away as not, or buy an airplane, or who knows what? She had a monthly income, enough to live on without worry, but not enough to be considered wealthy."

"In her name alone?"

"Yes." Marnie looked at her hands then as she said, "You probably already have heard that she had been married several times before Dale, and then there was Frank, Van's father. When we set up her trust fund, Ted, my attorney, made sure that the money would always be in her name alone—'irrevocable,' I believe he called it. It reverts to me, not part of her estate."

"Insurance? Life insurance?"

"Yes. Ten thousand. I was the beneficiary," Marnie said, looking at her hands. "She never changed that over the years."

Tony nodded. "Okay. I'll see if there's anything I can find out. No guarantees about success. I worked in homicide for twenty years, and there were a lot of times when we believed we had a murder case but without proof. A lot of times when the proof we could produce was not enough, not convincing. A gunshot is easier to deal with, you can trace the gun to an owner usually and go on from there. Same with a purposeful hit-and-run with a motor vehicle. Paint damage, certain dents, other clues lead to the car and the owner. That's how it works when there's a real murder weapon of any sort. But a fall called accidental doesn't have tangible evidence. It could have been helpful to have been at the scene, but two weeks later just adds to the likelihood that nothing can be proved. The investigators most probably won't even talk to me about it. Can you accept that this might lead to a dead end?"

"Will Comley was here," Marnie said faintly. "He'll most certainly talk to you, and I don't think he's quite the fool people seem to think he is."

She had ignored the question, and Tony didn't repeat it, suspecting that she would ignore it again. Tony thought she was right about Will. Tony had seen how he looked over those who had entered the bar the night Will had given him a history lesson.

"There's only one drawback to talking to Will," Tony said. "He'll know I'm looking into it and put two and two together. The news will spread. Do you care?"

"He talks," Marnie said, then surprised him by adding, "but I don't think he discloses anything official. He has his own line in the sand."

"I'm not official."

"From something Dave said I believe Will respects and looks up to you. I suspect he'd treat you as an official."

"I'll keep that in mind," Tony said, unconvinced both

that Will wouldn't gab out of school, and that he would treat Tony like anything but an outsider.

"Can you come to Portland with me tomorrow?" Van asked. "I can introduce you to Freddi and collect the art while you two talk."

"Is Dale likely to be around?"

"Maybe. I don't know. But I'd like to rattle his cage a little, let him know we're not buying anything he's selling."

Had Van grasped the significance of the other meaningful parts of that contract? Had Marnie? Neither one had brought them up, asked about them, and he wouldn't either. At least not yet. If that contract was determined to be valid, Marnie could protest every sale that Dale might try to make, resulting in endless fights, possibly court fights. She might lose each fight, but there could be costly delays, and few customers were likely to want to get involved in such family disputes. That possibility would depend on how the phrase *unreasonably withheld* was interpreted, and what kind of arbitration would be decided upon. But the possibility would have to be explored.

The other clause was more important. In the event of Marnie's death or incapacitation, Dale Oliver would be named executor of the art estate and have total control over all of it. Tony hoped her attorney would go into both clauses on the following day.

The trust reverted to Marnie, and the insurance, which no doubt she had paid for, had gone to her. Selling art was problematic. If Dale had simply wanted out of a bad marriage, he could have walked out. Tony knew all about that. There could have been another motive, he knew, but at this point money didn't seem to have been a consideration. If Stef had learned something Dale Oliver had not wanted revealed, it was likely to remain buried forever. Meanwhile, Tony decided, he would go to Portland, meet Freddi, and see where it led.

He nodded to Van. "I'll go with you." He finished his coffee, then stood. "Let's leave it for now. After you talk to your attorney and I talk to Freddi Wordling, we'll know a bit better where we stand. Now, I'll help you place those dowels where they belong, check out your windows and doors, and take off."

Marnie stood and said, "Tony, I don't expect you to donate your services. But I'm at a loss as to what a fair compensation should be. I'll need your guidance."

"If I start running up expenses, I'll let you know." He didn't believe it was going to happen any more than he believed there was a chance to prove Stef had died by murder.

9

TONY DROVE THE next day so Van could talk without being distracted by traffic. "Just talk," he said when they started. "Your life with your mother and Marnie, whatever comes to mind. I'll interrupt if a question occurs to me. Okay?"

"Free association," she said in a low voice. "That's what you want?"

"Something like that. Do you mind?"

"No, of course not. It's just a little awkward. I studied psychology for a while along with medicine, a double major, before I decided to concentrate on medicine. An assignment was to write three pages of free association, no editing allowed. What a mess of gibberish I ended up with." She laughed lightly. "There was probably a point to it, but I don't remember what it was, or I left before finding out."

"Why did you leave psychology?"

She hesitated, then said slowly, "I realized that what was

really on my mind was an attempt to understand Stef. I think most people go into psychology for a similar reason, either concerning themselves or someone close to them."

Traffic on the coast road was always heavy during the summer months. SUVs, campers, cyclists, family cars, formed long lines of slow-moving traffic for much of the distance before Tony would turn off and head inland. Now and then they had a spectacular view of the ocean, then woods closed in, while on the other side it appeared that the Coast Ranges mountains crowded the road, or bare cliffs gave way to more level land with a few houses or even fields now and again. Van saw little of it that morning as a long-forgotten memory surfaced, brought to mind by her words about psychology and her reason for abandoning it.

Free association, she reminded herself, and began to talk again in a low voice. "I rebelled, of course, as an adolescent. I had always adored Stef, someone exotic and exciting, unpredictable, who could be great fun or apparently forget me altogether for periods. Since there was always Marnie, more a mother than a grandmother, that was okay, too. Stef was this exotic woman who lived with us. Then I began to question everything about her—the men, her dyed hair, outlandish clothes, obsession about painting, everything. The studio door was kept closed, but sometimes she locked it, not often, but enough to make me believe she was painting pornographic pictures. I was convinced that she was making dirty pictures, and I watched like a spy for a chance to get inside and see for myself."

Van turned to face the side window and her voice dropped even lower. "I had a chance one day. I thought she had gone out and the door wasn't closed all the way, not latched. I just pushed it open a little and she was in there, sitting on the floor, crying. I couldn't see what was on the easel, but I saw her in that big shirt she always wore, cross-legged on the floor, crying. I backed off fast. I was pretty scared by it."

Van's pause was longer this time as she gazed blindly out the side window. "I heard her go out a few minutes later and I hadn't heard the studio door close. I went inside and looked. It was a nude study of a girl, me. Not idealized, not prettified, but me. I can't describe it, or how it made me feel, just in shock, I think. She saw things that I had not been aware of or had not let myself know or admit. I think it might have been a masterpiece."

Now she looked at Tony, at his profile, his hands on the steering wheel. They were in the Coast Ranges and she had not been aware of leaving the coast highway. "She was a great artist," she said quietly, "and her gift, her talent, a compulsion to paint the truth she saw, terrified her. That's what I realized when I was studying psychology, why I no longer felt a need to continue with it. I suddenly felt that I understood Stef. It had been at least five years since I saw that study, alternately feeling crushed or afraid, before my perspective switched. You know, like looking at the two vases that suddenly become two profiles, something like that. I think Marnie has understood for many years. That day when Stef rushed out, it was to buy a can of spray paint, black spray paint. The next time I was in the studio that portrait had been painted over completely. There was nothing but a black canvas."

Tony nodded. "That ability to translate raw emotion into visual art that forces others to share the same emotion must be extremely rare. She had a perfect eye for what is there, and for seeing the reality behind the facade. That could be a terrifying experience, to see that much and feel forced to convey it through painting."

"I think for most of her life she was hiding. Hiding her

real art, her fears, herself. All that makeup, those awful clothes, all an effort to hide herself. That's why she didn't want to sell most of it, it was too revealing. I think that so often after a painting or a series of paintings that were disturbing, frightening, she would turn to more conventional ones, as if trying to escape the compulsion. It became a pattern that never really worked for her."

Tony glanced at Van and again nodded. Hers was a remarkable gift, too, he thought, to have reached such an insight, such acceptance.

"Speaking of patterns," he said, "Marnie mentioned that she recognized the pattern of Stef's behavior with Dale. What does that mean?"

"She's had more experience with it than I've had," Van said drily, "but apparently when Stef was through with a man, there was always a big fight, then an apparent reconciliation, then she kicked him out. She had to be the one to give him the boot, so if it seemed that he was leaving of his own accord, there had to be the reconciliation first. I saw it a few times, but, as I said, Marnie's watched it many times. Dale was hubby number four," Van said with a shrug. "There were others on an even more temporary and less formal basis, but the pattern held every time as far as I know."

"You both believe she was following that script with him?"

"Absolutely."

Tony remembered the fleeting expression of satisfaction that had crossed Stef's face when Dale appeared the night Tony had dinner there. It had not been satisfaction over the strawberries. They had been a bit too tart, just as Josh had complained.

For several minutes neither spoke again, then Van began

to talk about her childhood, how Marnie took her to California at least twice a year to spend time with her father. "I expect the same will happen while I'm doing my internship," she said. "Marnie will bring Josh to Chicago now and then, just so he won't forget me. We all know how an internship will go, the kind of hours I'll put in, without much time off. I'll be sure to get an apartment where they'll have room to light." A wistful note was in her voice, as if she were already missing her child.

"I just hope he doesn't get sick," she said in a much lower voice, almost as if speaking only to herself. "It's so important to have your mother there if you're sick. Stef always was. For days on end she paid hardly any attention to me, but if I got sick, she hardly left me. She told me stories, spoon-fed me if I didn't want to eat, held me, rocked me, even when I was almost as big as she was. That meant a lot. It does, I think, to kids. Marnie was always there, a constant, but it was so special for Stef to be there when I was hurting, feverish. I wanted my mother, and she was there."

A memory surfaced and she became silent, recalling Stef's reaction when she announced at fifteen that she intended to become a doctor. "How could you bear it to be around people who are hurt, in agony, even dying? It might kill you to see and feel that much suffering!"

That was important, Van had come to know much later. Stef couldn't remove herself, be objective in the face of suffering. She felt it and couldn't escape it.

The silence in the car was prolonged when Van became silent.

Tony broke it by asking about Stef's art at the gallery. "Was any of it ever for sale?"

"Actually, Freddi sells quite a lot of it, most of it older work, but she's happy with the situation. She was very fond of Stef, and she also seemed to understand and have no trouble with her holding back the most powerful work."

"When she called to tell you that Dale had priced everything, did she know the reason, the insurance business?"

"I don't know what she knew. She didn't mention it. She was pretty upset, though, and seemed to expect Stef's furious reaction. I think that's why she didn't want to bring it up with her, but preferred to let the family do it."

They were nearing the outskirts of Portland and traffic had increased. "You know where we're to meet her?" Tony asked. "How to get there?"

"We're okay. We'll go straight into town, and I'll direct you when and where to turn. The café is a few blocks from the gallery in the downtown area."

The gallery was on Eighth near Broadway, and parking was a problem until he pulled into a parking structure within a few blocks of the restaurant. The plan was to talk over lunch, then go to the gallery, where Dale might be on hand. Tony was looking forward to seeing his reaction to the removal of Stef's work.

Freddi Wordling, sixty-one, was a little plump, had a pleasant, round face with a broad, generous mouth and many laugh lines at her eyes. She wore little makeup and had short raven hair without a trace of gray. She was married to a successful architect with a large firm behind him; they traveled extensively and were sailing enthusiasts. Tony had learned this on the drive from the coast.

"I strongly recommend anything with crab," Freddi said after the introductions. "I'm having crab salad and iced tea."

Van and Tony ordered the same, and Van said, "Marnie told me in no uncertain terms that this meal is on her. And I obey my grandmother without question."

"Beware the wrath of Marnie Markov," Freddi said, smiling. "How is she holding up?"

"It's been hard," Van said. "She'll be all right. Steel spine, all that."

The waitress served their tea and a basket of bread with butter. Van looked at her hands and excused herself. "I've been at the mercy of grubby little hands and want to wash mine."

After she left, Freddi studied Tony quite frankly, then said, "I warned Van that Dale is bound to object to having the paintings removed. Are you prepared to deal with that?"

"It's what I'm here for. Who's in charge at the gallery? You or Dale?"

"Fifty-fifty. He's business, I'm art director and manager. My former partner wanted to retire and found Dale, who was eager to buy in."

"Do you object to having the paintings taken away?"

She shook her head. "Dale said he has a contract that gives him the right to decide, however."

"That contract will be contested. Have you seen it?"

She shook her head again. "I learned about it a few days ago, the first I had heard anything about it. I haven't seen it."

"Let's wait for Van to go into that," Tony said. "I understand that you've been showing Stef's work for a long time."

"About twenty years. I saw some of her work that long ago in Marnie's shop, tracked her down, and talked her into letting me show it and even sell a few things."

"She wasn't showing it before that?"

"Only in Marnie's shop. We never had a formal agreement, only our word. That's why I find it disturbing if she signed a contract with Dale. I'd like very much to know the terms, what she agreed to."

"You know she had no insurance for the work at the house?"

"I know. I tried to talk her into letting me have an appraiser come over, but she dragged her feet and never did anything about it." Freddi picked up a piece of bread and spread butter on it, then put it down. "Mr. Mauricio, just who are you and what's your place in this? Marnie told me you used to be a New York City detective, retired now."

"True. Marnie and Van asked me to look into this matter for them."

"What matter?" Freddi asked bluntly.

"Neither of them believes Stef's death was accidental," he said slowly.

He watched her expression change from simple curiosity to disbelief, then a more thoughtful look. "They think Dale killed her?"

"Yes."

"Dear God!" she said softly, and looked away from him.

They remained silent until Van rejoined them, followed almost instantly by the waitress with their salads.

Then, with the salads as yet untouched, Freddi leaned forward and asked Tony, "How can I help you?"

"I told her why I'm here," Tony said to Van. To Freddi he added, "By answering some questions. Clear up a few details."

"Of course."

Over the next hour, eating their lunches as they talked, Freddi answered without hesitation the questions he had for her.

"You say the art at the house can be appraised and insured. Are you certain about that?"

"Yes. It would be minimal insurance since so much of the work has never been offered for sale, but there's enough that has been sold to form a basis for estimates, at the very least. I'm sure that some of it is museum quality, and a good appraiser is likely to come to the same conclusion. I also recommend that all the artwork be removed to a storage facility, one with good climate control. It needs to be sorted, arranged by date and or medium. Pastels with pastels, oil with oil, and so on." She looked at Van and added, "As executor of the art estate, it will be up to Marnie to decide, but if she decides to do it, I can send an art major out to help. It will be a big undertaking."

Van nodded. "I'm sure she'll want to do it. It's always been a worry, having it so haphazard the way it is."

"Did you know why Dale Oliver decided to price everything in the gallery a few months back?" Tony asked.

"No. He claimed that if Stef realized its value, she would come around. I doubted it, and her reaction justified my doubts."

"It wasn't so that he could get insurance?" Van asked.
"That's what he said."

"No. She knew she could get minimal insurance anytime she agreed to do it."

"Just one lie after another," Van said bitterly.

"Do you know anything about a possible big offer for the work titled *Feathers and Ferns*?" Tony asked.

Freddi nodded. "That's a real offer. Seventy-five hundred. Dale thinks it can go higher. The gentleman is a millionaire, based in Seattle, and he was quite taken with it. He's called a few times to ask when it will be available."

"Would that be considered a breakout sale?"

Her nod this time was a bit slower in coming. "I think so. It happens that way sometimes. One big sale and others want to get in on the ground floor while they can still claim to have recognized an emerging genius before anyone else. That sort of thing."

"Why were you willing to let her hold back so much of the most valuable art?"

"She needed to distance herself from it before she could let go," Freddi said, again speaking slowly and thoughtfully. "It's like that with some artists. Their art is too personal for a long time, but with distance, they often tend to denigrate it in some ways, to disown it even. That happened with Stef. Some of the recent sales were of work she refused to let go as recently as eight years ago, and then began to scorn. I knew it would happen again and again. I was willing to wait." Freddi looked down at her salad and said in a lower voice, "I thought we had time enough."

"Has Dale put prices on the art still in the gallery?"

"Yes. He said he had the right under the contract she signed. Now you tell me something about that contract. You said it would be contested. Why? What's wrong with it?"

This time Van answered. She told the terms of the contract, then added, "She spelled her name wrong, both names, Stefany and Markov. It had to be deliberate. We think she was mocking him, laughing at him."

"She had no intention of honoring the contract?"

"No. She was furious when he priced her work earlier, as you know. She knew he was lying. She wouldn't let it slide. You know what she was like."

Freddi nodded. "I was pretty upset when he came back from the coast after . . . after. They had loaded the paintings in the van and they were still there. He brought them inside, and a few days later, right after the memorial, he began to price and hang some of them. I found that upsetting."

Van pushed her plate back. "Freddi, when the dust settles, we'll want you to come out and decide what you want to show, to price it according to your own judgment. We don't want that arrangement to change. But it might take a long time for the dust to settle. I'm sorry."

"Thank you," Freddi said. "Her work should be shown, appreciated, enjoyed by the world."

"There's one more thing to go into," Tony said. "Van, this might be hard to take. You want to go wash your hands again?"

"I want to hear it all. Go on."

"It's that last day," he said. "The account I've read is that Dale was on the phone to you, Freddi, when Stef had her fall. Will you tell me about that phone call, what you could hear?"

Freddi closed her eyes for a moment. "He called me to say they'd be leaving in a few minutes. He mentioned that he was standing by the window checking out the weather and hoped it wouldn't start raining. He said they'd be bringing in about ten items, six charcoals and a couple of landscapes, the early ones, and something else that he didn't name. He sounded very pleased and said she was coming around, just as he had predicted. That she was in the studio selecting a recent painting or two. That's when I heard her scream and he said something like 'Jesus, what's going on?' I could hear his footsteps, then a door opening. He yelled her name and the phone banged down. They say he dropped it on the concrete. Everything was indistinct then, his voice calling her name. It sounded hoarse, far away, and I couldn't be sure of what he was saying or crying. It stopped when he ran back inside the house to call for help. I kept my cell on and used the office phone to call 911, but I didn't hear anything else from him. I was transferred to a dispatcher in Newport."

Van was pale but she did not move or utter a sound as Freddi spoke, or in the small interlude of silence that followed.

"Back up a second," Tony said after a moment. "You heard her scream. Can you describe that scream?"

Freddi looked puzzled, shook her head. "A scream. Loud, piercing, high-pitched. Just a scream."

"Like a scream in a horror movie? Something like that?"

"Yes. Exactly like that."

"Okay," Tony said. "Maybe we should wrap this up and go get those paintings. Is there a place to park at the gallery?"

"In the rear there's a loading area. The van is there, and if Dale's around, his car will be there. I'll go with you, if I may. I walked over, but I can guide you through our maze of one-way streets."

Van paid the bill, and after they collected Tony's car, Freddi directed him to an alley behind the gallery and to the loading area, where a silver BMW convertible was parked.

"He's here," Freddi said, her voice tinged with apprehension.

"Good," Tony said. "Let's get started."

They entered through the back door, to a hall with two closed doors and one open. Dale called out, "Freddi, there's something I want to . . ." He appeared in the open doorway and came to a stop.

"What are you doing here?" he demanded, glaring at Van and Tony alternately.

"I've come to get Stef's paintings," Van said.

"No way. I talked to my attorney this morning, and he said that contract's good as gold. She signed it and that's that."

"Mr. Oliver," Tony said pleasantly, "Van is going to collect those paintings, and you have two options. You can take a swing at me and I'll floor you. Or you can call the police and lodge a complaint, and while you're doing that, I'll ask Van to call the local newspaper and TV stations and get some media over here to witness a circus. Which game do you prefer? Go ahead, Van, start loading the car while Mr. Oliver and I decide what to do next. Ms. Wordling, you don't have to be part of this. Perhaps you'd like to go to your office and make yourself busy with whatever you have to do."

"I'll help Van with the paintings," Freddi said, and they left together for the front of the gallery.

"I'll charge all of you with larceny," Dale yelled, but he did not move from his office door.

"Okay," Tony said politely. "Meanwhile you should know that Ms. Markov has also consulted an attorney, and this matter is headed for the courts for a decision about the signature on that contract, which looks suspiciously like a crude forgery."

Dale flushed and said furiously, "She signed it! I watched her sign it."

Tony shrugged and went to the back door to open it as Van and Freddi came through carrying several paintings each. "There are a couple more," Van said.

"We'll wait," Tony said, keeping an eye on Dale, who had not moved. The flush had left his face, and his cheek was drawn so tight there was a visible tic.

It took only a few more minutes to be done. "Did you put the sheets over the artwork?" Tony asked Van, who nodded. She had brought them to cover the paintings on the way home. "Then we'll be on our way. It was a pleasure meeting you, Ms. Wordling," he said, glanced one last time at Dale, and walked out with Van.

In the car he said, "Help me find my way out of the downtown maze, and then I'd like to stop for a quick cup of coffee, if you're up to it."

"Am I ever!" Van directed him for the next several minutes, then asked, "Would you really have floored him?"

"Sure."

"I wonder, why didn't he call the police?"

"I imagine his attorney told him exactly what I expect Marnie's told her, that the contract is going to take a little time to research, and it's a toss-up about the outcome."

A few minutes later she guided him to a coffee shop she was familiar with, and seated with steaming coffee in place, Tony said, "Van, I asked a question last night that got no answer. Maybe you can give me one now. At least for yourself."

She nodded and waited.

"I asked if you know beyond doubt that Dale killed Stef, if there's no way to prove it, can you accept that?"

"Oh." She looked past him. "He would get away with it, wouldn't he? Handle her art, go on as if . . . as if he's innocent." She lifted her coffee, took a sip. "Too hot," she murmured. Finally she turned her gaze back to Tony. "I don't know. The thought makes me feel filthy inside. I just don't know. But, Tony, I do know this much. Marnie will never accept it. Never. She devoted her life to Stef, knowing and accepting everything about her, and she has a terrible guilt burden, feeling that she failed her in the end. She will never accept it. She would want to kill him herself. And, Tony, she's capable of it, killing him, if that's the only way to make him pay for it."

"Is that a little harsh?" he asked gently.

She shook her head. "I heard her talking in her sleep. Indistinguishable words, the way they are so often in sleep talking, but then she said quite clearly that she wanted to kill him. It shocked her awake. I heard her say it twice, and she meant it."

For a long time neither spoke again. Then Tony said, gazing past her at the street, "I've seen a lot of people so hurt, so angry and bitter at what they knew was an injustice, that they wanted to kill. Some of them did kill, but nothing was resolved. The hurt didn't go away, and they paid a horrific price, either through the law, or more often by what it did to them mentally, psychologically. Taking the life of another person is the ultimate expression of hopelessness and futility, and Marnie has too much to live for to admit to either. A lovely granddaughter she's immensely proud of and a delightful great-grandson she adores and will nurture to adulthood exactly the way she did you. She's not a killer, Van."

Van felt immobilized by his words, the gentleness of his voice, which, while somehow remote, suggested pain and a deep hurt of his own.

A silence persisted until the waitress asked if they would like refills. They both shook their heads and soon afterward left the coffee shop to start the drive home.

10

ALL TONY WANTED to do that late afternoon when he let himself into his apartment was nurse a long drink and stretch out his legs in the sun on his own tiny balcony. His hip had started to throb painfully, the way it did now and then, and his knee ached as if in sympathy. He had no more than taken out a bottle of bourbon when there was a knock on his door, and opening it, he found Chief Will Comley on the doorstep.

"Evening, Chief."

"Got a couple of minutes?" Will was wearing his mufti outfit that he called his uniform although it was not an official uniform. Mufti shirt and trousers, it was close enough.

"Sure. Come on in. Care for a beer? I'm having one." The real drink could wait, Tony decided. Beer would do for now.

"Don't mind if I do. Off duty until later, dinner pretty soon, guess a beer wouldn't hurt anything."

Tony nodded toward the small kitchen. "In here, and then out to the balcony and some sunshine for me."

"Portland's a bum deal in the summer, and winter, too, far as I'm concerned," Will said. "Too big, too noisy, too much traffic, too much bad air, too hot in the summer, too cold in the winter. Get spoiled, living away from it, out here where it's peaceful and quiet. Least most of the time."

Tony didn't comment as he brought two bottles of beer from the refrigerator and opened them. Will's way of telling him he knew where Tony had been that day? "You want a glass?"

"No thanks. This is good just like it is."

They went out to the balcony and Tony did stretch out his legs. It felt good. He made no attempt to fill the silence that lasted another minute.

"I talked to Dave a while ago," Will said. "He tells me you're taking a little time off to look into something for Marnie. She's a fine woman, Marnie. Friend to pretty near everyone along this coast. You know, people say I tell everything I know, but that's 'cause they're not paying much attention to what I say. Won't anyone mention that I ever talk about my business, my official business, I mean. Just town gossip that's already spread around a little, or something that folks really ought to know. Surprising how much people begin to tell you if you're known to like to gab, or you tell them what they already know."

Tony made a noncommittal grunt and waited. Will had just told him why he'd spread it around about Tony's background. Tony thought he might enjoy this elliptical way of divulging information.

"Some time ago, ten days maybe," Will said, "Van came in to the office and asked me to open a real investigation of her mother's fall. I told her there wasn't any need. Thought she was feeling a little guilty about her boy's truck being the cause of Stef's tumble. People feel guilty like that. You must have seen it plenty of times yourself in the line of work."

Tony nodded. "It happens."

"Well, today I had a little talk with Marnie, too. They both think the husband killed her. That Portland fancy dude. The medics, the rescue team, they've seen plenty of falls. Every year we get two, three tumbles off cliffs, off trails, you name it, people go where they have no business being and fall off. They said it was just like the others, accidental fall. Steep stairs, that little truck, her carrying a big painting so she couldn't really see where she was stepping. No mystery about it." Will took a long drink and set the bottle down on the floor. "But now Marnie's asked you to look into it, and it makes me wonder if there was more to it. You know? Just have to wonder."

Will glanced briefly at Tony as if waiting for a comment, and when none came, he said, "Anyway, seeing how both Marnie and Van think it bears looking into, seems like the least I can do is offer some help, if there's anything I can do to help you. Way I figure it, the only criminal experience I've had is to happen to catch a couple of kids breaking and entering once and hand them over to the sheriff. But you've had the experience. You know what they say, once a priest always a priest. Way I figure it, once a homicide detective always a homicide detective."

Knowing it was a long shot, against the rules, Tony said, "You could help by letting me have access to some databases."

"Marnie mentioned that. I've been thinking it over, and if you were authorized, no problem. You know how that goes. But if I deputized you, that would make you official. I don't have any budget for more than one deputy, and the job's already filled, though. Nothing in the rules against having a deputy who isn't on the payroll, far as I can tell, anyway."

"Deal," Tony said. "You were on the scene the day she took the fall, weren't you? Will you tell me about it?"

Will nodded, then told about it succinctly. He had been back by the motels when he heard the sirens. He got to his car, tuned in to the police calls, and learned that the sheriff was being called, that the rescue team was on the way, and he followed the medics to the house.

"They're trained to start an intravenous drip, administer CPR, you know the emergency things they do, but there wasn't any point this time. She was dead. Twisted in a way that suggested a broken neck, she'd bled from the mouth, open eyes, no pulse. She was dead, all right, but they can't pronounce anyone dead and had to wait for Doc Cranshaw to get there to do that. One of the medics hustled the husband inside and kept him there to wait for the sheriff. The dude was on his knees by her, calling her name, like that. Broken up. He'd been afraid to try to move her he said. Marnie came and I hustled her inside her house and stayed with her until Harriet McAdams got there a minute or two later. Then I went to her back door and watched that passage between the houses. No one was going up the stairs for quite a while, and I stayed up there until they did, then I went out to go to the studio when the others did. Closed door to the house, nothing upset or out of order, and I went back down. The doctor got there about then, and the medics got her body loaded on the gurney, and that's when they found the toy truck under her. She was barefoot. I figured that stepping on the little truck must of hurt and made her jerk and fall. The sheriff found the cell phone near that planter box on the side of the door. Dead battery by then."

"Another beer?" Tony asked.

Will nodded. "Guess I can be off duty a little longer than usual."

Tony went inside and brought back two more beers. "Was she fully dressed, except for bare feet?"

"Yes. Red pants, some kind of pink top. Just no shoes."

"What about the painting you said she was carrying? Where was it?"

"Looked like it went over the railing at the side of the stairs. The frame was broken and scuffed up."

"Was anyone taking pictures?"

"One of the deputies had a digital camera, and the other one had a big camera, probably a department camera. I didn't get a copy of the pictures, didn't think to ask for any, and would have had no use for them anyway. Marnie said her lawyer plans to get a copy of the autopsy. I guess pictures will be part of it."

"I hope so," Tony said without a lot of hope. If they had already decided it was an accident, no one would have done a lot to preserve anything from the scene that might serve as evidence.

He had a few more questions, but there was little more for Will to tell. He had not been inside when the sheriff asked Dale anything, had not been invited to sit in, he said with a shrug. He gave Tony the names of the medics, all of whom he knew pretty well, and the sheriff and his deputies' names. "If you want to ask them questions, I'd start with one of the medics, Johnny Ashford. I don't know about the sheriff and his crew, how likely they are to tell you anything."

From his tone and manner Tony thought it was probably not at all likely. Will finished his beer and heaved himself to his feet. "I'd better get myself off to dinner or Susan will send a search team. In the morning come by the office and I'll swear you in and we'll tackle that computer. If I knew how to do it, I'd just transfer information to your computer, but I don't. You have a laptop?"

"I have a laptop and I know how to transfer files. Chief, thanks. For your time, your assistance. It's been helpful." They were walking through the living room to the outside door.

"You think he did it?" Will asked as Tony opened the door.

"Just started asking a few questions, Chief. Let's give it a little time."

Will nodded. "Fair enough. Anytime before noon tomorrow." He held out his hand, and as they shook, he said, "See you in the morning, partner."

Returning to the balcony, Tony remembered what Van had said about changing perceptions: the vases suddenly become two profiles. Will Comley had suddenly changed from a town gossip to an officer of the law, a colleague.

Tony grimaced as he stretched out again and raised his bottle. He wished he had made that drink he wanted while he was on his feet, but he didn't want to get up again to get it. The beer would do while he considered Chief Will Comley.

He was not the fool he appeared to be with that unruly hair falling onto his forehead, his roly-poly body, amiability, and talkativeness. He was shrewd and noticed things and remembered them. Tony would keep that in mind. But whether colleague or partner, he still wasn't certain how much Will would talk, what he would say, and to whom. As for the question he had asked on his way out, Tony answered under his breath. "Sure, the son of a bitch killed her."

AFTER JOSH WAS in bed that night, Marnie and Van talked about the next few days. It would take a little time, Marnie said, to determine the validity of the contract, and it might end up in court. Also, getting the autopsy would take a little time. The sheriff would not be in a rush about it.

Marnie had called Freddi and now outlined the steps she had advised them to take. First, rent the storage facility. A number of them were in the phone book. "I think some people like to store furnishings, valuables, for months at a time while properties are vacant over the winter months," Marnie said when Van expressed surprise. "After we have the space, Freddi will send two young men, an art major and a practicing artist who always needs some extra money. They'll bring a truck and what she called spacers and some covers. After everything is secure and sorted, then the appraiser and insurance agent. She thinks it will take several days or maybe a week just to get things moved and arranged."

"I'll go to Newport and take care of the storage unit right after I drop off Josh at day care," Van said. "I think Tony wants to talk to you alone, so it will be a good time for that, too. He drained me dry today both going and coming back. I might have told him when I began to lose my baby teeth."

"Did he say a word about himself?"

"Nope. Mr. Ziploc Mouth, that's him."

Marnie smiled slightly. "I'm not surprised. He was limping pretty badly by the time you got here."

"I know. A hip injury sometimes flares like that, especially when the patient drives a few hours. He didn't say a word about it."

"Did he say what he wanted to look for tomorrow?" Tony had asked permission to come around and look over the houses, but Marnie suspected that Van was right. He also wanted to talk to her alone.

"Not a word," Van said. "It's impossible to even guess what that man is thinking. He could decide we're a couple of nutcases that he'll humor for a while, just to keep Dave off his back. I'm glad you got Tommy Gannet to come help move stuff today. I was afraid you'd tackle it alone."

"I no longer move furniture." Tommy Gannet was an amiable young man who lived with his mother, and who did whatever odd job needed doing, from yard work to gutter cleaning, hauling, moving, minor repairs . . . His mother had had a card printed for him that said NO JOB TOO ODD. That day he had shifted a few things from one house to the other. Now the paintings of the navy ships and the maps were on the wall in the rear house, and nearby was Marnie's favorite reading chair and lamp. Her bookcase was there, also. In her old bedroom, long used by Stef and whomever she was paired with at any given time, Marnie now had Ed's beat-up desk and her own bedspread and another chair she favored.

Although the rear house looked more like her home again, for days she'd had a persistent feeling of Stef's presence somewhere out of sight. A rustling sound, her running footsteps, a door opening, closing. Marnie had long been used to that feeling concerning Ed. She could not even guess how many times she had looked up from a book, started to share something she had read. Or felt him near her in bed. Never visible, never more than a feeling of his presence. Now there were two ghosts.

If Tony was thinking nutcases, she thought, at least he was right about one of them.

That night when Marnie went to her bedroom, she ran her fingers over the old rolltop desk. It had belonged to Ed's uncle, and Ed had kept it after Oscar died. He said it suited him just fine, just his style and period. Marnie got out her key chain with a key for the one drawer with a lock. For many years that drawer had not been opened, but that day, to move the desk, she had opened the drawer and removed the handgun in it. Now she put it back, but stood looking at it for a time.

Ed had picked it up somewhere and kept it with him. "A good old, simple six-shooter," he had said. "If you can't take someone down with six bullets, you might as well give it up and wave the white flag."

She closed her eyes remembering that day when he had shown her the gun. He had insisted on going up into the hills behind Newport, to an isolated, remote logging camp long since abandoned, where he had made certain she knew how to load the gun, knew about the safety, how to use it. Then he had been incredulous at her marksmanship. "I was driving a tractor by the time I was twelve," she had said. "Remember? Farm girl. And Dad taught us how to use guns. I'm better with a rifle, and okay with a shotgun. Dad was a gun freak."

Ed kept the gun in a bedside drawer until Stef began to toddle about and get into everything, and then it had gone into the locked drawer. He had carefully cleaned it, stored the bullets in a pouch, and wrapped the gun in an oiled cloth. The gun and the bag of ammunition were in a pale chamois pouch. It had not been taken out again until they moved the desk first to the rear house, then again to the front house, and now once more when the desk was moved back. The gun had never been registered, had no known history, and no one else in the family even knew it was there.

Marnie touched the pouch lightly, then sat on the side of her bed. It had been a shock to see it again so soon after the question posed by Ed's voice in her dream. He was within her, parts of him would always be with her, she thought then, but whose answer had it been? Her own or his? Was the gun her or his answer to the question?

She wanted Dale dead, never able to seize any of Stef's work for any purpose. She felt as if part of her daughter remained in everything she'd painted, that throughout her life her only means of communicating any of the things that had tormented and driven her had been through art. Each piece of her art contained something of Stef. For Dale to take it and exploit it for personal gain was an abomination. He had destroyed her physically, and by possessing and using her art he would destroy whatever was left if not of her soul, then something akin to a soul.

Was the gun the answer? She came back to the question and finally shook her head and stood. Not now, she thought, gazing at the gun for a moment before closing the drawer and locking it once more. She couldn't decide now. She would wait until the paintings were safe and secure, until Tony had a chance to do his work, but eventually she would decide, and if the gun was the only answer she had, she would use it.

11

AFTER VAN LEFT with Josh the next morning, Marnie went to the spare room that held the overflow of art. She knew what she was looking for, and although paintings were jumbled together, leaning one against another, filling the room to capacity with barely enough space for a path among them, she felt almost certain she knew where to look for the pair of paintings she was seeking. They would be close to a wall with others placed in front of them. Stef had treated some of her work that way, stopped working on it, then, as if it was too painful or too something, she hid it among the many paintings in the downstairs room. The painting with the broken frame was close to the hall door, and it seemed fitting that it was broken. The picture was of a wind-sculpted Sitka spruce, nature's bonsai, twisted as if in arthritic pain, with scant, miniaturized needles, but the size of the trunk indicated a great age. The spruce was growing on such a rocky ledge there seemed too little soil to anchor the roots. The painting was titled *Endurance*.

She passed it by and began to move other works. Few of the paintings in here were framed, and they were all sizes, small canvases eclipsed by large ones, in no order whatsoever. Few were dated, many untitled.

She found the pair she sought and pulled them out to the front, into the light. Gazing at one of them, she drew in her breath and nodded. The special beach that Stef had loved most of all. In the painting was a small beach enclosed by black basalt cliffs, higher and more forbidding in the painting than in real life, the way they must have appeared to a child. By each of the tide pools was a little girl, spectral, indistinct, surreal in the midst of stark realism. The tide pools were as finely wrought as a photograph, the glint of light on shiny rocks, sand caught in crevices, a bit of seaweed so real it might have been touched, felt wet. The little girl was translucent, impressionistic. Kneeling at one tide pool, squatting at another, sitting cross-legged, upright . . . All different, the same child in five different stances. Stef as memory, as ghost child, recalled by Stef the adult artist, then hidden away.

The beach was the beach of Marnie's nightmare. The child was Stef of the nightmare. Marnie shuddered, gazing at the painting. It had the quality of prescience, ghost child eternally racing from tide pool to tide pool.

Searching forever, she thought, a futile, endless search, never satisfied. The companion piece was titled *Treasures*, but she felt now that it had been done in an effort to answer the question *What are you searching for?* It was beautifully done, a bottomless treasure of tide-pool life, but it didn't answer the question, and the ghost child would spend eternity searching.

Marnie stood, transfixed by the painting of her dream child, her nightmare child, until she became aware of the sound of the doorbell. She jerked as if from a dream, backed out of the room, and closed the door.

Tony had arrived.

"Good morning, Tony," she said, admitting him to the house.

"Good morning, Ms. Markov."

She held up her hand. "Please, just Marnie. We're not used to such formality around here. What can I do to help you?" As she spoke, Tipper sniffed him, then wagged his tail in a belated greeting.

"I'd like to wander about a few minutes, if that's all right. Get the feel of the house, see the storage room with the rest of her paintings, just look around and then ask a few questions. I don't want to take up too much of your time."

"Time's not a problem," she said with a shrug. "Take as long as you like. I'll give you the key to the studio outside door, and when you finish wandering, we'll have coffee. Go wherever you want." She handed him the key. "Stay, Tipper," she ordered, and the little dog sat at her feet.

"Thanks." Tony started with the upstairs of the house, looked into the two bedrooms without entering, glanced inside the bathroom and smiled slightly at the array of ducks and boats lined up on the edge of the tub. The door on the opposite side of the wall was to a closet for storage. It was crammed with art supplies, framing material, canvases . . . He closed the door and went on to the studio. The floor was vinyl, as he had known, paint-spattered and stained, but clean and dustless. *Ladies in Waiting* was still on the easel, apparently untouched since he had last seen it. He continued on through the room to the outside door and out to the passage. The floor was painted with heavy green deck paint, as were the steps down. The treads were fairly wide and it wasn't as steep as Will Comley had made it sound. Railings and newels were the same green. Looking out toward Dave's house, he could see only the uppermost part, visible through the greenery of shrubs and trees. Unless Harriet McAdams had been on the roof, nothing that happened here could have been seen by her.

He started down the stairs, stopped to examine a few chipped spots on the rail close to the top of the stairs. From there, looking down, it appeared that the stairs had been an afterthought, ending on a concrete walkway a little too close to the door of the house. He continued down and at the bottom looked at the door, a raised doorstep, the end of the stairs. A large redwood tub of plants was to the right of the door, but not enough room had been available for a matching tub on the left.

Her body, twisted and broken, must have been visible from the house door when it was opened. And the cell phone was dropped. Visualizing the scene, he saw Dale opening the door, seeing his wife's body, dropping the phone. Why then hadn't it been fully visible? Why off to a side far enough not to be noticeable at once? The only way it could have ended up by the tub, nearly three feet from the door, was if it had been thrown there. He shrugged and went around the stairs to where, from the chipped railing above, it appeared that the painting had gone over the side. More concrete, but nothing to indicate now that anything had ever fallen there. If there had been paint chips, they had been blown away or swept away.

He returned up the stairs, back to the studio, locked the door behind him, and went down into the house. He saw that Marnie had gone out to the deck, and he continued into the hall, to a big master bedroom, Marnie's room now, he guessed, and did not enter, but did enter the room across the hall.

"Jesus Christ!" he said under his breath, surveying the clutter of paintings. A lifetime of paintings was in the room. One in the forefront held his attention a long time. It was in the mode of *Feathers and Ferns*, what looked like a bottomless collection of starfish, sea urchins, crabs, tiny fish, sand dollars, other tide-pool life, all meticulously rendered, merging, morphing one into another in a way that at first glance suggested a surreal blending of marine colors, sea green, pinks, tans . . . It was titled *Treasures*. The painting next to it was titled *Searching*. A child, a searching child, and what she found, he thought studying them. They belonged together, that much was clear, and Tony decided that if and when they went on sale, if he could afford them, he wanted them both. He made a note to himself to tell Freddi he wanted them.

Finally he turned his attention to the picture with the broken frame. It was in oil, beautifully rendered, realistic enough to suggest that the tree was suffering. Even in oils she'd had that ability to share with a viewer whatever she had felt about her subject. Pain, suffering, patience, endurance, they were all there. The painting itself apparently had not been harmed by the fall. It could be reframed. He could see no traces of green on the frame, but that meant little, he knew. A good forensics lab might well find such traces. Something had hit the rail hard enough to chip it, and the painting had been found below. No mystery. He shrugged, left the room, and closed the door behind him. He returned to the living room, through to the deck to join Marnie.

"I brought out the coffee," Marnie said. "It's nice out here this time of day. We seldom get much wind up here, but later, when the sun gets lower, it can be too hot. Coffee, and in a few minutes, I thought we might want a sandwich."

"Marnie, you don't have to play hostess for me," Tony said. "Relax."

She laughed and nodded. "I guess that's how I sounded, didn't I? Just all polite and Sunday-school nice. But I do want to make some sandwiches. It really is lunchtime, if you didn't notice." She suspected he had no idea that his wandering about a little had lasted an hour. She poured coffee and motioned for him to take one of the mugs that they always used out on the deck. She believed they held the heat better than regular cups.

"I saw my attorney, as you know," she said. "Like you, he said it's going to take a little research about that contract and it might end up in court. He'll get the autopsy as soon as he can. And if Dale or his attorney gets in touch with me, I'm to refer them to him." At Tony's nod, she continued, and told him what Van was up to, their plan for the storage of the art.

"Good," he said. "That's a valuable collection that should be protected."

"Now it's your turn. Your questions."

"Just a few. Was Stef in the habit of going barefooted in the house?"

"No. Why?"

"She was barefoot that day. Did the sheriff go into her room, look around? Do you know?"

Marnie nodded. "He asked me to go with him, see if there were signs of anything out of order. It looked about like it always did when she was planning to go away for a few days. Clothes on the bed, not packed yet, but nothing really out of order."

"I didn't see that painting, the broken one, up in the studio the day I had my mini-tour. Where was it kept usually?"

"Downstairs," Marnie said promptly. "I can't imagine why she took it up only to take it down again. It's an early painting, from when she was still interested in using oils, twelve or more years ago." Before he could ask another question, she said, "That was her pattern, too. She claimed not to be finished with a work for a long time, then moved it downstairs."

Marnie hesitated. "Sometimes she put the new one behind others, almost as if to hide it. Others, those out front, were mostly conventional works, and if they were sold, usually it was all right with her because by then she had rejected them, renounced them. But the ones she put in the back, deliberately put behind others, seldom were." She hesitated again, then said slowly, "She was afraid of being rejected. Any area where it meant a good deal to her, her husbands, her art, anything, as long as the tie was still strong, she feared rejection and avoided it by being the one to end a relationship, or by not turning loose of her work. Later, it mattered little to her what happened to it. She scorned those who bought work that she had rejected as not being good enough."

"Did she also have the pattern of getting revenge on the men she broke with?" He watched Marnie closely, not knowing if he had stepped over a line with her.

"No. But they seldom did anything she felt was outright betrayal. If she sensed the end of a relationship approaching, she was the one who ended it. It was that simple. I think I've made her sound like a monster, but she really wasn't. She had a habit of falling in love repeatedly, and it never lasted. Perhaps she was forever looking for the perfect relationship, the perfect mate, and thought again and again that she had found it. Perfection, the ideal in her mind, was not humanly possible. Not in her art, not in her life, but she kept looking for it, kept thinking this time she had grasped it."

"Okay," Tony said. "When you talked to your attorney, did he go into what might constitute a reasonable withholding of permission to sell a painting? What that arbitration clause means?"

Marnie felt a mild surprise that Tony had remembered it. "He said that it would be decided by an arbitrator, and most often that would be someone well schooled in the field in dispute, or a small committee of like people, knowledgeable people in the field. He also said that it would be hard to prove any legitimate offer was not a reasonable one."

With those words he had dashed any hope she'd had of making it so costly and time-consuming for Dale to start selling the paintings that he might have been tempted to give it up.

"One more thing," Tony said. "After the breakup of a relationship, did she ever maintain a friendly attitude toward her former partner?"

Marnie shook her head emphatically. "She put them in storage, exactly the way she did with her art that she rejected. Out of sight, out of mind, scorned." She paused briefly. "I don't know how she would have been able to work with Dale, knowing he was a partner in the gallery, that he would profit from any sale they made. She might not have been able to keep her work in the gallery after that. Is that what you're getting at?"

"I don't know what I'm getting at yet." But Tony did know that if that had been the way it had worked out, it might have provided Freddi a reason to back up Dale's story about the phone call, what she heard. How anxious would she have been to keep Stef's work exclusively in her gallery? Either party could have backed out of the contract by writing a letter to that effect, and if Stef had lived, it appeared that she had intended to do just that. Would she have backed out of the gallery at the same time? Just something to keep in mind, he decided.

Tipper had been close to Marnie, but now rose, stretched, and went inside the house.

"The sun's getting too warm for him, isn't it?" Tony said.

Marnie nodded. "Time to go in. Time for lunch. And you can tell me what Will said. I believe he was going to pay a call on you."

Tony grinned as they gathered up mugs and the carafe. "At your bidding. As of this morning, I'm his deputy with access to certain databases. Why am I so sure that you're not surprised?"

Marnie smiled and did not respond.

12

AT A FEW minutes after six that late afternoon Tony pushed his chair away from his kitchen table, closed his laptop, and stood, grimacing a bit with the motion. He was cramped from an uncomfortable chair, the wrong height of a table to serve as a desk, concentrating too long on the monitor screen, just cramped. He stretched and eyed his apartment with disfavor. Cramped, just like him, with hardly enough space to do anything but the absolute essentials. Minimum cooking space, tiny living room, bedroom without an inch to spare. As soon as the summer people left, he thought, as he had been thinking more and more often, back to house hunting. Or at least find a bigger apartment, one with a view. From his back porch he could see a few trees and houses. What was the point of living on the coast if the view could have been from any city window in the world?

He smiled wryly at his own use of the term *summer people*, considered mixing a drink, decided against it, and instead headed for the door, for a walk down to the little isolated beach, the sun-drenched ledges made for sitting. It was a good place to think and watch the play of light on water, breaking waves, compare it to the painting by Stef.

He missed his old partner, Manuel Martinez. At this point they would be talking about every aspect of this dismal affair. He could imagine all too clearly what Manuel would be saying along about now. "It's a fuckup. We ain't got no case and we ain't gonna get one. He's home free. Let's take him for a little ride and beat the shit out of him and move on." Justice served in a fashion, as much justice as was likely to come out of their investigation.

Tony knew enough about Dale Oliver to write a short, credible biography. And not a damned thing that he had learned would be helpful, he added to himself, crossing the access road to the motels. He started down the twisting path through the rocky cliff.

That day the tide was lower than it had been on any previous visit. More tide pools were exposed, more beach, but he knew it was the same beach that Stef had depicted, the same surround of black cliffs. He picked out his own ledge, sat down and stretched out his legs, leaned back, and began to sort the facts he had learned about Dale Oliver.

Son of Delmar and Mary Oliver. There was one sister. Delmar had been an engineer at CBS radio for twenty years; Mary had worked in a frame shop. So Dale had been exposed to art of some kind at an early age apparently. Home in Newark, school in New Jersey, eventually an MBA and a job as business manager at a Ford dealership in Newark. No criminal record, a few driving infractions, nothing serious. Married four years, divorced. Mother died when he was in his early twenties, father died five years ago at the age of eighty-four. Dale's sister apparently had been a beautiful girl, Miss New Jersey, had gone off to Hollywood and a minor film career, then nothing more about her.

Tony didn't know how much the pair had inherited from their father, but it appeared that it had been enough that Dale had quit his job and a year later showed up to buy into the gallery in Portland. Now he was heavily in debt, apparently living high on plastic.

Later, Tony had already decided, he would find out a lot more than he had already learned. He had always been a careful investigator, pursuing every lead, following up on every hunch, every clue, no matter how irrelevant it first seemed. He had been a meticulous planner with every detail in mind before he moved in, and he had rarely ever been wrong, even if convictions had not followed. Also, he knew where the lines were that he should not cross, and he knew how to cross them in his data searches, and he would no longer hesitate to take those steps that would put him on the wrong side of the lines.

With what he had gathered already, little more than background and conjecture, he was not even tantalizingly near having enough to take to the next level of a district attorney or grand jury. Even if he had the resources of a major police department at his command, he doubted that he would ever have enough. He had the familiar infuriating and hopeless feeling that it was dead end, had been dead end from day one, and nothing he learned would change that. Time to take the guy for a ride and beat the shit out of him. Move on.

He sometimes wondered if taking that kind of action

would have helped, would have assuaged the bitterness and hopelessness that had overcome him again and again. He no longer knew why he had stayed on the job as long as he had, how he had kept moving on knowing the system was broken and that nothing he did was going to fix it. Even when he and Manuel had gathered enough evidence, what had been irrefutable proof to make their case, there were the plea bargains, the deals behind closed doors, years of appeals, missing witnesses, or those who had died. Again and again the guy was home free.

He had not wanted to get involved ever again, he thought bitterly. All he wanted to do was work with his wood, make things, watch the waves break, sleep at night. He especially did not want to dwell on any of this; inevitably it led to that last day, seeing that terrified kid with shaking hands, holding a gun pointed at him. Watching the gun waver, the kid as still as a statue, listening to Tony, wanting to believe, desperate to believe it was going to be okay, he was going to be okay. Then the cowboys arrived with their guns drawn.

Tony shook himself and closed his eyes. *Not again. Jesus, leave it alone! Let it be. It's over, done with.*

He was startled by the sound of someone coming down the trail, and he pulled his legs back, prepared to stand, yield the beach to the newcomers. No one had ever come down before while he was here, and he had assumed that few others knew about this little hidden place, few others found their way down. He regretted that he had been wrong.

He was more surprised when he heard Van's voice. "Josh, stop that. Slow down or you'll fall." She was laughing.

Josh came around the last twist of the path and stopped when he saw Tony, then rushed forward again. "Hi," he said, dashing past him and onto the beach. He was already at the first tide pool when Van came into sight.

"Tony! Oh, dear. I'll gather him up and head down to the public beach, leave you some privacy."

"Please don't. In fact, that was going to be my line."

"We can both stay," she said. "It's one of our favorite places when the tide's going out, like now. Josh loves it, and I always did, too. I promised him that at the next low tide we'd come if it wasn't too dark."

"It's the beach Stef painted, isn't it?" Tony said, waving toward the tide pools, and Josh rushing from one to another, just like the memory child, the spectral child of the painting.

Van nodded, made her way past him, and chose a rock at the end of the cliff, next to the shore, and sat down. "Marnie used to bring me here, and before that she brought Stef. Now it's my turn with Josh. Our little secret beach, that's what we used to call it. We made up stories about it. Pirates landing at night to bury treasure, shipwrecks with survivors for us to rescue."

"Spies sneaking ashore?"

"Oh my, yes. And sea monsters. Mermaids with magic lutes. I had no idea what a lute was, but the mermaids had them anyway." She laughed softly. "Our secret beach, like a secret garden where imagination can take off."

"Mom! Come on! Look!" Josh yelled, waving his hands.

"Speaking of monsters," Van said, smiling. She got up and ran lightly on the packed sand to where Josh was by a newly exposed tide pool. They both knelt by it.

Tony watched them for several minutes, mother and child sunlit by the lowering sun, their black hair shining, both of them beautiful. Then he was watching only Van, her grace, her beautiful body, the way she gently held a crab, then put it back in the water. She laughed with Josh at something and rose from her kneeling position. With her head back slightly, her slender body a silhouette against the bright sky, she could have been posed as an idealized woman, strong, self-confident, utterly feminine, and beautiful.

Sitting in the car, listening to Van's voice as she talked about her childhood, about Stef and Marnie, about school, had stirred something in him, he realized. Now, seeing her at play with her child, hair shining in the lowering sunlight, made him realize how much he had been thinking of her, how much he had noticed and recalled over and over.

Abruptly he rose, and after one last look, he began to pick his way back up the trail to the road above. "Forget it," he told himself sharply. He also told himself that the ache somewhere deep within him was hunger. He'd had no dinner and it was getting late.

MARNIE HAD WAITED until after dinner to tell Van about her phone conversation with Freddi that afternoon. When Van and Josh came in from the little beach, he had to get in the tub immediately, Van had said, and finally with Josh in bed, Tipper there with him, Marnie and Van sat with their coffee.

"Freddi will send her two young men over tomorrow," Marnie said. "I told her they might as well stay here in the front house. They might not find anything else on such short notice. And it will be convenient for all of us. She vouches for them absolutely, and they'll bring sleeping bags. They've both done work for her, and one of them at least is awe-struck, according to her, by the prospect of handling Stef's work in any way."

"Sounds good," Van said. "I'll lead them over to the place I rented and let them go at it."

"She said something else quite interesting. A man named Joe Werner, the dot-com millionaire, called her today and said he'd like a sneak preview of the retrospective going up next month. He'd like a chance to pick out the three that he'll want and ensure that no one else bids on them."

Van was mystified. "What does that mean?"

"That's what I said. It appears that he told Dale that he wanted three, *Feathers and Ferns* definitely, and two to be decided when he has a chance to see the other recent paintings. One is for the corporate offices, one for a home he's building, and one for a downtown-Seattle condo. Freddi knew nothing about it until he called. Mr. Werner told Freddi that he was willing to go to thirty thousand for the three, two not yet chosen."

"Good God! Stef wouldn't have agreed to such a deal! Her recent work? No way!"

"Of course she wouldn't," Marnie said quietly. "She wasn't given the chance to turn it down."

"What did Freddi tell him?"

"She stalled. Told him that we had to have an inventory done, arrange for insurance, just the truth I guess. Then she called me. You were out collecting Josh when she called here."

Van did the numbers in her head. Seventy-five hundred was what Dale would have made as agent, plus whatever his share of the gallery proceeds would have been. But you don't kill someone for that kind of money, she told herself. Slowly she said, "It wasn't the immediate money, was it? He saw the door opening, other sales following."

Marnie nodded.

His story, if questioned about it, would be that Stef had agreed. He had said as much to Freddi on the phone that day, Van remembered. He had said she was coming around, he had sounded pleased and happy. Who could disprove it? His word against what Van and Marnie knew to be the truth. It would appear to be just a family feud over control of the art, control of money, greed. Van bit her lip and did not make that argument to Marnie, who probably had come to the same conclusion already without any prompt.

Van jumped up and paced through the room, touching a chair, a lamp, whatever was in her path, thinking, seeing nothing she touched. For a moment Marnie was stunned by her action, so like Stef at that moment, she thought. So like Stef.

It might all come down to that damn contract, Van was thinking. If some damn judge, one who had never met Stef, had no way of knowing what she had been like, and, uncaring, decided in his judicial wisdom that she had signed the contract, and if she had been playful about her name, it made no difference, it was nevertheless her signature, and the contract was in fact valid. Dale would win it all. Tony's persistent question rose: can you accept that? *God damn it! No!*

She stopped moving and looked at Marnie, who was watching her. Slowly she crossed the room and went to her grandmother, where she knelt and took her hand. "Marnie," she said softly, "if Tony can't find the proof, if there's no way to let the law take care of it, we will. You and I together, we'll see to it that he doesn't get away with it."

Marnie closed her eyes. How warm Van's hand was holding hers. She began to stroke Van's hair. It was soft, resilient. Silently she said to herself, *No, my darling. You have*

142

a wonderful future before you. Those beautiful hands will touch so many people, heal just by their touch, and you have a beautiful child of your own. Whatever comes will not involve you. She pressed her granddaughter's head to her breast and stroked her soft hair.

13

By Friday that week Tony knew a lot more about Dale Oliver than the superficial information his first searches had provided. He knew that periodically Dale faced the serious consequences of lapsing in credit card payments, the lease payments on the BMW he drove, and even his rent. He had been an adept credit card juggler apparently, signing up for new ones with lower interest rates as often as possible, but that was no longer a possibility for him. His credit rating had dropped too low. Twice it appeared that an influx of new cash had arrived just in time to avert what no doubt would have been catastrophic to anyone living on image.

Tony had tracked down Dale's sister, whose film career had consisted of several commercials. He found two of the commercials on the Internet and knew why a film career had never been in her future. Beautiful, with a good voice, but a wooden body. She couldn't act. Married young to a producer, divorced, married again to a history professor at UCLA, three children. Nothing, he decided, and gave up any further poking into her past.

But something about Dale had to be real beyond his debts. A lot of people lived on plastic, not a crime in modern society, rather it might even be considered the norm.

Where had he gotten cash on at least two occasions? Gambling? Lottery? Selling possessions? "Put on a mask and held up a bank," Tony muttered, and it was as plausible as anything else he had come up with. With a real ongoing investigation, he brooded, all the possibilities would be checked out. Pawnshops, gambling tipsters . . . Had Dale bought pricey cuff links that he had since sold? Gifts to Stef? Sold. The Rolex sold, replaced by a fake? On impulse he called Freddi Wordling in her Portland gallery.

"Tony Mauricio," he said when she answered his ring. "Are you free to talk a minute?"

"Why don't you give me your number and I'll call you back as soon as I can."

He gave her the number, leaned back in the uncomfortable chair to wait. Leaning back didn't help, and he rose and walked to the sink, back, out to the balcony, back. When she called in five minutes, he took the call on the balcony, where he could see houses and trees.

"Just a couple of quick questions," he said as if assuming his right to ask, and her duty to answer. "I don't want specifics, just a general idea. Have the gallery profits increased since Dale joined?"

She laughed. "That's an easy one. No. In fact they're down, but so is the rest of the economy."

"Did your former partner have an audit when he put his share up for sale?"

"Yes, of course."

146

"Have you had an audit since then?"

This time her response was delayed. At last she said, "No. Why do you ask?"

"Was auditing part of a routine in the past, annual audits, something of that sort?"

Again she was slow to respond. "Tony, I asked why you're asking about audits. What are you getting at?"

"Curious. Do you know if Dale Oliver is a gambler?"

"For heaven's sake," she said, her tone suggesting impatience and irritation. "What are you getting at?"

"I'm fishing," he said honestly. "Freddi, have you considered having an audit done, an outside audit? Would you consider it?"

Slowly she said, "I don't like the implications you're making. I haven't considered such an audit. The business manager is assumed to keep the books in order, as was always the case in the past. I don't know if I would consider bringing in an outsider, what the implication there is. I don't want to appear to be making an accusation based on nothing but a drop in business, which I can attribute to the economy. I think I'd like to talk this over with my husband."

"Good enough. Mind you, I'm not making an accusation, but I am trying to close some gaps in what I know, no more than that. Thanks, Freddi."

She would do it or not, he thought after disconnecting. If yes, it might shake Dale a bit even if nothing was out of order. If not, no harm done. Except Tony still wouldn't know how Dale had pulled himself from the edge a few times as he had done. Tony returned to the kitchen table and eyed the laptop, then reseated himself. Might as well complete the picture, he decided, find out something about Dale's father, and how he had accumulated enough of an estate as an engineer at a broadcast network to let his spendthrift son buy a partnership in a business with his inheritance, if that had in fact been the case.

He Googled Delmar Oliver and was surprised at the large number of entries he found. He started a new search for information.

He was concentrating again on his monitor half an hour later when his phone buzzed.

Van was on the line. "Tony, I want to see you. Right now if it's possible. I just picked up the autopsy from the attorney's office. We need to talk."

"At your house?"

"No. I want to talk to you alone. Can I come over to your apartment?"

He glanced at his tiny kitchen, shrugged. "Sure. I'll be here." He gave her his address and she said five minutes.

He put away his laptop and started a pot of coffee. She was prompt. She glanced over the apartment but made no comment, and he brought out coffee mugs and poured for them both.

"Out there," he said, motioning toward his small balcony. He had put an end table between the two chairs. At least they didn't have to put mugs down on the floor.

"I already looked through it," Van said, taking the autopsy report from her bag, handing it to him. She held her coffee in both hands as he read it.

It was thorough, a good autopsy, better than he had expected, he realized, and reminded himself that even in these small coastal communities, professionals were doing professional work. He didn't linger over the three pictures that were included. When he was finished, he put the report on the table and lifted his own mug.

"I was hoping it would prove that she was already dead when he pushed her down the stairs, or threw her down,"

Van said in a distant voice, an impersonal voice, as if speaking of a stranger. "She wasn't. She was alive, the bruises and abrasions demonstrate that." She was gazing straight ahead, where nothing but fir trees and houses were to be seen.

Tony had hoped the same thing and agreed. She was alive when she went down the stairs. Dead people don't bruise, suffer cuts and scrapes that bleed. There was no mention of a bruise on either foot, and there would have been, he felt certain, if there had been one. All that meant was that she had not stepped on a toy truck. It didn't change anything. No alcohol or drugs had been involved. All her injuries were consistent with a fall down stairs and hitting a concrete surface. A head trauma would likely have proved fatal, but a broken neck that snapped her brain stem was the immediate cause of death.

"We'll never be able to prove a thing, will we?" Van asked in that distant voice, gazing straight ahead at nothing.

"I don't know. But that report doesn't help."

"We know, Marnie and I know, beyond doubt that he did it, and no one is going to believe us. I don't think you believe us. He'll get away with it."

"I believe you, Van," Tony said quietly. "I know he did it, too."

She swung around in her chair to face him. "You know? What do you know?" Her composure, self-control, whatever had imposed distance, evaporated as she cried, "Tony, for God's sake, tell me how you know! What you know!" Impassioned, her eyes blazing, she set her coffee down on the table, spilling some, and she looked ready to spring upright.

"Easy, Van. Knowing and proving can be oceans apart. What I know is that anyone tripping and falling doesn't scream the way Freddi described the scream she heard. A victim of an attack who sees it coming and is terrified screams like that, not a falling person who goes down without warning. She might gasp, cry out, but she wouldn't pause long enough to scream like that. If the falling person is holding something, it just gets dropped, or else tossed in a reflexive way. It wouldn't get banged down on a banister hard enough to chip paint and break a picture frame. Reacting to a fall is pure reflex. Fast, unthinking reflexes and instinct take over. A quick grab for support, protecting the head, an attempt to stop falling, is what you would expect, not a head-over-heels, unchecked tumble."

Van was staring at him, wide-eyed, not moving. She moistened her lips. "That's all?"

Tony set his own coffee down on the table, rose, and took the few steps to the balcony rail, where he stood with both hands on it. "He said he heard her scream and he ran to the outside door by the stairs. He had told Freddi she was in the studio. Why didn't he go there, up to the studio? For a scream to be heard by Freddi, with the studio door closed, the back house door closed, it had to have been loud and prolonged, and it should have sounded as if coming from the studio, not the bottom of the stairs."

Van came to stand near him at the rail. "Why isn't that enough?" she demanded. "You can demonstrate that his story is a lie, it didn't happen the way he says. What more do you need?"

"Proof," he said harshly. "Incontrovertible proof. This is all conjectural, hypothetical, subjective, an opinion. It isn't evidence that a prosecutor could take to a grand jury. A defense attorney would tear it to shreds with expert testimony from half a dozen witnesses. But it would never get that far, to a trial. This is the starting place for an investigation, not the end place. You form a hypothetical case and go dig for evidence to support it. If you can't find that evidence, you don't have a fucking case. Period."

She was taken aback by the intensity of his words, the harshness of his voice, and she moved away a step, then returned to her chair and sat down again. She watched him at the rail. He was rigid with frustration or anger, it was impossible to tell which was more galling, and she wondered how many times he had dealt with such a situation, knowing who committed the crime, unable to do anything about it, watching a criminal, a killer, walk away from it.

She picked up her coffee and sipped it. "Tony, I'd like to fill you in on what's been going on at the house and what else the lawyer had to say today."

His broad back visibly relaxed after a moment, and he turned toward her. "Okay, shoot."

"The two men Freddi sent over finished moving all the artwork to storage, and it's going to take them about a week now to sort and tag it. They'll use those little round stickers with numbers and catalog everything. Number one, title if there is one, and name the medium, oil, pastel, whatever. If no title, a brief description will go with the number— 'landscape in oil,' 'figure study in charcoal,' that sort of thing. Freddi said it will make the appraisal go faster if they do it, and they work cheaper than an appraiser will. So a week for that, then at least two weeks for the appraisal—apparently some research will have to be done. After that, insurance should take another day or two at most. We're talking about the next three to four weeks, if the others can get to it promptly, and that's how long the attorney intends to put off taking that contract to court."

Tony returned to his chair as she talked. He was listening intently.

"Mr. Gladstone," Van said, "he's the attorney. He said a court decision could be issued within weeks or it could take months, no way of predicting when a judge would move. He thinks that if the appraisal comes in very high, there might be taxes to pay on the collection. Tony, he was talking about a couple of million dollars, that an appraisal for thirty years of art could be that high. And until all of this is settled, not a single piece of that art can be sold."

"I wouldn't even show any of it, if I were you." Tony was wondering how desperate Dale might be to pick up another piece of change during the next two months, what this would do to discomfort him. He hoped Freddi would go ahead with an audit, let the bastard really start squirming and sweating.

"He also said," Van continued, "that Marnie should have him rewrite her will, to name me as executor of the art estate, just in case something happens to her."

Her eyes were wide and apprehensive as she said this. "He asked me when I have to report to the hospital for my internship, and he wondered what would happen if I asked to postpone it for a year." She swallowed hard, then ducked her head to look at the cup in her hands.

"Do you know if you can ask for a postponement?"

She shook her head.

"When do you have to check in?"

"September, the day after Labor Day."

For several seconds neither spoke again. Then Van said, "If I'm fully engaged in my internship, and I will be immediately when I get there, I won't be able to participate in any legal fight, or anything else going on here. And if Marnie—" She stopped and looked away from him. "He frightened me, Tony. What he was implying frightened me."

152

"Van, remember what I said? The conjecture is the starting place, not the end. Okay, I've got the starting place, give me a little time before we decide I've come to an end. I'm following up on a couple of things. There'll be weeks, possibly months, before anyone can make a motion toward that art, and I'll be using that time in going from point A to B, and onward. Meanwhile, let's talk about how much of this you'll bring up with Marnie. As for the will, she should write a new one. The situation has changed drastically, her will needs updating. No other reason has to be given or even hinted at. There's the trust that's reverted, two houses to consider, executor, and so on. Routine stuff for the legal profession."

Van took a deep breath. "That's right, of course. And there's no reason for her to see the autopsy, those pictures. I'll just say I handed it over to you and tell her the conclusion we reached, no details."

"Good. I'm leaving it up to you to decide how much you should tell her about my own opinion. Would it help or hurt her?"

Van studied his face, then shook her head. "I don't think it would help, not right now. Later, just not yet." She was afraid that Marnie would decide to take her own action if she knew Tony was as certain as they were that Dale had murdered Stef, and that Tony might not find enough evidence to prove it.

"It would be good for her to know something about the timeline, that four or five or even more weeks will pass before any decisions are made about the collection. That it can't be touched for at least that long."

Van nodded, grateful for this kind of collusion, collaboration, whatever it was, and that it was also rational and practical.

"Do you want more coffee?" Tony asked. "Wine maybe? Or a beer? Anything?"

"No thanks. And especially thanks for leveling with me, Tony. I really appreciate that, more than I can tell you. Now I want to ask a favor. Will you let me help? Anything I can do, gofer, transcriber, look up something, anything. I want to help." She smiled a little half smile. "Maybe just talk to you now and then."

"Or listen to me blather," he said with a grin. "If there's anything, I'll let you know. Fair enough?"

"Yes," she said, rising from her chair.

He stood also and reached for the cups to take in with him. Van put her hand on his arm, and he felt as if an electric current had touched him. For a moment she looked startled, and she quickly pulled her hand away. Without looking at him, she picked up her own cup and walked into the apartment. Tony did not move for another second or two, then followed her inside, walked ahead of her to the outside door, and opened it. He moved aside so that when she left, she would not brush against him.

Again, she avoided looking directly at him as she walked from the apartment and to her car at the curb. Midway down the sidewalk, she turned back partway and said goodbye.

In her car, as she inserted the ignition key, she realized her hands were shaking. She closed her eyes hard and drew in a deep breath, another, aware that he was still standing in the doorway watching her. Under her breath she whispered, "Oh, my God!"

He watched her fumble with her key, watched her drive away, closed his door, and walked back to the balcony. "Forget it!" he said aloud. "For Christ's sake, just forget it! Keep away from her!"

He sat down and gazed at trees and saw her hand on his arm, felt the warmth of her hand on his arm, and he closed his eyes. His own hand went to the spot where hers had been. It stayed there.

14

THE HOUSE FELT different, emptier, lonelier, as if Stef had
gone with the paintings, leaving a vacuum that no music or
radio, no television program in the background, could fill.
Marnie hated it that she was allowing Josh to spend the late
afternoon watching his programs, but she felt powerless to
turn off the set, let the silence intrude once more. Usually
Van made him take a nap when he came home from day
care, but Marnie had not wanted him to go upstairs, be up
there alone while she was downstairs alone. She had closed
the door to the downstairs bedroom, closed the door to the
studio, but the emptiness of both rooms seemed pervasive
and was more haunting than the other rustling sounds had
been.

Get used to it, she told herself sharply, wishing Van would
return, no matter how dreadful it would be to hear about

the autopsy. Just a voice, she thought, not the unreal, disembodied voices of cartoon characters; a human voice would drive away the silence that was so invasive.

She thought about the coming months, with Josh upstairs by himself at night, and she shook her head. She wanted him close to her. She thought again about the empty room across the hall from hers. It could be a bedroom for Josh. She went to the other chair in front of the television, sat down, and said, "Tomorrow we have to go shopping, you and I. Want to turn that off and talk about what colors you want in your room?"

His look was skeptical. "What room?"

"I think when your mother goes to Chicago, we might move you down here, across from me, but we have to buy furniture and paint and drapes and things like that first."

He jumped up and turned off the television. "Yellow. And red."

"We'll see what the stores have. And twin beds so you can have a sleepover pal now and then. Would you like that?"

"Yeah. Can I have my own television?"

"No. A desk, a toy chest. What else? A bureau for socks and things. You might want some posters. It's going to take a lot of shopping, I'm afraid. And Sunday is your mother's birthday so we have to buy her a present."

"And make a cake. Can I help make a cake? Chocolate, with lots of chocolate icing, and candles. A lot of candles."

Thirty, Marnie thought with a pang. Thirty candles. She nodded. "Lots of candles. What kind of present do you want to look for?"

His face furrowed in thought. "No clothes," he said after a moment. "She has enough clothes. And no books."

Marnie smiled and nodded. "Maybe we'll have to look around for your present."

Tipper raised his head, cocked his ears, and then Marnie heard the car also. "I think she's back. You be thinking about a present, but no talking about it. Okay?"

He nodded and jumped to his feet. "It's a secret." He ran to the door to greet Van.

"We're going to paint my room and get twin beds so I can have Petey over to sleep. And make a chocolate cake for your birthday. But I can't tell you about the secret."

Van looked past him at Marnie, who spread her hands helplessly. "It's a secret," she said ruefully. "No party Sunday, just us, and a cake. Maybe I'll ask Tony over. He must get lonesome, knowing so few people around here."

Van looked drawn, strained, Marnie thought, and realized how hard all this was on her, too. And now the autopsy on top of the rest. "Let's have a glass of wine out on the deck. Or do you want a Bloody Mary or something else?"

"I'll settle for wine," Van said. "And you can tell me what he's talking about."

"Can I have a Coke?" Josh said.

"Of course not," Van said. "We don't even have any in the house."

"You can get some."

"No way, and you know it."

"Okay." He turned the television back on and sat down in his own chair again.

Neither Marnie nor Van said a word about it and went on to the kitchen to pour wine, then out to the deck.

"That little monster knows we want to talk," Van said. "I think he's a step ahead of me almost all the time these days."

Marnie agreed silently. Ahead of them both. "Tell me," she said quietly.

Van repeated what she and Tony had discussed and

finished by saying, "I think Mr. Gladstone was right about the time involved, and he's also right about your will."

"I suppose so," Marnie said, gazing at the unquiet ocean spread out like a rippling blanket fringed in white, frothy lace. "I'll go in next week and take care of it." Like Van, she had wanted the verdict to be that Stef was already dead when Dale threw her down the stairs. She closed her eyes, thinking of her child tumbling down, over and over.

"Tony said he's following up on a couple of things. Maybe Sunday we can get him to tell what they are," Van said. "Now, you tell me what Josh was talking about, painting a room, twin beds."

"I kept thinking of him upstairs alone after you leave and just thought it would be better if he's down here. We'll paint that room and get posters, whatever. Make it his own space. He wants yellow and red."

"Oh, God. Don't let him do it. It will be like a circus tent or something."

"We'll see. By tomorrow it might have changed to pink and purple." Marnie smiled slightly, remembering when Stef had wanted black walls, black floor, black everything. Marnie had put her foot down and said no. A week later the color scheme had changed to dark blue and white, then something else, and something else again. It had ended up stark white with garish posters and lavender drapes and bedspread.

Van sipped pinot noir and thought about having Tony over for her birthday dinner, and the disquieting feeling that had washed over her when Marnie suggested it. She had to face him. Put it out of mind that with her hand on his arm, she had felt such a strong, immediate desire for him. Never, she told herself firmly. He wasn't interested, and she didn't have time, not now, not with a year away coming. Never, in fact. She didn't want a man in her life in the near future, or possibly ever.

He had felt it. She knew he had. She had seen the change come over his face, had felt his arm grow rigid. Reacted to her surge of hormones? A strong whiff of pheromones? He had felt something as strongly as she had. And he had made no motion toward her, had instantly rejected that surge of sexual chemistry. He wasn't interested, she told herself again, and wanted to believe it. He knew it wouldn't work as well as she did, and he had not made a motion toward her, had rejected what he probably had seen as a pass. She drank her wine.

"I told Tony that I want to help in any way I can," she said, and heard the strained quality in her voice. "I don't know what I could do, but if anything comes up, I want to be on hand."

Tony had read the autopsy again, this time more slowly and carefully. He studied the three pictures. One a full-body shot with only the bottom steps in the frame. One a close-up of her head and shoulders. And the third one from a greater distance, showing her and the entire staircase. As Will had said, it was obvious from the close-up that she had been dead. Her head was twisted in such a way that a broken neck was equally obvious. In the full shot of her body and the stairs, she looked smaller, childlike, with one bare foot still on the bottom step. A broken, discarded pink-and-red Barbie doll, he thought, and shuffled the pictures together.

From the multiple bruises and abrasions, it was clear to him that what he had said earlier was in fact correct. She had tumbled head over heels down the stairs, had not stiffened and tried to stop her fall, had not slid down on her back or her front, had not done any of the things a fully alert person might have attempted to stop falling. She had been unconscious.

Would the doctor back up that conclusion? Cranshaw, he reminded himself. Dr. Cranshaw. But even if he did, so what? The counterargument would be that she had hit her head, knocked herself unconscious. Or she'd had a dizzy spell, a fainting spell. It wasn't enough, he knew. More than enough for him, far too little to make a convincing case.

He turned away from the table, surveyed his kitchen and living room with hatred, and knew he had to get out, go somewhere else. Find a restaurant, maybe in Newport, where he could get seated, have something to eat, put all this out of mind for a while.

And especially put Van out of mind, for a long, long time. She kept getting in the way of thinking. She had seen those pictures, had known what they implied. No doubt she had participated in autopsies during her training, but that was her mother in a twisted death pose, and she had handled it better than anyone else he could think of. He had seen witnesses crumple and collapse when faced with such pictures, and she had handled them. She knew. Marnie knew, and he did, that Dale had murdered Stef, and she was handling that. No hysterics, no hair pulling, just looking to him to prove it, waiting for him to wave the wand and make things right. And he didn't have the magic, didn't know the spell that would work.

He was in a savage mood when he left to go find a restaurant, to just get away from it, be somewhere else. Maybe find a woman somewhere. His laugh was bitter when he thought of that. He didn't want any woman. He wanted Van.

———

He had driven to Newport in maddeningly slow traffic, summer people out in droves, had put in a reservation at a restaurant that couldn't seat him until eight-thirty, had walked in old town by the bay until then, had eaten, and now, back in his apartment, it was still only ten-thirty, much too early to think about bed. He turned on the television, turned it off, and finally got out his laptop and resumed his search for information about Delmar Oliver.

It was interesting, he realized an hour later when he stood to stretch and make a pot of coffee, cursing himself as he did so. He knew he didn't need coffee at that hour, but he made it, and when it was ready, he drank a cup and thought about what he had learned.

Delmar Oliver had been a genius of radio drama, apparently, a sound-effects genius. You wanted a mob scene, he could provide it. Airplanes landing or taking off, got it. Kids at play, street sounds, gunfire, screams, whatever the script called for, he was there with the sound effects to put the listening audience on the ground of the action.

Delmar had arrived at the midpoint of what had come to be called the golden age of radio dramas, from the thirties into the fifties, when they went into a gradual decline with the advance of television.

Delmar was said to have had a huge collection of old program records, a collector's dream collection. Tony had not yet been able to find out what had happened to it after his death five years ago. Possibly Dale had sold it, accounting for his sudden wealth, how he had bought into the gallery.

Tony had copied several links to follow up on, and he started, with a second cup of coffee at his elbow. A guy in Idaho whose Web site malfunctioned. Someone in Rhode Island who was offering digitized programs from that period. But since digitized programs seemed readily available,

Tony passed on that. He went on to the next link, a company called Audio Magic Studios in Portland. It was midnight when he visited that site. "In stock," the come-on read, "dozens of authentic Delmar Oliver sound effects! What isn't in stock, we can provide. Try us!"

Tony clicked on some of the sound effects offered. A train whistle, people boarding, crowd noises. Closing his eyes, he could see the scene, almost smell the station. He tried another one or two and was impressed. Sound magic. And the man who ran it was, it appeared, a fan of Delmar Oliver's and had acquired some of his sound effects. Tony wanted to talk to him. He made a note of his name, Kent "Bud" Budowsky, and the telephone number to call the next day, then remembered that he had not turned his own phone back on after muting it in Newport.

When he turned it on, he found a message from Marnie inviting him to dinner on Sunday. "Not a party, and you are ordered not to bring a present, but please join us if you're free. Anytime in the afternoon. Hope to see you then."

His first reaction was to plead a previous engagement. He had to smile at his own inane excuse. "Right," he said under his breath. A date with a seagull. He had to face Van, he knew. She was more or less a client, or something akin to one, and he was doing a job for her and Marnie. He would have to see her now and then, and it would not get easier. He appreciated it that he was talking himself into the dinner that was not her birthday party, and he knew he would go. Get it over with. Establish a professional relationship and be done with it.

When he looked at his monitor again, he knew it was hopeless. He no longer could concentrate on the screen. He kept thinking, *Now she's thirty, or will be on Sunday.* And he was fifty. And a beat-up fifty at that, with a bum hip and bad knee. He couldn't wish the years away, go back to forty, or have her advance to forty. Thirty and fifty. Period. At forty he had been married to a woman he didn't love and who didn't love him; he had no wish to repeat those years. And at forty she would have an established medical practice, a child who would be fifteen, in high school, and he would be sixty.

He turned off his laptop, went out to his balcony, and wished he had a cigarette. He had not smoked in fifteen years, and suddenly he was craving a cigarette. And the nights out here on the coast were too damn cold not to have on a heavy jacket. He was all but snarling when he went back inside and got ready for bed.

THAT NIGHT AFTER Marnie said good night and went to her room, Van put down a book she had not been reading, pulled on a sweater, and went out to the deck. Many town lights were already turned off, and nothing was visible beyond the few remaining. Too many thoughts and images were swirling in Van's head for her to have concentrated on words on paper, but neither had she wanted to talk. Now the images and thoughts surged with a new urgency.

No matter where she started, the image of Stef, of her mother tumbling down the stairs, imposed itself and made anything else vanish. Van knew what the autopsy meant. No paint under her fingernails, no abraded fingers to indicate she had tried to check her fall. Thank God she was unconscious, she breathed, and had not suffered the terror of the fall. The abrasions and bruises on her arms, her face, everywhere, said it was not a slide, but a head-over-heels tumble. Van saw again the injuries the autopsy had meticulously listed. Scrape, abrasions on both arms, on her feet.

Her face, bruised, one cheek abraded. Van closed her eyes, but the image only grew sharper.

Tony knew it was murder, she told herself in an effort to see something else, think of something else. And, she added, he knew there was no way to prove it. No witnesses, and Freddi there to back up Dale's story. Tony knew, and his talk of other leads was just talk. There was no way. She saw again his rigid stance, his fury that once more a killer would succeed, would get away with it.

Her own instant denial when he posed his question again. Can you accept that? No! She would never accept that! "I'll kill him first," she said under her breath. She remembered her own vapid and empty words to Marnie that they would stop him together. Slowly she shook her head. Marnie wanted to kill him, she had said it twice. "I will kill him myself," Van said quietly. "I will kill him for what he did to my mother."

She was cold suddenly. Shivering, she hugged her arms about herself, and slowly she nodded. She would do it. She would kill him. She had to kill him.

She had dedicated her life to medicine for fifteen years, she thought then. To be a physician, to help the ill, cure them when it was possible, alleviate their pain, talk to them, comfort them. To do no harm. She bowed her head, and instantly the image of her mother tumbling head over heels down the stairs erased everything else. Poor skinny Stef, all nervous energy, given the gift or curse of seeing too much, feeling too much, unable to resist the compelling need to express what she saw and felt, terrified by the truths she revealed through her art, communicating those truths, those raw emotions, to anyone who gazed at her work. Compelled to do it again and again, suffering through the process again and again, unable to stop.

What relief it must have granted her when she painted a work such as *Feathers and Ferns*, or the lovely if conventional landscapes, but the escape had always been short-lived. Maybe that's what let her keep painting, Van thought, the hope that she would return to such work more often. Like a candy treat, to be handed out rarely, but always a possibility, a reason to keep going.

The image of her mother tumbling down the stairs returned as strong and clear as ever, and this time it included Dale Oliver standing watching.

Tears were hot in Van's eyes as she rose and went inside. She had to kill him for doing it. It was not a question, not a hypothetical, not an idle thought. She was going to kill Dale Oliver.

15

TONY WAITED UNTIL ten on Saturday morning to call the Audio Magic Studios. Expecting to get voice mail or a "leave a message" answering-machine response, he was pleased when the phone was answered promptly. It sounded like a kid on the line saying, "Audio Magic."

"Is Mr. Budowsky in? May I speak with him please."

"This is Bud. What can I do for you?"

Tony rolled his eyes, imagining a kid in his bedroom, probably in his underwear, on the other end. "I'm trying to track down some of the original Delmar Oliver recordings. I understand that you might know something about them."

"I sure do. What do you want to know?"

"I'm trying to find out what happened to the collection after Oliver died, five years ago. It seems to have vanished."

The kid laughed. "Right. Vanished into the collection of a collector. They were all sold to a collector."

"Is that when you acquired the originals you mention on your Web page? Are they part of the collection?"

"No, sir. My grandfather gave them to me. He worked with Delmar Oliver for a long time and he made the recordings and gave them to me. I have the original recordings, you know, old reel-to-reel tapes, and some pictures, stuff like that, probably worth a fortune to certain collectors, but I'm holding on to them. Granddad told me if he'd known how much they were worth, he could have sold them and made out," he said cheerfully. "But he said what would he do with a fortune at his age, so he's glad he gave them to me for nothing. He's going on ninety."

"Mr. Budowsky, would it be possible for me to come by your studio and have a look at some of that material, the pictures, find out a little more about them?"

"Sure. But they aren't for sale. I'm selling digitized copies, not the originals."

"I understand. Do you know who bought the Oliver collection?"

Bud hesitated a moment. "I can't remember now, but it'll come to me. So much money got involved, you know, people bidding against each other. When do you want to come?"

"Monday. Around noon, if that's good for you?"

"Make it two and you're on. I have some work to finish in the morning. What's your name?"

Tony was grinning when he hung up. Kent "Bud" Budowsky might be a kid, but he seemed to know what he was talking about, and he wasn't shy about talking. What did it mean to him when he said a fortune was involved? What constituted a fortune to a kid?

The next call would take a little more thought, he decided, standing and stretching. Outside, a fog had settled in, the way he had been told it often did in the summer. "We go to the valley to get warm, they come out here to cool down," Bill the bartender had said. "Winter, it's the opposite, they come here to thaw out, and we stay home."

Francine Oliver Capek, Tony was thinking, three kids, Dale's only sister, married to a university professor. A failed actress, beauty queen, coheir to Delmar Oliver's estate, which had included his original radio drama recordings from the forties on into the sixties.

He knew what he wanted to ask her, but it could get touchy. According to Bud Budowsky a fortune had become involved, and how touchy it could get might depend on the definition of fortune. He sat down again and placed the call to Francine Capek, and this time a real kid answered. He sounded to be about the same age as Josh.

"Yeah, she's here." Then he yelled, "Mom, it's for you."

Tony introduced himself when she came on the line. "I'm an investigator. I'm sorry to interrupt your weekend, but we're looking into what could be a case of fraudulent representation of certain artifacts, and we believe you could have information that might help in our investigation."

"What fraud? What artifacts are you talking about?"

"Mr. Delmar Oliver's original recordings of radio plays dating back half a century ago. We need to track them down in order to determine if what's being offered for sale presently are in fact what the seller claims, that is, Mr. Oliver's personal recordings."

He gazed out at the fog as he lied and waited for her reaction.

"I don't know anything about that. Dad's estate was settled five years ago, and as far as I know, those old tapes were sold along with almost everything else in an estate sale. I don't have any way of knowing who might have bought them or anything else about them."

"Are there records of buyers from that time?"

"Not that I know about. Mr. . . . ." She already had forgotten his name, he was pleased to note. She might mention this call to Dale, but no name would go with it. Let him wonder who was looking into it.

"All that happened while I was busy giving birth to my son," she said. "You should get in touch with my brother, Dale. Dale Oliver. He handled it. He took care of the sale and everything. It was a difficult time for us, my father had just died, and I was due to deliver a child. Dale stepped in and took over."

"Those tapes must have brought in a sizable amount of money. Was it reported to probate court? We could look up the records."

She laughed. "There was very little, not enough to make a hassle about. A small house to sell, and it had fallen into disrepair, personal things, those old tapes, that's all. Dale said you can download all those old programs now, so they had little value. My lawyer said Dad's will was perfectly clear, and as I said, there was little to divide between my brother and me. But you really should talk to Dale about this. I can give you his number, if you like."

Tony took down the number she provided and thanked her. She wished him good luck in his investigation. After he disconnected, he stood at the door to his balcony and regarded the fog. The son of a bitch stiffed his own sister. Charming Dale. Unless the fortune Budowsky had mentioned consisted of no more than a few hundred, or even a few thousand dollars, it appeared that Dale Oliver might have picked up a neat bundle, and with it and half the proceeds of even a small house sale, possibly enough to buy into a business.

Why buy into a business with such a small margin of

profit, though? He considered it a long time, got no satisfactory answer, and let it go. Maybe he'd ask Dale someday and find out.

He didn't want to spend time staring into fog that was like a dancing wall, drifting slightly to reveal trees that appeared ghostly, then closing in, hiding them again. Nothing was going to happen until Monday, he decided, and he might as well get in some real work. He went to the shop.

Dave had started a set of four chairs. He had turned out the legs and roughed out the seats. Tony set to work sanding. He missed Dave's tuneless hum, he thought once, then forgot him again. The buzzing of his cell phone roused him from a near trancelike state that he usually fell into when he was working with wood, a meditative state that left him feeling relaxed, peaceful. The mood was shattered when he saw that it was Freddi calling, and also that it was ten minutes before six.

"Hi, Freddi," he said into the phone.

"Tony, I'm glad I caught you. Jordan and I've been talking over things that you brought up, and he agrees that it would not be out of line to order an audit." She paused. "I don't like talking about things like this on the phone. Will you be coming to town in the near future?"

"Monday," Tony said promptly. "An appointment for two in the afternoon. Anytime at either end of that."

"Let's make it lunch again, noonish. Same place as before."

After the brief conversation, he looked at the work he had accomplished and had little memory of doing it. That also happened. "The elves came and did it," his father used to say, and Tony could agree. That was how it often felt; someone, something, came in and took over his body, freed him to think. That wasn't the right word, since he could not recall a single thought that had crossed his mind, but he didn't know exactly what was right. Something took over.

He imagined that Dave would make one of his characteristic grunts, this time of satisfaction, when he saw that the elves had come in and done the work.

Tony cleaned up the bench, washed his hands, and thought about dinner. And shopping, he remembered. He had to shop for a few things.

Driving to Newport, he remembered a shop he had wandered into the previous night, a shop that sold items made in Oregon. Laurelwood bowls, vases, and toys. Nothing for Van, he had been ordered not to bring a gift, he reminded himself, but he would look into the shop again.

In the shop later he went straight to the display of toys that had caught his eye before, and there it was, a wood puzzle that when put together formed a train, an engine and three coaches, with wheels that worked. It might be too difficult for Josh alone, but he visualized Van and Josh at the tide pools, and he knew that she would help him make the train.

He had dinner in a bay-front restaurant, where visibility stopped just outside the windows. The bay had vanished under fog. He wondered, as he had before, how many hours Stef had spent gazing at the bay, if she had felt the peace that had pervaded her painting, and if she had felt the chaos of her harsh landscapes or the cruelty of *Ladies in Waiting*. What had she felt while painting? Had painting been a release? Or a magnification of whatever emotion drove her to paint it? Had someone or something taken over and freed her?

Recalling the brief conversation they'd had about process, and Van's account of seeing her on the floor in tears, he knew she had not been freed while painting. It had tormented her, and she had been compelled to do it in spite of that.

174

He cursed Dale Oliver under his breath, and he thought once more of his former partner's judgment call to take the guy out and beat the shit out of him because he was going to get away with it.

"No, he isn't, not this time," Tony said under his breath. "Not this time."

MARNIE HAD SAID to come anytime in the afternoon, which he interpreted to mean that dinner would be fairly early. Probably little kids such as Josh didn't approve of late dinners by candlelight. At least he hadn't when he was a kid. He arrived at the house a little after five on Sunday.

"Tony, it's good to see you again," Marnie said, admitting him. "It's cold, isn't it? That fog is always cold, and it's coming in thick. We'll get some wind in a day or two and it will be summer again."

She eyed the plastic bag he was carrying and shook her head. "Van said no presents. You shouldn't have brought one. She meant it."

"It's for Josh," he said quickly. "I thought that might be all right."

Marnie sighed. "You win. No one can object to a present for Josh." She led the way to the living room, where a low fire was burning. The ocean was not visible that day, and what could be seen of the town was surreal, a fantasy town with soft outlines.

"I'll take your jacket," Marnie said. "What can I get you to drink? Van and Josh are out crawfishing, but they'll be along soon."

"Crawfishing? Here?" There had been crawfish in upper New York in the summer, and he and his buddies had spent many hours in pursuit of them.

Marnie laughed. "Crawfish thrive in Silver Creek, in most

little creeks in the state, I guess. Josh decided they were a necessary part of a birthday dinner."

Tony thought of the little creek falling from the mountain behind the town, spreading out to a shallow expanse of icy freshwater, emptying into the Pacific Ocean. It did not seem the right place to find crawfish.

Marnie glanced at his feet. "You can probably catch them down by the creek, if you'd like." He was wearing sneakers, good enough for the trail, no good for real hiking. "If you go out through the back, there's a path you can take to the trail by the creek. They won't be far."

"Another secret place. There seem to be a lot of them."

"There are. And we know each and every one of them."

She ordered Tipper to stay and went to the door with Tony. "That silly dog can't go down there. He won't stay out of the water, even after getting caught in the rapids for quite a spill. I thought we were going to lose him."

Marnie watched Tony go out to the deck, through the gate, and find the path. The path had been cut by the Huddleston kids, their father had said. Later Marnie and Ed had kept it up, and she had taken Stef down to the creek to crawfish many times, and when it was Van's turn, she had taken her. Their secret place. Then Marnie was thinking of the time that Stef had taken Dale down, and how furious he had been when they returned. His expensive suede shoes were muddy, ruined, he claimed.

The trail was easy going down, but Tony suspected he would pay a price on the return trip. Not too steep, and someone had cut steps into stone for a part of it, but still, going back would be uphill, and his hip objected to uphill climbs. After making one last zigzag turn, he saw Van and Josh. They were down another hundred feet, Josh wet almost to his waist, Van slightly less wet.

Silver Creek rushed to the ocean in a series of rapids and shallow falls, followed by small, still pools, then another series of rapids and falls. Up here the growth of wind-stunted trees was scant, the shores rocky, with wide, smooth places, good for sunbathing when there was sunshine.

"Hi, down there," he called.

Van looked back over her shoulder, smiled, and waved him on down. She was carrying a small pail. Josh hardly glanced at him. He was in one of the still pools concentrating on a rock that he was approaching in water up to his ankles. Why wasn't he freezing? Tony wondered.

This new stretch was steeper than anything above it, and Tony slowed as he made his way down to join them. Josh upturned the rock, pounced, and let out a jubilant cry. He was holding a bright-red crawfish. He waded out of the water and added his catch to the pail. Then they both moved several yards up the trail to the next pool, where he began to examine the rocks closely.

"Hi," Van said as Tony drew near. "Appetizers or something." She held up the pail for him to see. It looked like a lot of crawfish in it.

"I had no idea this was here," Tony said, motioning toward the trail. "How far does it go?"

"All the way down, under the bridge and on to the public beach, or you can stay on it and go on to the motels. We hardly ever crossed the highway in the summer. This was our preferred way down."

She had pulled her hair back in a ponytail, held by a rubber band, and her cheeks were flushed.

"Are you freezing? Is he?" Tony asked, pointing to Josh.

"He wouldn't admit it. When his lips get blue, I blow the whistle on him. I did the same thing when I was his age, and I never admitted to being cold either."

"We played in the snow with ice in our socks, down our mittens, and swore we were warm," Tony said. "Do you start downstream and work your way up? That's what we did as kids."

She looked at him in surprise and nodded. "Marnie said that they spread the word and hide if you start searching upstream."

"True. They do."

Tony looked away first, and they became silent, both of them watching Josh sneak up on another rock.

"One more, Josh," Van said. "We have plenty already."

He didn't acknowledge her, continued to approach the rock stealthily, then flipped it and let out another cry of triumph.

His lips were turning blue, Tony saw, as the child left the water and came to toss his latest catch into the pail.

"Home," Van said. "And don't run."

"Tell the wind not to blow," Tony said as Josh dashed off ahead of them, back up the trail.

"He's part mountain goat," Van said with a laugh.

Going to the house, Van set the pace, mindful of his hip, how he had limped after driving to and from Portland. Where the trail got too narrow for them to keep a little distance from each other side by side, he dropped back to walk behind her. *Okay,* Van thought, *we can be pals or something. Crawfishing buddies.*

He watched her easy stride, the ease of her body where the trail steepened, her grace. She moved like a dancer, or a trained athlete. He suspected that if he were not along, she would be right with Josh all the way up.

Twice they nearly caught up with Josh when he stopped to investigate something, then he was out of sight again in a flash.

As they went up, Tony knew that he was walking more and more slowly, but it could not be helped. Stabs of pain shot from his hip through his back, down his leg. Van was adjusting her pace to accommodate his, he also realized, and cursed under his breath.

"Josh," Van called, when they neared the house, "take your shoes off on the deck and go straight upstairs." To Tony she said, "I'll warm him up in the tub and clean him up. God only knows what all he's been handling. Worms, bugs, anything that moves and is smaller than he is."

"Boy things."

She laughed again. "I was just like that, according to Marnie."

When they reached the deck, she set the pail down and took off her wet shoes. Tony picked up hers and Josh's and they went inside. He put the wet shoes on the hearth by the fire.

"Success," Van said to Marnie. "I'll get Josh in the tub and change my wet jeans, then I'll clean them."

"I'll clean them," Tony said quickly. "I'd like to do something useful."

He cleaned the crawfish. Marnie had already set the table, and when Josh and Van returned, warm and dry, they all sat down to eat.

"I haven't had crawfish since I was about ten," Tony said. "That's when my dad began to show me how to use his tools, and I guess I never went crawfishing very much after that. I had forgotten how delicious they are."

And the cake was also delicious and brought up memories of his own mother in the kitchen putting icing on such a cake, his anticipation of having the pan to scrape clean. Josh was disappointed that only three candles were on the cake.

"You said a lot," he grumbled to Marnie.

"These represent a lot," Marnie said. "Thirty candles would melt the icing and it would run like a river down the sides of the cake. Each candle means ten, so we have ten, and ten more make twenty, and ten more make thirty. See?"

He seemed awed by the number thirty and looked hard at Van, as if trying to understand how anyone could be that old.

Only after the table was cleared did Josh see the bag on the coffee table and go to investigate.

"I said no presents," Van said sternly. "Really, I didn't want you to bring anything."

"It's for him," Tony said. "Open it, Josh, take a look."

He dumped the box from the bag, studied the illustration on the cover, and began to tear it apart. "It's a train!" he yelled over his shoulder. When he opened the box, he found a jumble of wooden puzzle pieces. "I thought it was a train."

Van joined him and looked at the box. "It's a puzzle. A train puzzle. When it's put together, you get the train. Let's empty the pieces on the floor and see how hard it's going to be."

They both sat on the floor cross-legged and began to examine the puzzle pieces.

"Tony, do you want coffee?" Marnie asked. "I do. And it's ready."

They had coffee at the dining table and watched Van and Josh start to piece together a train. Marnie smiled softly, glanced at Tony, and then, aware of his expression, she thought, *Oh, dear.*

Soon Van stood and joined them. "He's got the hang of it. His job." She looked at her watch. "Half an hour and it's off to bed for him. Tony, can you stay a little longer, give us a little talking time?"

He nodded, and Marnie said, "Well, let's take more comfortable chairs by the fire."

When she rose, Tony got to his feet, and a stab of pain hit him in the hip, raced through the groin and down into his leg. He stopped the motion midway, and Van made an involuntary movement toward him, quickly drew back, and exchanged a glance with Marnie. Tony finished straightening up and without a word turned and walked toward a chair across the room.

"I'll put on fresh coffee," Marnie said.

"Josh, how's it coming?" Van asked, and went to sit by him on the floor.

Giving him a minute, Tony thought bitterly, and he needed a minute or two. It had been bad, as bad as it ever got, and only slowly was subsiding. Soon Marnie was bringing the coffee carafe, and Van was helping Josh gather up puzzle pieces. As they started for the stairs, Josh detoured to approach Tony. "Thanks for the train puzzle, it's really cool." He showed Tony one of the coaches, complete except for the wheels.

"Well," Marnie said as soon as Josh and Van were going up the stairs, "he's learning, isn't he? No prompting necessary, thank you."

"He's a great kid," Tony said.

"Van's a great mother. She told me you're following up on a lead or two, and we're hoping you can tell us a little about what they are, when Van comes down. Meanwhile, tomorrow I'll drop in on the boys to see how the inventory is coming. They'll make a printout or two and be ready to leave. Also, I plan to see Ted Gladstone and tell him to go ahead with a new will."

"Marnie, I'd suggest that when you call Freddi, tell her there's no rush. Anytime in the next few weeks is fine for an appraiser. Are you okay with that?"

"Yes, but why?"

"Let's squeeze Dale a little and see how much he squeals."

Silently Marnie went to the fire to put another small log on, alarmed at how suddenly the image of the gun in her desk drawer had flooded her mind with his words. She needed time for the will, she had come to realize, time to make certain it got written and signed, and she had not thought of it right away. What else was she overlooking? She needed a little time. *Slow down everything for now,* she told herself. *There's no rush.*

Van rejoined them. "He loves the puzzle. He decided to paint the train red when it's all put together. Thanks, Tony. One of the best presents I never got."

Moving carefully, Tony leaned forward. "Here's all I have so far. Not much, but it's how a real investigation goes. You plod along, pry into this and that, and most often come up empty-handed, but it's got to be done. I'm in that stage. I'm looking into how he got enough money to buy into a business, and wondering why it was one that doesn't offer greater return. Tomorrow, I'm off to Portland to see Freddi. She's having an audit done, and there's something else on her mind, but I don't know what it is yet. And I'm seeing a guy about some original tapes Dale's father had when he died, tapes of radio drama shows from the forties into the sixties. He was considered a sound-effects genius."

"Let me go with you," Van said quickly. "I know my way around Portland, and I'll drive and act as assistant or something. I'll take notes. If Freddi wants to talk to you alone, I'll take a walk and you can call me when you're ready."

Marnie nodded, and after a moment Tony did, too. "Okay, assistant."

"I know about those radio shows," Marnie said. "Out here television was late in arriving, and the reception was terrible when it did. We listened to the radio in the evenings. There were some very good dramas, and some that no doubt were dreadful, but we listened to them, anyway. Some were really scary, *Lights Out, The Inner Sanctum,* things like that, but some were as fine as any dramatic presentation possible, real plays with real characters in real situations. I loved them. And to think Dale's father was involved in producing them. Boggles the mind."

They talked a while longer, planning the coming day, and Van and Tony agreed to take his Acura instead of her much older Nissan, but that she would do all the driving. He hesitated at that, reconsidered, and said fine, dreading the moment when he would have to stand again, and yearning for a long, soaking, hot bath. When that moment came, both women made a point of not watching. It was bad, not as bad as earlier, but bad.

After he was gone, Van said, "He's in real pain at times. It must have been from coming up the trail. That can be hard on a bad hip. I wonder if a hip replacement is an option."

Marnie's gaze was searching when she looked at Van, and she thought again, *Oh, dear.* It was swiftly followed by another thought: *She could do worse.*

16

Van had insisted on leaving at nine-thirty to give them plenty of time and to allow for a coffee stop at some of the most magnificent old-growth rain-forest trees to be seen. She would provide a thermos of coffee.

That morning Tony came to fully appreciate the view of the drive up the coast, the wild surf and cliffs, the sudden stretches of beaches, well-spaced turnoffs where the vista expanded dramatically up and down the coastline, stunningly beautiful in both directions. As driver he'd had to concentrate on the road and never before realized how little he was seeing. He stretched out his legs and enjoyed being a passenger. The soak the night before had helped, and so had the codeine tablets he kept for just such a time. He had decided that morning to keep a couple of the tablets with him, just in case, and now they were in a little pillbox in his pocket. Pain was a private affair, and he despised how he had revealed it the night before. It seemed to be a plea for pity, and that was contemptible.

Traffic was heavy on the coast road, but he didn't care. Van was a good driver, patient and relaxed. After they turned off the coast road, heading inland, he told her what little he had learned about Delmar Oliver and Kent "Bud" Budowsky and his grandfather. "He sounds pretty young but he seems to know his stuff. What does a 'fortune' mean to a kid?"

"To me it meant I could get an old junker of my own to drive," she said promptly.

He laughed. "Did you ever hear any of those old radio shows?"

"I don't think so, not that I remember anyway. TV generation, and now it's computer generation, or iPod generation. What next?"

"Implant generation. Straight into the brain."

"Now that's a real horror story."

It got warmer with the passing miles, and when they stopped for coffee, he took off his Windbreaker and she took off her sweater. Here, the rain forest was almost overwhelming with its exuberant growth. Magnificent trees, giant ferns, brambles, all crowding one another, greenery on top of greenery, with lichens and mosses covering everything firm enough to support them. It was a green world. Even the air seemed green. *Another time,* Tony thought, gazing at it, *take time to linger, explore a little.* That day's stop was regrettably brief.

"It's going to be hot in Portland," Van warned, back in the car. "Up to ninety today."

She proved to be prophetic. It was nearing ninety when she parked a block away from the restaurant at ten minutes before twelve. "I'll go in with you, and when Freddi gets there, if she wants this to be confidential, I'll get out. You have my number."

But Freddi waved her down again when she made the same offer at the booth. "You might as well hear it, too. I have no idea if it will help, but Jordan and I both thought it might be relevant to have the audit." Freddi looked tense and angry, her words were clipped.

They ordered, and as they waited, Freddi said, "We talked about it Friday night, and Jordan pointed out that our business went into something of a slump over two years ago, before the economy began to tank. I hadn't given it that much thought since it's really an up-and-down kind of business to start with. But then I started to think about several different things that might or might not be connected."

She drew back when the waitress returned with their lunches.

That done, Freddie resumed, "Anyway, I called Hiram Delacroix, my former partner. His wife has Alzheimer's that's progressed to the point where she needs around-the-clock care in a facility. He knew it was coming, and he knew how expensive it would be, the reason he sold in the first place.

"The point is that Hiram was trying to plan for a very costly few years. Dale seemed a likely prospect. MBA, a sizable down payment, three hundred thousand, with five years of annual payments, was the arrangement they had. Partnership, profit sharing, a salary, it was a mutually satisfactory deal for both of them. Two years ago Hiram called me and asked how the business was doing, and I told him things were slow. That was the gist of the whole conversation, and I didn't give it much thought at the time. But it was very uncharacteristic. Saturday morning I called him back and asked if there had been a reason for that call, if there was a problem. He said there might be, but he figured it wasn't my problem and hadn't wanted to bother me with it. It seems that Dale was late in his payment that year, and again this year. He hasn't caught up yet." Freddi sipped her tea. "He owes Hiram over forty thousand dollars. He told Hiram he had a CD coming due in a few months and he'd make it then. That was in March, and he still hasn't caught up."

The Crab Louie was delicious, but Van was eating mechanically, tasting little of it. And Tony was watching Freddi so intently, it was a wonder that she didn't start squirming, Van thought. They remained silent as Freddi continued.

"Anyway, that was one of the things. That same year, two years ago, over Christmas, one of our regulars came in looking for a new work by a relatively unknown artist named Moira Koogan. She does charming children's fantasy paintings, fairy-tale characters, things of that sort. This customer had bought two of them for her own daughters and wanted another one for a niece for Christmas. Moira hadn't brought in anything in months and I didn't have anything to show. I know Moira makes little enough for her work, a couple of hundred or two-fifty usually, but there's a market for them and she always needed the money. Most artists do. Few can support their art on sales, and they have to have outside jobs to keep going. She clerks in Nordstrom's. Months after the inquiry about her work, I happened to run into her while I was shopping and I asked if she had given up, thinking to encourage her not to. She could have a future as an illustrator for children's books. She confided that since Dale had found her an outlet, she was making two thousand a year at least, and if she could keep up with the demand, it would be three or four thousand. She was happy about it."

Freddi obviously was not happy, her distress was clearly written in her pained expression.

"Freddi," Van said hesitantly. "I don't understand. What's wrong with that?"

"Wait," Freddi snapped. "I kept looking at my artists, my

regulars, and there's another one who dropped out. He's at the same place in his career as Moira, a time of exploration, of trying out this and that, finding strengths and weaknesses. Finding a personal direction. I called Loretta over at Blue Skies, and she wasn't sure, but later she called back and said it's the same there. Two of her young artists are gone. She knows where one of them works and tracked him down at his job. It was the same story. Dale has found him an outlet."

Freddi leaned forward at the table and said furiously, "That bastard is building a stable! Collecting a group of dependable artists who can produce art on a regular basis. Sign them up for the next four, six, whatever number of works, pay them up front, and as soon as it appears they're reaching the first goal, provide a new contract, a new advance. It's a death trap for them. They spend the money just about as soon as they get it and face months of work without another cent coming in. They seldom can afford to buy back the contracts, if there's even a clause that permits it. The work is scanned, sent to Photoshop, and is ready to go into production as print cards or, more often now, e-cards, glanced at and discarded, deleted. Forgotten."

"They don't have to keep signing new contracts," Van said. "I mean, it isn't as if there is enough money involved to live on."

"Often there's a binding option clause that can be hard to break without legal help, and they can't afford that. And if they do manage to get out from under, they realize that they have to start over. They've picked up bad habits that have to be broken, working too fast with too little thought, skipping the final touches that can make or break a painting, no exploring, just more of the same kind of thing, over and over. The little bit of money hasn't meant a thing, and the years have been a complete waste. Worse," she said bitterly, "something they loved to do, needed to do, turns into nothing more than assembly-line work, drudgery that they end up hating."

Freddi took a long drink of iced tea. "Sorry, I'm just so goddamn mad I can't bear it. One more thing. Late last fall, a couple of weeks before Christmas, I went out to the coast to see what Stef had been up to over the past few months. I did that often, since she would paint something and stash it away without anyone having a glimpse of it. Anyway, there were two recent paintings, either of them superb alone, but together altogether stunning. I begged her to let me show them, not to sell if she didn't want to go there, but more like museum pieces that people could look at and enjoy. She was reluctant, but finally agreed. I had them up two days, only two days, and she came to town and took them away. She was upset with her decision, said it was a mistake. And that was that.

"A few days after Stef's death, I had a call from an extremely wealthy woman who comes in now and then, usually looking for garden sculpture. She reminded me that over the winter she had been in and had been intrigued by a pair of paintings by Stef. Those two that I had up for only two days. One painting is a little girl at tide pools, and the other is tide-pool life. This customer wasn't looking for paintings at that time and moved on. But she said she had been haunted by that wild little girl, and in her mind's eye she was darting from one pool to the next. Finally, in March or April she had come back, only to find them no longer on display. I wasn't there that day and my assistant Bonnie Jean didn't know what to tell her and turned her over to Dale. When she called me, it was to ask if we still planned a big show of Stef's work, with both pictures included, and if she still had a preview privilege."

Freddi shrugged. "I told her the estate ordered an inventory and an appraisal and it will all take time. I'll let her know."

"He made the same promise to them both," Tony said.

"Of course," Freddi said. "The dot-com millionaire knows he wants *Feathers and Ferns*. Plus two others to be decided. She knows she wants a painting that's haunting her that happens to be one of a pair. Won't it be interesting if it turns out that those two catch his eye also?"

"Dale wants them to bid against each other," Tony said, "run up the price all around." He believed the dot-com guy would fixate on the tide-pool painting as soon as he saw it. It was a gorgeous piece of work that would go beautifully with *Feathers and Ferns*, and no longer even a possible purchase for Tony. A bidding war would simply clinch the fact. He was sorry that he would never see it on his own wall.

"I'm surprised that she even displayed the painting she called *Searching*," Van said. "That was a self-portrait of herself as a child, really personal to her."

"I saw it at the house," Freddi said. "I talked her into letting me show them both. She was so upset, it was as if she had not been able to sleep until she got them back."

Freddi began to make wet rings on the tabletop, moving her tea here, there. Watching it, she said in a deceptively low voice, "He's been backstabbing, double-dealing, double-crossing, conniving, plotting, lying from the day he got here. I'm not going back until Wednesday, when the auditor gets there. He advised me to get in touch with the security company, to change the locks, and he'll bring a strapping young man, he said, who will make sure Dale doesn't remove anything. I won't tell him in advance, of course."

Freddi looked at Tony, then at Van, and her fury, although under control, was still there. Quietly she said, "If there's any discrepancy, anything at all out of order, I'll have him charged and I'll make certain that the media have the story."

After Freddi left, Van leaned back and blew out a long breath. Gravely she said, "I believe he's made her angry."

Tony nodded and equally gravely said, "I believe she wants to blow him out of the water." He looked at his watch. "How long will it take to get to the Audio Magic shop?"

"I'd like to allow half an hour. It's all the way across town in the northeast, and I don't know those streets."

"Time for a cup of coffee. You want one, too?"

VAN PULLED UP to the curb outside Audio Magic Studios at a few minutes before two. It was blistering hot, the sky cloudless, the sun like an acetylene torch.

"He said two, so let's wait in the car," Tony said. The air-conditioning was straining, but it was doing its job.

This was a warehouse, industrial district with wood-products wholesalers, plumbing supplies, packaging . . . No pedestrians were in sight. It was close to the airport and also close to Interstate 205. Van began plotting her route home, on the interstate, a Portland bypass highway that connected to I-5 miles south of the city. On down to Salem and cross the Coast Ranges from there. That way she could avoid most of the early onset of rush-hour traffic, she decided.

A bicycle appeared and drew near on the sidewalk. The rider wore a helmet and was in shorts and a T-shirt. His arm and leg muscles bulged and looked oiled, they were so wet with sweat. He stopped at the car and Van rolled down her window.

"Tony?" the young man said, leaning over, peering in.

"Come on in. I'm Bud." He motioned toward the studio entrance, then pedaled a few times to reach the door, dismounted, and unlocked the studio. He entered and was leaning his bike against the wall when Van and Tony followed. He hung his helmet on the handlebar, ran his hand through his hair, which was plastered to his scalp, then said, "Bud Budowsky," rubbed his hand on his shorts, and held it out.

It didn't help much. It was wet when Tony shook it. "Tony Mauricio, and this is my associate Dr. Markov."

Bud looked Van up and down, grinned, and said, "Hi, Doc."

She grinned back. "Hi, Bud."

They were in a small, dun-colored entry foyer. A single door was on the left side and a staircase on the right. The space was stifling and airless.

Bud opened the door and motioned for them to come in. Cool, fresh air swept over them as they entered the room. It was spacious, with a pair of desks right-angled to each other, a computer on each of them. Simple straight chairs had been scattered about seemingly randomly, and sound equipment was everywhere. Speakers hung from the ceiling; turntables, DVD players, tape players were on various surfaces, tables, desks, shelves. A freestanding CD rack was filled to capacity, and shelves were filled with cassettes. Something Tony thought was a mixer took a lot of space on one side of the room. The walls were covered with photographs, sometimes overlapping in the profusion.

"You guys want a cold Coke?" Bud asked, opening a refrigerator.

Tony said no thanks, but Van said, "I'd like a Coke."

"You got it," Bud said. "Hot. I had to get stuff in the mail, and, man, it's big-time hell out there." He handed a can to

Van, popped a second one, and drank. It seemed he was going to down the entire contents before stopping.

Tony was looking at a photograph. From the twenties or thirties, he guessed. Five or six people at a table, a pitcher, glasses. The same people were in other photographs. He recognized Orson Welles. A couple of the others looked vaguely familiar.

"That's the original crew at Mercury Theatre," Bud said, joining him. "Orson Welles started it up in New York State. GE had its own radio station and they aired a show as a tryout or something, but people loved it and they kept going. Later, after Welles did *War of the Worlds* back in 1938, the Campbell's soup people began to sponsor it and they called it the *Campbell Playhouse*, but it was the same group. That broadcast of *War of the Worlds* caused a nationwide panic, it was so real. That's what radio can do, make it so real you want to go hide in the basement. My grandad worked on sound effects. He said old Delmar came along right after that, and he was a genius. Those were the golden years of radio dramas, the thirties and forties."

Bud leaned in closer to a photograph and put his finger on an unkempt-looking man standing near a microphone. "Look at that beer belly." Then he singled out a woman turned halfway away, talking to someone else in the background. "And she looks like she's a hundred years old. But it doesn't matter. It's the voices that count, and with the right sound effects they become a young couple eloping, or Fred and Ginger dancing cheek to cheek. Audio magic. Hey, Doc, you ready for another one?" He held up his Coke can.

"I'm fine," Van said.

He got another can from the refrigerator, and before he started drinking again, Van said, "Bud, what exactly do you do here?"

"Oh, I thought you knew. See, when I was a little kid, eight or nine, Grandad had me out somewhere one night, and driving home, he found a radio play running. We listened to it, and when it was over, I said something like I was scared out of my skin when I saw that guy on the airplane wing. Grandad laughed and laughed, and he said, 'You're a radio man, my boy.'"

Van glanced at Tony, who was grinning, and she waited for Bud to get around to answering her question.

"He had moved in with us in L.A., and he began to let me listen to his old reel-to-reel tapes of shows. I couldn't get enough. Then when old Delmar moved out there and bought a little house, Grandad would take me along when he went to visit with him. They talked about the good old days and I listened to Delmar's tapes. I went off to Caltech and Delmar kicked. Grandad asked a neighbor to let him know when a yard sale, estate sale, something like that, was posted. He planned to buy a few things Delmar had. But when the estate sale came up, there wasn't a tape in sight. They were all gone. That was when he gave me his collection. He said I was the only one who knew about them, what they meant, and he wanted me to have them before they vanished into thin air. Anyway, a couple of months later he heard that the whole collection was for sale by Dale Oliver. Lots of those guys kept in touch, you know how they do, old-timers. Anyway, bids poured in, and the price began to climb. Pretty soon there were only two guys bidding. One made screws and nails and junk like that, but apparently it paid off real big, and the other one owned feedlots and he was loaded. The feedlot guy dropped out at seven hundred thousand and some change. The screw guy ended up with them."

"Good heavens!" Van murmured, and Tony said, "Wow!"

"Collectors," Bud said. "My bunch is worth more, they go back to the very beginning. They're in storage, climate controlled and everything."

"But how does that explain what you do here?" Van asked after a moment, during which Bud chugalugged his drink.

"Getting to that. While I was at Caltech, before Delmar died, Grandad came across a cassette, Delmar's sound-effects library. His house was a mess, tapes everywhere, cassettes, stuff scattered all through the house. He had no idea what all he had, but Grandad found the cassette and asked if he could buy it. Delmar said no, but he could have it. He had no use for it anymore. And when I said I intended to start this studio, Grandad gave it to me, so I had a base to start with. I do sound effects for groups putting on radio dramas around the country. They never really died out all the way, but television killed them for the big time. University groups, independent stations, community stations, local public broadcasting, groups like that, still put them on now and then, and I provide the sound effects. I do documentaries, too, and sometimes commercials, anything that needs sound effects."

He emptied his can, burped. "How it works is, they send me a script by e-mail. They say how much time they have, one act or two, whatever, and I read through it and start to gather the right sound effects and eventually put together a disc that's just sound effects, nothing else unless it's music for background. That sound-effects library is the starting point, and I'm adding to it all the time. Anyway, when it's done, I e-mail the sound effects to them and send them a disc. They read their lines with the effects disc running, and they follow the cues on my disc, you know, footsteps, a door opens and closes, and the dude says hello or something. They usually record a final disc of their own with everything in place, sound effects, the spoken parts, music, and they're ready to air it."

This time when Bud paused, Tony said, "I think we've taken up enough of your time, Bud. Thanks a lot. It's been illuminating."

Bud said, "I want to show you my soundproof room, where I make the final disc, and show you some of the other kinds of broadcasts, things like *Vic and Sade*, and creep shows like *The Inner Sanctum. Arch Oboler, Lights Out. The Lone Ranger.*" This was directed at Van.

She shook her head, smiling. "We have to go. You sell broadcasts on CDs, don't you? I would like to buy a couple for my mother. She used to listen to them."

He wanted to give her two or three, but she insisted on paying and let him pick the shows. Soon afterward, she and Tony left.

"Your conquest," Tony said on the way to the car. "He adores you."

"What a beautiful hunk he is! I bet he runs marathons, rides eighty-mile jaunts and back, swims back and forth across the Columbia. He's gorgeous!"

The heat was as intense as it had been, possibly even more intense. At the car they opened all the doors, turned the fan to high, and set the air conditioner at its maximum, then stood back to let the superheated air escape. After a few seconds, Tony said, "It can't be worse inside, out of the sun."

Back behind the wheel, Van said, "What a windfall that was for Dale and his sister."

"She never saw a penny of it," Tony said. "He told her the tapes were worthless because those old programs can be downloaded now."

Appalled, Van said, "His sister? That shithead! That scumbag! God, he's slime!"

"All the above. You know where his apartment is?"

"Yes, why?"

"Let's go around there, close by at least."

With regret she thought of the escape route she had planned and she headed for downtown Portland.

17

AFTER DRIVING SILENTLY for several minutes, Van said, "All this today, whatever we've learned has just verified what we already knew, hasn't it? He's slime and sociopathic, not a touch of empathy, evil all the way through. But we haven't gotten any closer to proof. Isn't that true?"

"It's true." Tony studied her profile as she drove. Both hands on the wheel, watchful of surrounding traffic, keeping her eyes on the traffic all around her, she exuded confidence. She was an exemplary, alert driver, but he suspected her real attention was focused on the problem of proving Dale Oliver guilty of murder.

"And you intend to get into Dale's apartment to try to find something that will help with proving he's a killer. Isn't that also true?"

"Van, the less you know about my intentions the better. I just want you to point out his apartment, drop me within a block, and take off. We'll meet again at that same spot. I'll call you when it's time."

"No. Don't freeze me out, Tony. I deserve better than that. Don't try to protect me. I'm not a child. Are you going to try to get into that apartment?" Her words were spoken quietly, but they had an underlying unyielding quality, a hardness. She continued to look straight ahead.

"Van, it's called breaking and entering and it's a felony. I don't want you to get involved."

"I'm involved all the way." She glanced at him. "He killed my mother. I think that contract will be ruled legal eventually, and for now we're buying time. The audit, appraisal, just buying time. But at the end of that time, he'll have won exactly what he set out to get, complete control of my mother's artwork. Tony, I told you that neither Marnie nor I will let that happen. Believe it. If he can't be stopped legally, we'll stop him. I'll kill him myself if that's what it takes."

"Van, listen to me. Killing for revenge never resolves anything. It's a lose-lose game from start to finish. You don't bring back the dead, and you don't relieve the grief. You just spread it further in a broader circle." His voice was low, intense, and more bitter than she had ever heard it.

For a time neither spoke, then she said quietly, "If you can find proof to let the legal system work, great, and I want to help in every way I can. Just don't freeze me out of the process. If you have a key and use it, would it still be a felony?"

"Still illegal, invasion of privacy, illegal search, but not as serious as breaking and entering."

"I have keys. It takes two, one for the outer door, one for the apartment door. Stef gave them to me years ago. Sometimes she asked me to stop by and pick up something for her. I still have the keys."

"I'll be damned. You're the best associate I ever had. Okay, no more holding out."

She glanced at him again, nodded, and smiled faintly. "Deal," she said. Then, turning again to the increasing traffic, she warned him that it was going to take nearly an hour to get to the apartment, and that was cutting time short. "It will be after four, and Dale might show up early on such a hot day. There's not a thing I can do about it. Stop-and-go traffic until we cross the bridge into downtown Portland."

"I'll be as fast as I can," Tony said. "I won't waste time trying on any of his Armani suits."

She looked at him quickly to see if he was grinning, laughing at her. So much for telling him how to run his business, she chided herself.

It was five past four when she drove by the apartment complex, which took up half a block. "That's it," she said. "Second floor, this corner of the building. There's a big parking area in the rear with entrances on both streets."

"Let's take a drive through, see if his car is already there."

Covered parking spaces in the rear were about half-filled, but Dale's convertible was not there.

"You'll be my lookout," Tony said. "If and when he shows, call me. I won't answer and my phone tone will be muted, but it will vibrate, and I'll know. See if we can find a place where you can see both the entrances to parking."

She drove down both streets, but there was no such place. Then Tony said, "That café has an upper level, and I think it would work for you." It was not quite opposite one of the parking lot entrances, not ideal, and if Dale entered and parked at the other entrance, probably she would not see him. Tony didn't think he would do that, but would park closer to his own apartment. She parked nearly a block away, gave him a small key ring that had two keys, and they walked back. She entered the café and he strolled into the parking area.

He let himself into the building, took the elevator to the second floor, located the exit with the stairs icon, then opened the door to Dale's apartment.

Upscale, spacious, decorator perfect. He gave it a swift scrutiny and looked instead for a home office, or at least a desk. A small bedroom proved to be an office, equipped with a table with a scanner, fax machine, paper cutter, one extra chair, and a desk. Quickly, using a paper clip, he unlocked the desk. A deep side drawer served as a file case. There were eleven of the contracts Freddi had described, and swiftly he looked over several of them. They appeared to be identical boilerplate contracts, not really negotiated, without changes, just accepted and signed as written. He skipped the contract signed by Stef, but stopped at a contract Dale had with a greeting-card corporation. Using his digital camera, he took pictures of them all. He closed the drawer and turned his attention to the center drawer. Passport, trip to France and Italy nearly five years before, an unlabeled envelope that held two driver's licenses, with matching credit cards.

"Jackpot," he muttered, and turned on a desk light. He positioned the licenses and credit cards under it and took several pictures. He replaced them in the envelope and picked up an address book.

"Mega-jackpot!" he said softly. There were two pages of passwords, some identified, most not. He took a lot of pictures of them, then started snapping shots of the addresses that followed. He stopped when it occurred to him that the computer operating system might have a general computer password. He turned it on and, while waiting for it to boot up, resumed snapping pictures of names and addresses.

Windows finished loading and he went into the properties screen, and there it was, the system password. He took pictures and also wrote it down in his notebook. He was closing his notebook when his cell phone vibrated in his pocket. Moving fast, he turned off the computer, put the address book back, and closed the drawer most of the way. He left it open just a little, then opened the file drawer enough to suggest it had been an oversight. Let Dale worry about it, he thought, turning off the desk light. Let Dale wonder if he had been careless, or if there had been an intruder.

He slipped out of the apartment and was at the door to the stairs when the elevator stopped and the door was opening. The stairs door was closing after him by the time the elevator door opened all the way.

On the sidewalk once more, he spotted his Acura coming toward him and waited for it. Van stopped, he got in, and she drove out of the neighborhood.

"Good timing," he said. "Thanks."

"I didn't get to finish my iced coffee. What did you find?"

"Iced coffee! That's a great idea. One more stop to get iced coffee to go. I'm parched."

"For heaven's sake, what did you find?" she demanded.

He told her all of it except for the passwords. He never told his associate every single little thing, he thought, and waited for her response.

"What does that mean, fake driver's licenses and credit cards? What for?"

"Don't know yet. I'll be doing a lot of snooping and might find out something, or not. I didn't read his contract with the corporation but I have pictures, and I'll download them and have printouts to look at."

She scowled at him. "More of the same, just more of the same."

"Van, this is how it works. You plod along for weeks, months, gather crumbs along the way, and there's always a possibility that one of the crumbs might be the important key. No predicting it, though. You just plod along."

"Right," she snapped. A second later, she said, "Tony, I'm sorry. It's just so, so fucking frustrating."

"I know, Van. Believe me, I know."

She stopped at a coffee kiosk, and while he ordered two iced double espressos, she called Marnie to say they were still in Portland and would be pretty late. It was a quarter to five and she was not looking forward to the highway with its stop-and-go traffic, or gridlock.

They were both silent as she eased into the traffic heading toward Highway 26 and the coast. It had not been a wasted day, Van realized. She had learned a valuable lesson, to keep things as simple as possible. She had been devising one incredible scenario after another: lure Dale into a trap, pretend to go along with whatever he wanted, drinks with poison in his, tinker with his car, and they had become so complex that she had abandoned them all and started over time after time. But watching Tony stroll casually into that parking lot as if he belonged there had made her realize how simple it would be for her, after all.

Years ago, Ralph Coleman, her mentor/lover, had told her she needed a handgun for self-protection. She was keeping terrible hours, driving alone late at night, and it would only get worse in medical school. He had taken her to a gun shop and advised her to buy a .22, easy to use, small enough to keep in her handbag, and it would be enough, he had said. He had helped her with a permit and had taken her to a firing range, where she received instructions and practiced using her new weapon.

He was history, she thought grimly, but the gun was now

in a locked box on her closet shelf. She felt as if those thirteen months with her lover had been a dream, someone else's dream. She had come awake pregnant and had looked at him in wonder. How had she been so malleable, so moldable, his to shape and direct, his to command? Love? She had thought so, but had come to know it had not been love, but rather an intoxicating infatuation, one that let her give up her self, her body, her thoughts, everything. Then she woke up from the dream.

And now she was wide-awake and planning on how to kill her onetime stepfather. It would be so simple, she thought. Park a block away, stroll into the parking lot, let herself in as if she belonged, and go straight to the apartment. If he was there already, she would shoot him on sight, make certain he was dead, and walk out. Simplicity itself. If he was not there, she would wait and shoot him the minute he entered. No talk, no arguments, no pleading. Shoot him dead and leave.

She didn't consider it murder. Every year she joined one of the volunteer groups that cleaned the entire coast of tons of trash accumulated over winter. What she planned was of a piece with that. Clear a piece of trash from a beautiful world.

Tony's bitter words came to mind, that killing for revenge never resolved anything. The memory of seeing her mother sitting on the floor in tears rose in her mind. Not revenge, she thought. Dale had to be killed or he would possess her mother's soul. She shook her head slightly. She didn't believe in souls, but something of Stef's being, her essence, had been the cost of her art. Over and over she had paid the high price demanded of her, and a piece of filth like Dale could not possess that part of her that lived in everything she painted.

The creed that she accepted and believed in, that would guide her throughout her life as a physician, came to mind. Do no harm. She would do no harm. She would prevent a malevolent, conscienceless killer from doing additional harm.

Traffic came to a stop and she sipped her coffee, then she said, "Those two pictures Freddi talked about, the little girl at the tide pools and the other one, they weren't a pair at first. Stef painted the little girl at least five years ago. I think it was an expression of herself as a child searching for answers. She was always different, according to Marnie, never part of any group, never really accepted at school, or in town. I think she saw things no one else saw from the day she opened her eyes. I think she was trying to still that questioning voice in her head and just pretended she had found what she was looking for. Or maybe she was trying to keep anyone else from ever questioning what the child was looking for."

"I thought kids never questioned the reality they experience," Tony said. "Like someone color-blind who doesn't know it, or question what he sees unless tested."

"But she questioned it as an adult, and as an adult came to know that the child had been searching without the words to tell anyone about it."

Tony nodded. He thought Stef died without finding answers. He glanced at Van, but she was intent on cars trying to change lanes ahead as traffic inched forward again, and he didn't say any more.

After another prolonged silence, feeling that she was stepping onto forbidden territory, she said, "I looked up that shooting incident in New York. A lot was written about it at the time, and there are several different versions of what happened. Will you tell me about it?" She didn't dare look at him again, but she was aware of his stiffening posture, his withdrawal.

Traffic moved and she inched forward again. Hesitantly she said, "There are such contradictory accounts that I began to wonder if any of them was right."

"It's okay," Tony said tonelessly. He looked out the side window. In a monotone he said, "A kid walked in on his father beating up his mother while a neighbor stood by drinking a beer. The kid got his father's gun and began to wave it around. The neighbor ducked out and called 911. I was a couple of blocks away and was the first responder. The door was open and I just walked on in. They were in the kitchen, her eye was swollen shut, her lip split and bleeding. And the kid was holding a handgun. He was desperate for a way out. He didn't want to shoot anyone, he wanted his father to stop beating his mother. Seventeen, intense, eyeglasses, and desperate for a way out. I was giving him an out. I said I'd testify against the father, his hands were bloody, and the law would deal with him. The kid was listening and I kept talking, how violence just leads to more violence. Stop now before someone gets hurt. Like that. Then the others came in with their guns drawn, and in a flash the kid slipped into panic mode. Scared thoughtless, all rationality gone, just pure panic. They began to shoot simultaneously, the team and the kid. He wasn't aiming at anyone, he couldn't have aimed at that point. He went down and so did I."

In a voice so low it was almost a whisper, Van asked, "How could they have blamed you? Some of the accounts said they found you at fault. How?"

"Internal review," he said, his face still averted, his voice still toneless. "They did what they're trained to do." He thought, but did not say: shoot first and assess the situation when they get around to it. "I should have disarmed the kid when I got there. I should have drawn my own weapon, shot him if necessary. What the team saw was that a kid had the drop on a cop and they reacted appropriately. Case closed."

"Good God! And one of your own guys shot you in the hip, shot you in the back."

Tony did not respond. The review found that twenty-six rounds had been fired, seventeen hit the boy. One hit Tony directly. A ricochet got his knee. One of the final questions before he was dismissed repeated in his mind: *Why did you go in without drawing your weapon first?*

"It had been three to five minutes from the time 911 was called, and no shots had been fired. I didn't believe any would be. I could hear their voices when I got near. That kid didn't want to shoot anyone." He lifted his coffee and took a drink.

"The family got a settlement, didn't they? It didn't go to trial, they just collected a lot of money. A newspaper story was that she had fallen and he was helping clean the blood from her face. The neighbor said that was right, he saw her fall. And the boy's mother confirmed that account. My God! How much is a life worth?"

After a moment of silence Tony said, "Let's play one of those broadcasts you bought from Bud."

"In my bag," she said, pointing to the big handbag she had put on the floor.

Tony pulled the CDs out, one written by Archibald MacLeish, staring Agnes Moorehead and Orson Welles. Too heavy, he decided, and loaded the other one, an episode of *The Inner Sanctum*. He and Van exchanged skeptical looks when it started with the squeaking, squealing door, and the ominous voice of the host. It was a ghost story. In spite of himself Tony began to listen; the broadcast play drove out the bitter memories of that day, that desperate boy he had not wanted to hurt. He could have taken him out, he knew, a disabling shot, not one meant to kill. He could have done that, but he hadn't wanted to hurt the frightened kid. Instead, he had gotten him killed.

The ghost story played: a small group of people forced to find shelter by a blinding snowstorm, an antiquated, run-down hotel, and the eerie happenings, since become clichés, but new in the forties, and effective, suspenseful, even frightening.

When it ended, Van said, "Wow! Bud's right, it sucks you right in. You participate, build scenery, get involved. Television and movies don't do that. You're just a passive observer."

They talked about the radio play, how good the sound effects were, how involved they had become, about the traffic that had begun to flow, how those who could do it flocked to the coast to escape the heat of the valley, and other things. They did not refer to the shooting incident again.

In the Coast Ranges Tony began to adjust the air-conditioning, then turned it off and they opened windows. The cool marine air felt heavenly, Van said. Tony agreed.

It was seven forty-five when they pulled into the driveway at Marnie's house. She met them at the door with Josh at her side. He grabbed Van in an embrace. "I want to show you something," he said, tugging at her hand. "And you, too, To—Mr. Marso."

Tony laughed as they went into the living room. "Hey, Josh, if your mother permits it, you could call me Tony, the way my pals do." Van's mouth tightened and she shook her head.

Ignoring her, Tony said to Josh, "The guys I put in jail always called me Mr. Mauricio, or sometimes Lieutenant Mauricio, but my pals call me Tony."

"Tony!" Van said indignantly. "That's a dirty trick."

"Mom," Josh said, "can, I mean, *may* I call him Tony like his pals do?"

"Since he said it's all right, I guess so," she said with a reproachful look at Tony.

Marnie ducked her head, smiling. She often thought that Van went too far in reacting to Stef's upbringing, went too far in the other direction.

"Come on, Mom and Tony," Josh said. "See, I have three trains put together already, and I'll get the engine done tomorrow. Gramma and I got paint today, red paint. I'll paint them, and when it dries, I'll take my train to school for show-and-tell."

"That's great," Tony said, examining the completed coaches. "It's going to be one good-looking train. I was afraid it might be too hard for you, and I was dead wrong. Good job!"

"You two sit down and relax," Marnie said. "Josh has eaten and had his bath, and it's just about bedtime for him. What do you want to drink?"

On the coffee table was a platter of crackers, cheese, cold cuts, olives, and shrimp. Van said a bourbon and ice water, and Tony said that sounded just right. She went upstairs to wash her hands, and Tony washed his in the lavatory off the kitchen. Marnie brought the drinks and they sat near the wide windows and watched the blue sky turn into a sunset mix of muted colors.

When Van took Josh up to read a story and tuck him into bed, Marnie said, "Did you find out anything new today?"

Tony told her what all they had done, what Freddi had said, about Bud and the search of Dale's apartment. She listened without comment. He felt that he could almost hear her thoughts: more of the same.

Marnie got up to take a lasagna from the oven, add vinaigrette to the salad, and slice a loaf of bread. Van came down and they had dinner.

Tony waited until coffee was poured, then said, "I know how disappointed you both are that things aren't moving faster, we're not getting the results we want, but this is the way it works. Look at it from Dale's perspective. He's being squeezed and the pressure will go up. He can't get his hands on the art, and his big bidding war is on hold for an indefinite period. He owes money to Delacroix, and if he fails to meet his obligations in a timely fashion, their agreement could be revoked altogether and he'd be out of the gallery. That's a standard clause. He knows that. On Wednesday he'll find out about the audit. We know he owes Delacroix about forty thousand, his apartment is expensive, and the lease on that fancy car is, too. If he's delinquent on anything, he's in trouble. The only option he has right now is to bring pressure on the stable of painters he's signed up, but that's problematic, too. I think that after Wednesday, he'll want to make a deal with you, Marnie, something to break the impasse and let that bidding war go forward. He'll probably see his attorney, instruct him to make proposals and do it fast. And you'll stall, send him to your attorney with instructions for him to stall."

"There's something else we could do," Van said, leaning forward. "Write a letter to Dale's sister, something like, did you know Dale made seven hundred thousand from those old tapes? Ask—" She looked at Tony. "What's Bud's grandfather's name? Do you have his address?"

"Jeez," Tony said. "You were born to conspire. Yeah, I have his name."

"I'll write the letter and get it in the mail tomorrow. Anonymously, of course." She looked thoughtful for a second, then said, "I wonder what he did with all that money? It wasn't even quite half when he bought into the gallery."

"He was in France and Italy for several months," Tony said. "And I imagine he lived like a Saudi prince while there, spending sprees, designer clothes, custom-made suits, the works. Maybe too many jaunts to Monte Carlo." Tony shrugged, not really caring how Dale Oliver had managed to get rid of close to half a million dollars in less than six months.

He sipped his coffee, regarded Marnie and then Van with a sober look. "I think he's going to get pretty desperate by the end of the week, and desperate people often do very foolish things. I don't know what direction he'll take, but I suspect it won't be very smart, and we'll have to be ready to deal with it."

18

THAT NIGHT VAN took her calculator to the kitchen table and played with numbers. Dale owed over forty thousand to Delacroix, but even if he got his bidding war and collected 25 percent as agent and another part of whatever the gallery would make, it would not be enough to cover his debt. Say he got the prices up to thirty thousand altogether, she thought, still not enough. Even if he got twice that much, it wouldn't be enough. He couldn't count on his stable of artists to all come through at once. They might bring in another ten thousand or so.

To kill Stef for a few thousand dollars was so outrageous, so hideous, it was pure evil. She felt that she couldn't contemplate such evil, such malevolence, and she went out to the deck where she watched the town lights go out until she was chilled. She continued to sit inside, huddled under a blanket for a long time, finally gave it up, took a hot bath, and went to bed and a deeply troubled sleep.

Tony was on his own balcony that night drinking bourbon and water. He had done the numbers in his head on the drive back to the coast, and it didn't add up, he thought. Van was right, all they were learning about Dale Oliver was more of the same, little or none of it admissible as relevant in a murder case. He used unsavory, but probably common, business practices in the art world, the problem with his sister was a civil matter to be settled in a different court, or by mediation or something, not relevant. If he had been involved in a scam at the dealership or adjacent used-car lot back East five years ago, let New Jersey handle it; it was not relevant to the murder of Stefany Markov.

He had seen too many cases crumble, he brooded, to believe that this would be any different. It would never get to a jury, to trial. No prosecutor would move it forward since it was based on nothing more than suspicion, and a shady past. There was no real evidence that would be admissible.

Tony knew he had done it, and that day he had learned how he had done it. He closed his eyes and watched the scene unfold in his mind's eye.

Dale was Delmar Oliver's son, he'd grown up knowing about sound effects, how they were produced and used. He tapes a scream lifted from television. Any night of the week you could hear a scream or two. No problem. He walks a dozen or so steps in his apartment, then tape records a door opening, followed by his own anguished cry. He probably practices that part many times until he gets it right. Again no problem. He drops something and gets that on tape. Not likely to have been his cell phone. Why risk ruining a perfectly good phone? He places his phone on the sofa, faced away from him, and goes to the other side of the room to utter more agonized words, her name a few times, then on to his little home office, not out of range of the phone, but distant enough for Freddi to almost hear his words, and he fakes a call to 911. He turns off the tape recorder at that point.

The day of the murder, he has his pigeons lined up, the various sound effects coordinated, a narrative background. He and Stef load some artwork in the van. He puts the little truck at the foot of the stairs. Stef goes up to shower and dress, and he picks up one of her paintings, an oil that isn't likely to be hurt and can be reframed. He takes it upstairs, out to the passage and stairs, and smashes it on the banister, tosses it over. Back to the bedroom where Stef has put on some clothes, but not her shoes. Doesn't matter, he decides, and clips her, knocks her unconscious. He carries her limp body upstairs, to the passage, and rolls her down the stairs. He wants her to have a lot of bruises, abrasions, a broken bone or two would be okay. Those injuries will hide the mark left when he hit her in the head.

He goes back through the studio, closes the door after him and goes downstairs, out to check, make sure she's dead. If she isn't, it's easy enough to finish the job, another twist of her neck, another smash of her head on concrete. Inside again, he starts the CD player, and using the sounds as his cues, he calls Freddi, ebullient, bubbling because, he tells her, Stef is coming along, has agreed to sell more work, recent work. The scream sounds, and he goes to the door and waits for the CD to finish. When it's done, he puts his cell near the planter where it's safe and will be found; his last call will confirm the time he called Freddi. He retrieves his CD and stashes it among music CDs in the van. Later he will reformat it or simply burn something new onto it. Then he waits for the cops and act two, where he plays the bereaved, shocked, and agonized widower. A little soapy water in his eyes makes that perfect, he is weeping for his beloved.

But the numbers didn't add up, Tony thought morosely. Dale needed money now, and Stef's art was more like a separate 401(k) that would pay off over the years. He got up to replenish his drink and put on his Windbreaker. The apartment had been hot and stuffy when he got home that night; now it had cooled off a little too much and he was nowhere near ready for bed.

He sat in his darkened living room, lit only by a sink light from the kitchen. He would find the right guy in Newark, pass on the information about the fake ID and credit cards, let them go on from there, or not. There had been a scam going, he recalled, with flooded cars from one of the recent hurricanes. The cars were toast, and most of them ended up crushed to a block of metal and shipped off to China, where the metal was reprocessed. But some were sold cheap at salvage auctions for usable parts, and some of them ended up in used-car lots, cleaned up, paint touched up a little, and they were sold as good used cars, only to fall apart within a couple of months. Dale Oliver might have been involved, but it made no difference here and now.

Dale might take the whip to his stable, Tony thought then. He had looked over Dale's contract with the greeting-card corporation, a multibillion-dollar business with an insatiable need for new original art, not only for individual purchases, but wholesale to stores, big-box stores, mom-and-pop stores, and for charities that sent out thousands, hundreds of thousands, of packages of cards, hoping for return donations, new donors to add to their base. Corporations, universities, sales forces, all sent out thousands of cards, and they wanted original art for print cards as well as e-cards.

The payment schedule in Dale's contract agreed to pay him five thousand dollars for every two to four original works of art delivered to the corporation, depending on the quality of the paintings. The corporation then had the art to recycle forever after. According to Freddi, her artist Moira was making two thousand, and her work was going for two hundred fifty dollars a painting. That meant that twice a year Dale got five thousand, paid her one, and pocketed four thousand. With eleven artists already in his stable, it could mean a yearly income of up to a hundred thousand dollars, but it would be staggered throughout the year, and there was no guarantee that each and every one of the artists would keep producing at that rate. It wasn't like an automated factory cranking out endless strings of spaghetti. And Dale Oliver needed money now, within the next week or so.

Tony sat up straighter and drained his glass. Stef had produced thirty years' worth of art, hundreds of paintings, he thought, and recalled what Van had said, that Dale mentioned that all art was exploitable, even *David* was available as a refrigerator magnet.

"He intended to add Stef to his stable!" Tony said under his breath, and cursed.

She signed her death warrant when she signed that contract. Dale would have known about her past men, her past marriages. He would have known she would ditch him, nullify that contract, and he killed her to keep that from happening. Thirty years of art to exploit. Four thousand dollars at least for every two or three paintings he delivered. In Stef's case, he would keep it all, and neither Marnie nor Van would ever know what he had done, and that meant five thousand for every two or three works of art. Her work, even her more conventional work, was superior to anything else in his stable; no doubt hers would be worth more. He could sell hundreds of paintings to the corporation. A few big sales, a museum piece or two sold, would make her other art more valuable, more expensive. That was Dale's out, his pot of gold at rainbow's end. If she hadn't played a game with her name on the contract, it would have been done by now, and he would have been out from under the bus.

But first she had to die.

Of course, Dale would deny that such was his intention. He said, she said. A draw. What a prosecutor would see was a suspicion, possibly a plausible suspicion, a hypothetical method, an equally hypothetical motive, and not a scrap of hard evidence of murder. Even a mediocre defense attorney would demolish a case like that without raising a sweat.

Tony brooded, lifted his empty glass, put it down. He didn't want to get drunk. He went into the kitchen, poured leftover coffee instead, and heated it in the microwave. It was bitter, but he sipped it, welcoming the bitterness as fitting.

The real question, he thought then, was what in hell did he think he was doing? Stef had meant nothing to him. An unstable woman, eccentric, thoughtless, often cruel, indifferent to anyone's opinion, a burden on her mother, and a trial for her daughter. And a brilliant artist who was tormented by the truth she was compelled to paint. An artist just reaching the height of her talent. What would she have done in the years ahead? But she had been nothing to him.

Her family meant nothing to him, acquaintances, no more than that. Van was forever off-limits, and Marnie, with a multitude of friends, needed nothing he had to offer except for this one task that he could not accomplish.

"Knock it off," he muttered to himself. He knew perfectly well what he was doing. He intended to apply so much pressure to Dale Oliver, coming from all directions, that he would be forced deeper and deeper into a corner until in desperation he would do something stupid, something that would justify Tony's shooting him.

He was planning to kill Dale Oliver. Not just beat the shit out of him. He was going to kill him. Possibly to make up for all the others who had gotten away with it. Possibly because of that desperate, scared kid holding a gun, the kid he should have shot and didn't. Possibly because his own guys had shot him in the back. Possibly because he had never shot anyone. Possibly because for twenty years he had been a good cop, knew exactly where the line was and was always impeccable about keeping on the right side of it. Possibly because he had come to hate and despise Dale Oliver more with every new bit of information that had come to light. He knew he had lost any shred of objectivity, a cardinal sin in investigations. He no longer could step back and look at this case with an impersonal eye. He had let his feelings take over. If this had happened when he was still on the homicide detail, at this point his captain, Mark Rosini, would have sent him off for a vacation. He had no intention of walking away.

The line he had observed for so long had vanished. Poof! Gone.

It was late, and he was tired down to his bones. He poured out the remaining bitter coffee, rinsed the cup, and turned off the light. In the bathroom, brushing his teeth, he looked at his reflection in the mirror and said in a low voice, "Welcome, Wyatt Earp."

Sleep refused to come. He lay with his eyes closed, pretending he was drifting off, and his mind kept going over the past few days, that one day in particular. Van had made the kid with his gun leap into his head again. His shaking hands, dead white face, big scared eyes magnified by his glasses.

His thoughts took a fast-forward to the day Mark Rosini had come to his apartment. Captain Rosini, longtime friend, his superior.

"Goddamn, Tony, you're looking better," Mark said heartily when Tony admitted him to the apartment.

Not quite a lie, but close. At least no tubes were in various parts of his body as they had been the last time Mark had visited at the hospital. Using crutches, Tony made his way back to a recliner chair and motioned toward the couch.

Mark perched on the couch. He was lean with a voracious appetite, the envy of those who claimed that looking at food made them gain weight. He was ten years older than Tony, not good in social situations, and was an extremely good captain. There was an awkward silence that Tony felt no inclination to break. Finally Mark said, "The guys send their best wishes."

Tony let it pass. That wasn't what Mark had come to say.

"Lincoln Doherty's been around," Mark said after another pause. Doherty was with the law firm that handled what the press sometimes referred to as delicate situations. "You know the family sued for ten million? They're about to settle for something like two."

Still Tony made no comment. A common enough practice. Get it settled and out of sight as fast as possible. Avoid going to court, no matter what. Bury it. He knew.

"And, goddamn it! They're trying to give you the shaft! I'm supposed to persuade you to take that desk job. Hell with that desk job," Mark said, and for the first time Tony felt Mark had left the script. He was winging it. "I talked to Sid this afternoon. He's sticking to his guns. He told Doherty to fuck off, meet again in court if that's what it takes. I told Sid anything I can do, any of the guys can do, we're there for you. I mean that job, if you wanted it, great with me. But to force it on you. They want to keep you in the chain of command, keep you quiet. Fuck that!"

"Thanks, Mark," Tony said. "I appreciate that."

Tony had been in law school with Sid Byerly for a couple of years. Sid had continued, and they had remained close friends. Sid was a successful trial attorney. He had come storming into the hospital while Tony was still groggy with dope and he had raged, "Not a word! For God's sake don't sign anything! Keep your mouth shut. Not even name, rank, and serial. They know who the fuck you are. This is my baby, Tony. Mine. Your own guys shot you in the back, for Christ sake! Goddamn cowboys! This one is mine, and don't you forget it."

Tony nodded at Mark. He knew Sid was sticking to his original demands. A good settlement, total medical coverage for the rest of Tony's life, highest disability pension, enough to live on comfortably for a year or two after he finally got around to the hip replacement.

"He'll get what he's after," Mark said. "He'll get all he's after. What's next for you, Tony?"

"I don't know," Tony said. "Out, away. That's as far as I've got. Someplace where I don't have to wonder if everyone I see on the street is packing a gun, where kids don't point guns at their parents. The cowboys are in charge, Mark, and I'm tired. Just tired. From the highest office in the whole fucking country to the box beds in alleys, nothing but guns, trigger-happy cowboys. They'll be sending newborns home from the hospital with their own little pink or blue first guns." He paused and said bitterly, "It sucks, Mark, from top to bottom it sucks. Even when we nail them, they manage to walk. I want out of it."

"Yeah," Mark said heavily. "I hear you. Soon as Rory gets

221

out of school, I'll be looking for that place, too. Let me know if you find it." Rory was Mark's youngest son and had recently started going to the university. "You know when you're likely to take off?"

"Soon as I get rid of them," Tony said, indicating the crutches. "And when Sid says go."

Mark rose from the couch. "I guess that's what I came by to say." He was awkward again. "I'll see you before you take off. But if you skip in the middle of the night, and I wouldn't blame you if it happened like that, well, you know."

Tony pulled himself up and took his crutches again. "I know, Mark. Couple of weeks, maybe a month. There'll be time."

"Yeah. Well, I'd better get back." Mark went to the door, then turned and gave Tony a big hug. "You take care of yourself, Tony. Get that hip fixed. Just take care."

"You, too. I'll let you know if I find that place."

Lying in bed, the scene in his head real, fresh, and alive, Tony closed his eyes tighter. They had both been near tears that day. They had known that was the real good-bye. There might be a little party later, dinner with the guys, something, but that was the final good-bye.

Cowboys, he thought then. He had become one of the cowboys. It felt right, where he belonged, where he had a role to play.

19

VAN ROAMED THROUGH the house restlessly after delivering
Josh to day care. Waiting for something to happen was the
hardest part, she told herself several times, but that didn't
help. Finally she decided to paint Josh's room, keep busy all
day, accomplish something.

Marnie was nearly as restless as Van. She walked to the
shop, where a folding screen had been put in front of the
alcove. Molly's two nieces were working. They smiled brightly
at her and continued helping customers. The shop was busy
with summer people looking for souvenirs, postcards, sweatshirts, whatever. She didn't linger and had no desire to talk
to anyone in town, accept condolences again, and the looks
of sorrow that appeared on nearly everyone's face when
people saw her. She walked back home.

Later she stood in the doorway of Josh's promised room
and for a moment felt disoriented because it was so bare. No

paintings lining the walls, filling all the space. She blinked hard and cleared her throat. Van stopped painting and turned toward her.

"Midge just called," Marnie said. "She wanted to know if we could make it to their place for the Fourth of July. She urged us to come. I said we would. Josh will love it. If you'd rather not, I'll call her back."

Every year Midge and Pete Fellows had open house for the Fourth with a potluck dinner, and when it grew dark, from their lovely big deck high on a bluff overlooking Newport Bay, the fireworks were a holiday treat. Van had loved it as a child and she knew Josh would also. This was the first year she felt he was old enough for the event, and already he was excited by the idea of fireworks, his own sparklers.

"That's good," she said reluctantly. "He really will love it and we should start doing things again, I guess." She resumed painting.

THAT MORNING TONY spent some time probing Dale's computer. He stopped abruptly and logged off. "What difference does it make?" he asked himself savagely. Dale had twenty-one hundred and change in his bank account, four credit cards, two maxed out, two close to the edge. He was making minimum payments only. He had two porno sites with their own passwords.

Tony went out to his balcony. Dale might not go for a negotiated agreement first; he might decide he had to take some action as soon as he found out about the audit. And he, Tony, had put Van, Marnie, and Josh at risk.

If Dale did decide to take action, it would have to be here in Silver Bay. No way could he lure both Van and Marnie to a meeting in Portland or anywhere else. And he wouldn't come here in his flashy convertible, dressed in a designer suit. The locals would watch him like a poisonous snake. He would use one of those fake IDs, an alias. Tony went inside to study the printouts of the credit cards and driver's licenses again, Daniel Olson and Dominick Orsini. Both had darker hair than Dale, Dominick's quite a bit darker, and he had what looked like a three- or four-day stubble of a beard. Olson had a bad haircut, with hair standing almost upright on the top of his head. His eyebrows were heavy and nearly black, and he wore black-framed eyeglasses. He also had a stubble of a beard. Of course, Tony thought. That cleft chin. Hide it.

The most interesting thing about the cards, Tony knew, was that they both were still active, with expiration dates one or three years from then. Dale had kept them active, had used them enough, paid them off on time, and kept them. For what purpose? To buy illicit items? In case of emergency? Just to have if the need arose to go somewhere else fast? To hide his movements?

Possibly if Tony continued to unravel the various passwords, he would come to the credit card activities, but he had decided it didn't matter. They were active, and that did matter.

He nodded, put the printouts away, and left his apartment to drive to the motel access road. In each motel, and the motel that called itself an inn, he told the same story. What quickly became evident was that Will had prepared the ground for him by spreading the word about Tony's past. He told people some things they should know, Tony reflected, remembering Will's words. In this instance he was grateful for Will's need to talk.

"I'm not wholly retired," he said to the four motel managers he talked to. "More like an extended leave of absence. Recently I had a call from a colleague back East who mentioned that a guy they were looking for might be headed this way. Since I'm on the spot, he asked me to let him know if the guy comes through here. Seems they want to ask him some questions about a possible white-collar crime or some kind of fraud back East, and they've had reports that he's been moving up the coast, maybe headed for Canada. He isn't considered dangerous, and they want to keep it quiet, but to be informed if he shows. I said I'd pass the word to the motels in the area. All I'd want is to be called if he makes a reservation or simply shows up wanting a room. I'll call the state troopers, if that's the case, and they will handle it very quietly. I don't expect it to happen. It's a real long shot, but no harm done in keeping an eye out for him."

There usually were a few questions along about then, which he parried with no trouble. No one questioned his right to make such a request.

"He's been using two different names, and we don't know which one he'd use if he turns up," he told them.

"Better not just turn up," Lorinne Hadley said. She was the manager of the Silver Moon Motel. "This time of year, with the Fourth coming, there usually aren't any spare rooms to be found. He'll need a reservation anywhere along the coast."

"Even better. That will give us some time to prepare for him." Tony gave them his cell phone number and the two names, made sure the managers spelled them right, and that was done.

Aware that Van would leave to pick up Josh at day care a few minutes before four, he waited until nearly three-thirty to drop in at the rear house on the ridge.

Marnie let him in and asked, "Anything new?"

"A little. Is Van around?"

"She's washing up. She painted Josh's room today. Come

on back, Tony." She led the way to the living room. The completed train was on the coffee table. "He's anxious to start painting it," Marnie said when Tony stopped to admire the train. "He wanted to stay home from day care and do it, but we said no. He loves his train, Tony. He's so proud that he put it together by himself. What a wonderful thing to give him. Did you have a train set when you were small?"

"Yeah," Tony said softly, remembering the train setup he, his sister, and his father had put together in the basement. Mountains, tunnels, houses on hills, a church . . . His mother had started to complain that it was a menace when she was doing the laundry. He was telling Marnie about it when he became aware that Van had come down, stopped at the door, and was listening.

"That was a long time ago," he said. "What I came to tell you is a little about those contracts. He has eleven artists signed up, and for every batch of three or four paintings he sells to a corporation, he is paid five thousand. He pays his artists one thousand and keeps four. He lives in an upscale, high-rent apartment, and payments for various things are coming due the first of the month." Just two days away, he realized. June was nearly over.

"He will be feeling more and more pressured," he warned, "so keep your eyes open. Don't let him in, and don't talk to him if he comes here. Just give me a call and I'll come over."

Marnie's mouth was a grim line, and Van nodded. "Inviting him in for coffee is not in our game plan," she said bitterly. "Not unless it's laced with strychnine."

"Tony, we're invited to a big potluck on the Fourth," Marnie said, as if eager to change the subject. "Some old friends always have an open house for it, and you'd be welcome as our guest to watch the fireworks over Newport Bay."

He thanked her politely and declined the invitation.

Marnie had a flash of memory. Stef had wanted Dale to join the group one year and he had said, "A potluck? How very Norman Rockwell." He had not gone.

Van looked at her watch and said she had to go, and Tony said he'd be on his way, too. He was thinking furiously. The Fourth of July, fireworks, people shooting guns, strangers all over town . . . What a perfect setting for Daniel Olson or Dominick Orsini. Sound effects guaranteed.

FREDDI CALLED VAN on Wednesday. "The auditor was already here when Dale came in. He turned white, I swear, dead white, and he began to say things like common decency required that I give him a little warning, to let him make sure everything was up-to-date.

"Sometimes he lets things slide until the end of the month, things like that. I told him I'd talked to Hiram Delacroix and I wanted to be able to reassure him that everything was all right with the gallery. Then the man came to change the locks, and I thought Dale would roll on the floor kicking and screaming or something. He was shaking, he was so mad, and he took off. So now he knows." Freddi was almost breathless.

When Van hung up, she repeated what Freddi had said to Marnie and added faintly, "The ball's in his court. His move."

It wasn't long in coming. Van had taken Josh to day care and planned to grocery shop after dropping him off. Marnie was making curtains for Josh's room, a train motif on a blue background to go with the primrose-yellow walls and blue trim. She rose to answer the doorbell that late morning.

"Ms. Markov?" her caller said. He was in his midfifties, she guessed, with nice gray hair, wearing a handsome pale-

228

gray sport coat and darker slacks, a white shirt open at the throat. He was well tanned and looked trim and fit.

"I'm Marnie Markov," she said, without opening the door to invite him inside.

"My name is Lionel Moulton, representing Mr. Dale Oliver in that unfortunate misunderstanding about a contract. May I come in to outline some proposals Mr. Oliver has agreed to put forward to resolve this issue?"

"Please, excuse me just a moment," Marnie said. "I'll be right back." She closed the door and went to the kitchen counter, where she had placed several of Ted Gladstone's cards. She picked one up and returned to the door, opened it slightly wider than before, and held the card out to the attorney. "This is my attorney's card, his Newport address and phone number. Please contact him with any proposals you may have."

"Ms. Markov, may I give you some friendly advice? A judge will not look approvingly on your refusal to even consider a compromise in this situation."

"I'm sure Mr. Gladstone will welcome such advice. Goodbye, Mr. Moulton." Marnie closed the door and stood with her hand on the knob while she took in several long breaths. She had never been so rude to anyone in her life, she thought with satisfaction when she returned to the kitchen and the phone there to call Ted Gladstone and inform him that Dale's lawyer might be on his way to the office.

Van was putting away groceries when Ted Gladstone called back later. She closed the refrigerator door and listened as Marnie took the call.

"He came," Ted said jovially, "and Dorothy followed my instructions and told him that I was tied up for the rest of the day and would be out of town until after the Fourth. She suggested that he should mail me his proposals and I'd get in touch next week after my return. She said he was in a snit."

"Thanks, Ted," Marnie said. "That sounds just right."

"I put a draft copy of your will in the mail," he said. "When you get it, look it over, and if you find it satisfactory, give us a call and we'll arrange a time for you to drop in and sign it. I think it's exactly what we talked about."

She thanked him again and, after hanging up, repeated the conversation to Van. They were both nervous, and she suspected that Van had done the same things she had done before going to bed the night before. She had gone through both houses, testing the windows, making sure the door stops at the sliding doors were all in place, making sure the doors were all locked, checking outdoor lights to make certain they were on. Also, after Josh had fallen asleep, she had called Tipper out and closed Josh's door all the way, something they never had done before. It was Tipper's time to be a watchdog, Marnie had decided. And finally, she thought grimly, she had done something Van could not have done. When Marnie went to her room the previous night, she had unlocked the desk drawer, removed Ed's old handgun, and put it in the drawer of her bedside table.

Van's .22 was now in a similar drawer in her bedroom, and it was loaded. It only added to her nervousness for fear that Josh might wander into her room and come upon it. She was watching him closely to prevent that.

"I'll call Tony and tell him about Moulton," Marnie said. Then she added, "I'll be checking locks and everything later. Let's do it together."

Van nodded and Marnie dialed Tony's number.

———

230

WHEN DALE STARTED to curse Moulton over the phone, the attorney interrupted and said, "Mr. Oliver, I did the best I could. I'll be out of the office until July fifth. Why don't you call my secretary and make an appointment for the afternoon then and we'll discuss this, if you wish."

He hung up and Dale snapped his phone shut. "Goddamn bungling idiot! You botched it, you bastard!" he yelled at the phone.

Idiots and fools! He was surrounded by idiots and fools! That idiot had let a stupid fishwife run the show! He'd warned him that Marnie was out to steal the artwork, that she hated his guts. She and Van both hated his guts for no reason at all, just jealousy and greed. They wanted the paintings for themselves. They wanted to cut him out, grab it all.

That asshole Moulton acted as if he were their goddamn lawyer, Dale thought savagely, thinking of the conversation they'd had when this mess began. "They were perfectly in their rights to order an inventory," Moulton had said. "Any judge would agree. As long as she is the executor of the art estate, that is her right, and her duty."

"She isn't the executor! I am!" Dale yelled.

"Not yet. Not as long as that contract is in dispute. Mr. Oliver, this is going to take time, perhaps a long time. Until the matter is resolved, she will remain in charge of the artwork."

"Crap! What if a tsunami wipes her out?"

"Ms. Vanessa Markov can continue to contest that contract, and, Mr. Oliver, if that tsunami catches her, too, the attorney for the estate can still contest it in the name of the child."

Moulton had continued in the same calm, measured tones, as cool as an ice floe, "Mr. Oliver, there is no way of knowing at this time how a judge will decide concerning the validity of the contract. He will, of course, do what the law demands, but he also is a human being who will weigh in all the circumstances involved. Ms. Markov provided a home for her daughter all her life, and she set up a trust for her to ensure her future economic security. Those are not the actions of a greedy woman, but rather those of a caring parent. You are number four in a series of short-lived marriages, and you have been on the scene for no longer than three years or so. Furthermore, you and the late Mrs. Oliver maintained separate residences for most of your married life. He will also add that fact to his considerations."

"Are you telling me I can't prove my case?" Dale demanded furiously. "She signed that contract. She wanted me to handle it."

"That, of course, is a factor in the equation a judge will take into account. However, I advise you not to make any plans at this time for the future dispensation of the work." Moulton rose from behind his desk.

He was being dismissed, Dale thought with his fury mounting. He stalked to the door of Moulton's office. "If the tsunami gets them all, then by default I'd be the executor, because no one else would be left. Is that how you see it?"

"That would be the only way I could state with certainty that you would be the executor," Moulton said coldly. "But, Mr. Oliver, don't hedge any bets by counting on an act of God to end this dilemma."

He should have pounded him on the spot, Dale thought angrily. He should have told him to shut the fuck up and found himself a different lawyer. One not so cool and superior, not so goddamn condescending. The only reason that bastard had even gone to Marnie was because he had planned to go to the coast on Friday anyway, to spend a few days with his family at their coast cabin.

And Marnie shut the door in his face. That bitch, he

thought savagely. She was out to screw him over, her and Van both. They'd turned Freddi against him, had her doing their dirty work.

All his life, ever since he was a kid, the women around him had been out to screw him over. Ever since his stupid sister won her first beauty contest when she was ten and he was twelve, he had been the invisible kid in the family. Things had been good before that. They all played games together. Christ! They even played with his old man's crazy sound-effect tapes, taking roles, reading the lines, laughing at the result when they played them back. Then that beauty contest.

His mother and sister, all they could think about after that was her next beauty contest. Screwing him over, all of them, and nothing had changed since then. One woman after another out for all she could get.

Even Jasmine, as good as he'd been to her, would have left without a wave of her hand. She had not been cheap. It was her fault he was in trouble now.

He got up and went to the bar in the living room to make a drink. All right, he told himself, he was in a jam, but he could handle it. His artists were too flaky to count on. They made promises to deliver and went camping or to visit family in Montana or some damn place. A sick kid, or someone needed to go to practice. Always something. Damn slackers. There was still one who might come through in a couple of days, and he had two more artists he had been talking into signing on, and they would bring in eight grand. In a few weeks, not this week.

He had to have twelve thousand dollars in hand when the auditor finished and made his report. Probably on Monday or Tuesday. Rent was due on the first and the lease payment on the car. Another three thousand. He had ten days' grace period for them both, but not a day more than that. He could handle all that one way or another, but it was that son of a bitch Delacroix who was being a pain in the ass. He had money, he didn't need any more right now.

Dale needed the gallery. He met people, rich people, people who counted, and they respected an art gallery owner, looked up to him, invited him to lunch, introduced him to others. Delacroix had the gall to refer to the termination clause in the contract. Not a direct threat, he was too cowardly to come right out and say it, but the threat was there, and if that miserly old man got serious, Dale would be out on his ass.

Dale sat at his desk with his eyes closed, drinking scotch. He could get out of the gallery problem if he had the money in hand. His wife had just died. He had been too distraught to think clearly, had made bookkeeping errors, had been careless. On-the-spot restitution, apologize, done.

It was the bitch scarecrow's fault. If she hadn't got cute with her name, this would be over. He had sold four of her paintings to Global Greetings, an easy ten thousand, and no one had missed them. His contact at Global wanted more as soon as he could deliver. Executive cards, he had said. High-class material for CEO types. Fourteen more right away, Dale had decided, and then slow it down, way down. And raise the ante. If Global balked, a zillion others were out there.

No cash advance on his credit cards was available, and he had sold or pawned just about everything with enough value to make it worthwhile. Pennies on the dollar that fed his rage every time he had to go that way.

The other two, he thought then. Olson and Orsini. He could get cash advances on them, ten thousand total. He had used them for Internet stuff, never in person, not since leaving New Jersey, and they both had bank accounts with enough cash to cover them and keep them active, just in case.

He sat drinking scotch, thinking of his Jersey days, the dealership, the used-car lot. He had been treated like some kind of low-life scum. No more. Never again! He thought about Ernie "the Get Guy" Kavitch.

Minutes later he drained his glass, looked up Ernie's number, and placed a call.

"Hey, Ernie," he said when the gruff voice he remembered came on the line. "Dan Olson. How're you doing?"

There was a long pause. He could imagine Ernie sifting through names for a match. Then Ernie said, "Danny! Danny Olson, where you been keeping yourself? Haven't seen you around?"

"West Coast," Dale said. "In the art racket. You know, buy and sell art. Buy a piece here, there, wherever it turns up. You know anyone with a . . . a piece of art to sell? Tacoma, Seattle, someplace like that?"

Another pause. "Maybe," Ernie said. "Give me a number. I'll call you back."

AFTER TALKING TO Marnie, Tony considered the time element. It was one-thirty. Moulton might get back to Portland in time to report to Dale that evening, or he could call him, or put it off until the next day. Then, once again, it would be Dale's turn to move. Tony was deep in thought when he left his apartment a few minutes later, to walk down to the motel access road, and his favorite spot on the coast, the basalt rocks overlooking tide pools. He regarded it as his thinking spot as he had come to dislike his small apartment more all the time.

The tide was going out he saw when he reached his chosen

rock. One day he would make it when the tide was inward bound, and a storm pushing it hard. He would have to stop much higher on the trail, but it would be good to see the waves breaking high against the surrounding cliffs, to be that close, yet safe. He had to get a tide table, he thought, and remembered that he had thought the same thing quite often, then repeatedly forgotten to pick one up.

Okay, Dale's move, he thought again, sitting where the wind didn't reach him, on rocks warmed by the sun but not facing directly into it. A good place to sit, to meditate, to plot.

Dale might have a grace period to pay his debtors, but it would not be for long, and the only way he could raise enough money was by selling a dozen, two dozen, possibly even more, of Stef's paintings to the corporation he had a contract with. He didn't know where the paintings were, so he couldn't go in and help himself. He would know that Marnie was using every stall available to keep him on the outside. The only way around that was to get rid of Marnie, and to do it before she had a chance to update her will, to name Van as the executor of the artwork in the event of her own death or incapacitation.

Tony doubted that Dale considered Van to be much of a hindrance. Her whole future as a doctor was at risk if she became involved in a prolonged struggle here. And she had not yet been designated a possible future executor of the art estate.

In any event, Dale would have to move soon, as soon as he could conceive of a workable plan. Tony believed he would make his move to coincide with the Fourth of July.

And he had to make his own plan to deal with that. He watched a retreating wave, the foam that formed, then vanished in the wet sand, leaving a new tide pool exposed. A new wave recovered the tide pool, retreated. Then another . . . He blinked as a little girl ran to the newly uncovered tide pool. He had not noticed any others on the tiny beach until she moved.

Abruptly he stood up and rubbed his eyes. They had been playing tricks on him. No one was on the strip of beach. Yet, he had been watching a wraithlike little girl with wild, wind-tangled hair darting from one tide pool to another. "Jesus God," he muttered, and shook his head. She had been almost transparent, quick as lightning dashing from pool to pool, and he had watched her, followed her actions.

He had so focused on her, so concentrated on her, that not a single thought had occurred to him. He had not come up with any plan of his own. He rubbed his eyes again. He did not want that painting in his house, he realized. He did not want that ghost child running from tide pool to tide pool anyplace near him, haunting his dreams. Let that spectral child haunt someone else.

He started back up the stairlike basalt rocks, away from illusions, from ghosts, back to the real world.

At eight that night Amory Gallingsworth called. He was the owner/manager of Surf's Up Motel, operated by him and his wife, and of course a cleaning crew, he had told Tony.

"He made a reservation," Amory said in a low, conspiratorial voice. "He said he's Daniel Olson, and he wants a room for the Fourth. Me and Ruth talked about all this and we've been holding one room open, you know, just in case, and he did it, called for a reservation."

"Good job," Tony said. He suspected that Amory and Ruth craved a little excitement, something to talk about later, be the center of attention for their fifteen minutes of fame. "One thing more. When he checks in, he'll give his car license number and make of car. I want you to call me as soon as you can and pass on the information. This is going to make all the difference, Amory. Many thanks."

"Oh, we want to help, Tony. We really do want to help. I'll call you the instant he leaves the front desk. The very instant he leaves."

"Uh, Amory, just don't do anything to make him think we're onto him. You know, act excited or treat him in any special way. Just be yourself. Okay?"

"You bet, Tony. Just another overnight customer. That's all, just another tired traveler. I get it."

Tony sat on his balcony after the call, but his mind kept drifting, he kept seeing *Feathers and Ferns,* and a little transparent girl searching tide pools, *Ladies in Waiting,* harsh, brutal landscapes . . . and finally he gave up trying to force his shutdown brain to function. He went inside and channel-hopped on TV, then he surfed the Web aimlessly until he decided to go to bed, put it all away for the night. Sleep. It was elusive, a long time coming.

20

TONY WAS IN the shop when Dave McAdams arrived on the morning of July 2. Dave grunted, cleared his throat, and asked, "How's it going?"

"Pretty well. I need thinking time. I'll finish up with those chair legs today, and think." No more surfing the Internet, no more sitting around brooding, just do something, he had decided, and he had gone to the shop.

Dave grunted again and nodded. He understood that. He did some pretty heavy thinking himself while his hands kept busy doing what needed to be done. He knew that feeling, that way of getting to the middle of a problem.

The day passed swiftly, leaving Tony as relaxed as a punctured balloon, and as thoughtless. It was strange, he thought a little later, no plan was in his head, no coherent plan of what he was going to do overall, but he knew what he had to do next. One step at a time, he told himself. Just one baby step at a time.

He went to Tom's Fine Foods and ordered fish-and-chips to go. It was nearly impossible to find a table or booth as the heat wave continued in the valley and the Fourth approached, sending more and more people to the cool coast for relief and to celebrate. He took his dinner home and ate on his balcony, and that night he slept well.

He had learned Chief Will Comley's habits almost as well as Marnie knew them, and he dropped in at ten on the morning of July 3.

"Got a few minutes, Chief?"

Will was delighted to be having company, as always. "Sure, Tony. Come on in. Let me get you some coffee. Anything new with Marnie's problem?"

"Maybe," Tony said, taking the extra chair, accepting Will's terrible coffee with a polite thanks.

At his "maybe" Will's eyes narrowed as he took his own chair behind his desk and leaned forward expectantly. "What do you have?"

"A very long shot, but what the hell, we're trained to pay attention to them all, aren't we? Long shots, sure things. They all need looking at. Isn't that how it goes?"

Will nodded emphatically. "That's how she plays, all right. Tell me about it." There was almost a pitiful, plaintive note in his voice, as if he really doubted that Tony had any intention of telling him anything important.

"That's what I'm here for," Tony said. He put his coffee mug down on the desk and leaned forward, lowered his voice a little, and said, "I think it's a break, but like I said, it could be a wash, and it's definitely a long shot. I need backup, help."

"Tony, you've got it! All the way, partner. Whatever it is, you got it."

"Thanks. You know I've been poking around in Dale Oliver's past, just routine, but sometimes routine pays off. I called a guy I know back East and asked him if they had anything on Oliver, and he called back later and said maybe. They wanted to ask him questions five years ago, and he sort of disappeared before they got to it. There was a scam going at a used-car lot connected with a dealership where Oliver was the business manager. Bummer cars, cars that had been flooded, cleaned up a little, were being sold to the locals. Seems some aliases were being used to cover up how the cars had been acquired, at salvage auction, and they were being passed off as individually owned vehicles from around the state. Two of the aliases, they believed, were being used by Dale Oliver. One called himself Daniel Olson, and the other one was Dominick Orsini. Along about then Oliver came into some money and he took off for a few months in Europe. Then he came out here. They didn't have enough to put out an APB and it was dropped."

Will's eyes rounded, and he said, "They really do that? Keep their initials like that?"

"As often as not. Anyway, this is where the long shot comes in. Chief, I think Marnie and Van are dead right about him, and that he really did murder Stef."

Will shook his head and drew back a bit.

Ignoring his reaction, Tony continued, "With that in mind I started to wonder if there might be a damning bit of evidence left in the house, something Oliver knows is there, but that no one has come across, or wouldn't recognize as important if they did. The house was filled with people after Stef was killed, and then Marnie ordered him out and

241

changed the locks. So he hasn't been back. It occurred to me that if he still had those fake IDs handy, he might use one, get a room here, get inside the house, and collect it. He wouldn't show up here as the fancy city dude with his big, splashy car and designer clothes. But he could come as someone else. Like I said, a real long shot."

Tony spread his hands, lifted his coffee, and even took a sip before putting it back down. Will Comley was leaning all the way back in his chair, the posture of a man who didn't believe a thing he was hearing.

How easy it was, Tony thought, to start with a germ of truth and spin, spin, to weave a web without end, ever expanding, ever more elaborate. He had seen it countless times with those on the opposite side of the table, even admired their skill, he had to admit, but now he was finding out how easy it was, that he had a talent for doing it. The words flowed and were plausible. Idea followed idea, and the web grew.

Softly he said, "I was trained to follow up on those long shots, Chief. Routine. Habit. Whatever. I followed up and talked to the managers of our own motels here, asked them to give me a call if either Olson or Orsini got a reservation or checked in. Olson called in a reservation for tomorrow, the Fourth of July, Chief."

Will jerked forward so fast he nearly sent his chair flying out from under him. "God damn! Are you shitting me?"

"Nope. Amory over at Surf's Up Motel gave me a call. He made a reservation, due in tomorrow."

"Hot damn! We'll nab him the second he checks in! We've got the son of a bitch!"

Tony held up his hand. "Not so fast, Chief. No reason for you to know it, but I took a few years of law way back, and in twenty years working in the New York homicide department, I learned a lot more about the law. You have to have probable cause. And we don't. For all we know right now, that guy might really be Daniel Olson, a traveling salesman or something. It's a common enough name. We have to give him a little rope."

"What do you mean?" Will heaved himself to his feet and picked up his coffee mug. "Let the coffee get cold. I'll put on a new pot. Won't take a minute."

He picked up Tony's mug and went into the attached bathroom to dump it all out. Then, putting on a fresh pot of coffee, he said, "So what's the game plan?"

"We'll let him check in. Amory will give me a heads-up on his license plate and make of car, and I'll pass the word to you. The car will be a rental, most likely, something nondescript that won't draw a second glance. And that car will need watching, Chief. The minute it moves, I'll need to know. I'm going to stake out the house and wait for him. If he shows, then we nab him, with probable cause. I'll give him time to lead me to that piece of evidence, and you'll be backup. We'll have him."

"What about Marnie, Van, and the kid?"

"They're all going to Newport to watch fireworks. Oliver knows that. He thinks the house will be empty, his chance to do what he has to do."

Will resumed his chair, almost quivering with excitement. "You want me to tail him, follow him up to the house?"

"It's going to be tricky, Chief. He knows you and you can't let him get even a glimpse. Traffic's really heavy all along that coast highway, and you have to keep him in sight. It's going to get tricky."

"What about your car? He'll see it up there."

"I'll park up at the turnaround, out of sight, and walk back. It might be a good idea, when he moves, for you to get on the other side of the highway, park on one of the side streets where you can see anyone heading up Ridge Road, and wait. When he passes, give him plenty of time. He has to break in, and it will take him a little time, and I'll be inside. Then you move in and he's dead in the water. How does that sound?"

"Sounds good, Tony. Sounds real good. Breaking and entering is probable cause enough to hold him, ask him some questions before we bring in the sheriff or anyone else."

Will got up again to pour fresh coffee, and they discussed the plan for a while longer. "I'll have to bring in Morgan, you know, to spell me if I need a break, want a bite to eat or something. If Oliver checks in late in the afternoon, he isn't likely to move until seven-thirty or so. That's about when they'll head out for Newport." Morgan Walsh was his regular summer deputy, an easygoing, middle-aged man who liked to ticket out-of-staters for parking infractions.

Before he left, Tony said soberly, "Chief, it's absolutely vital that not a word of this is leaked. Not to anyone. If he gets alarmed or smells a trap, he'll simply take off and we'll be where we started, nowheresville."

"Tony, believe me, I understand. I really do understand an operation like this," Will said earnestly. He made a zipper motion across his mouth. "I promise, no one, not even my wife, will hear a word."

They shook hands on it. "I'll buzz you the minute I hear he's checked in. Good luck, Chief. To both of us."

Walking back to his apartment, Tony decided it had gone as well as he might have expected, and maybe Will Comley really would maintain silence. He felt sorry for him, watching a car most of the night, spelled now and then by Morgan Walsh, but on the job. He didn't believe for a second that Dale Oliver would drive to Marnie's house. He would take the trail up and back, and his car would not leave the parking lot until the following day when he would head back to Portland, mission accomplished. But Chief Will Comley was a necessary part of the plan, Tony also knew, even if he could not have said precisely what the entire plan was.

IT WAS A long afternoon. Tony shopped at the local market, bought ham and cheese, tomatoes and lettuce, makings of a sandwich for the next day. Little held his attention that day, television, surfing the Web. He was getting more and more irritable about his apartment and wanted his books, which were still in storage in New York, wanted more space to move in, and something to look at besides damn fir trees when he sat outside.

The following day was more of the same, waiting for a call from the motel manager, willing Dale Oliver to come, to check in.

The call came at four in the afternoon.

"He just checked in, Tony," Amory said in the same low, conspiratorial tone as before. "He's in Room 8, driving a black Ford Escort, a rental, and I have the license number." He read it off and Tony made a note, thanked him, and called Will Comley.

"I'm on it, Tony," Will said. "We'll watch that car like a cat watching the canary. First move, you'll hear about it."

Tony made his sandwich, filled a thermos with hot water, readying it for coffee a little later. Then, in his bedroom, he unlocked his suitcase and took out his old shoulder holster and his Glock, which had never been fired in anger. He placed them on his bed, along with his lightest-weight Windbreaker. It was a warm day, too warm for any jacket, but he would need it.

He sat on his balcony, his mind almost a perfect blank, with no images, no thoughts, nothing, like being in a trance state where nothing was happening.

His telephone jarred him out of it, and he was afraid he had miscalculated, that Dale Oliver was playing by a different set of rules. It was Van on the phone.

"Tony," she said, "I'm going mad. Isn't there anything we can do? What are you up to? Harriet McAdams told Marnie that you actually spent a whole day in the shop! For God's sake what are you up to?"

"Take it easy, Van. Go watch the fireworks, relax, have a little fun. I'll come around tomorrow."

"Why don't you come with us? You need a little time off, too."

"Not this time, Van. I'll see you tomorrow."

"Oh, this is driving me crazy. Okay, tomorrow. But, Tony, we have to do something to force his hand. None of us can take this much longer."

"I know. Maybe it will come to a head soon."

Van stood holding her phone, puzzled by something she could not identify. Not anything Tony had said, something else. She had a memory jolt of a lecture, one of a series on patient/physician relations, a required course.

"You have to listen to your patients," Dr. Chadworth had said. "Really listen. If they're talking about symptoms, most often they'll tell you what's wrong, where you should focus. But more than that. Try to get to know your patients, listen to the way they talk, the timbre of their voices, learn to tell the difference when they're hopeful or fearful, impatient or willing to accept the treatment you decide is necessary. Learn to tell if they're down or neutral. Depression may be denied through the words they use and broadcast by the way the words are expressed. A transcript would reveal only the optimism, good cheer, but a good listener might hear an altogether different story. Body language might suggest despondency—"

"Mom, can we go now?" Josh asked coming into the room. "Petey has sparklers, too!"

"It's too early. Come on, you have to put on a clean shirt and wash your face," Van said, and pocketed her cell phone.

After Van's call, Tony filled his thermos with fresh coffee, strapped on his holster, and slid the Glock into place. It was still too warm for the Windbreaker, but he put it on. It was six-fifteen, time to get into position.

Traffic on Highway 101 was too heavy to try to cross. He turned right, heading south, down to the stop sign, made a left turn, and got into the traffic heading north to the first side street that led to Ridge Road. He drove past Marnie's front house without a glance toward it, up to the turnaround, and to the far side of the road, where he parked under the trees.

He ate his sandwich, not because he wanted it, but because he had learned on stakeouts that it helped pass the time to eat something, have coffee at hand.

A few minutes after seven he left his car, stayed back in the trees, and went down the road far enough to keep an eye on Marnie's house and driveway, and he waited for them to leave, to go watch fireworks.

From here he could see enough of the path to the Silver Creek trail that if anyone appeared on it—not anyone, he corrected—if Dale Oliver appeared, he would see him. He did not expect him yet, though. He waited.

In the house Van said to Marnie, "We should be on our way. It's going to take a few minutes to collect Petey and get his car seat in your car, get him settled in." Petey was Josh's best friend, and they had invited him to go with them. Before long neither boy would need a booster seat, Van thought with relief and some regret. They were both growing fast. They would be ready for the regular seat belts, make life a little easier.

"I'm ready," Marnie said. "I'll put the cooler in the trunk, and we're off."

She had made a chicken-and-rice casserole, her contribution to the potluck. Van got Josh strapped in and took her place behind the wheel, and they left. It was twenty minutes after seven.

Tony watched the car back out of the driveway, waited until it was out of sight, then went down to the house. He walked around both houses with no need to go inside, although he could have done so. He knew where they kept a spare key in the planter by the door. He headed down the path to the trail that followed Silver Creek to town and beyond.

Where the path joined the trail, he removed his Glock from the holster and slipped it into his Windbreaker pocket. Then he sat down to wait, to let his ears adjust to the noise of the rushing water, to distinguish that sound from all others. There were distant pops as fireworks were set off. No guns were being shot yet, but they would be, he knew. No aerial display yet, the sky was still too bright. The firecrackers echoed up the gorge cut by Silver Creek. He identified the various sounds, and he waited for Dale Oliver.

21

THERE WAS THE music of Silver Creek, fireworks popping, with an occasional sharp crack of a rifle now, a slight breeze stirring fir needles. And something else. Tony raised his head higher, listening, and slowly got to his feet, put his hand in his pocket to grasp the Glock. A rock dislodged, clattering a little. The sound of feet on the trail, muffled, not loud, but unmistakable. Someone was coming. He waited until the hiker got closer, then stepped out from the path, onto the trail itself.

Twenty-five feet away Dale Oliver stopped moving and stared at him. He was dressed in old jeans, a T-shirt, hiking boots. His hair was shades darker than his usual platinum blond, and he had a stubble of a dark-blond beard. He carried a canvas sack, the kind people sometimes took to the supermarket when shopping.

"Freeze, Oliver," Tony said, taking the Glock from his pocket, raising it. "Don't move a muscle."

"Who the fuck are you? You've got the wrong guy. My name's Olson. You crazy or something?" His gaze was fixed on the gun.

"Oliver, you've got one chance to come out of this alive." Tony's voice was strange to his ears, hard, icy, remote. "You do exactly what I say, and nothing more, and no talk. Put the sack down. Slowly. Just put it down."

Oliver made a quick motion as if to grab for something in the sack he carried and Tony said, "Listen, Oliver. Did you hear that click? That's the sound of a safety being released. Put the sack down. Now!" He spread his feet slightly and raised his other hand to the gun, assuming the posture made familiar to audiences by television and movies. There was no need for him to take the stance. He could fire the weapon with one hand. His big hands, the strength in his upper body, his arm, had proved that many times over on the firing range.

Dale looked at the gun, then at Tony's face, back at the gun, and knew he was staring at death. The guy was crazy. He wanted to kill someone. He was looking for an excuse, any excuse. Dale had seen that look twice, and both times someone had died.

VAN AND MARGARET Agee, Petey's mother, finished securing him in his car seat and Margaret leaned in to say, "Petey, you do exactly what Van and Ms. Markov tell you. Behave yourself."

Petey nodded and turned to Josh. "I have some sparklers!"

"He'll be fine," Van said. She handed Margaret a small

day pack that held Josh's pajamas, toothbrush, and clothes for the next day. He was going to spend the night at Petey's house.

Van got behind the wheel again and started back to Ridge Road, to avoid the slow traffic in town. The boys' voices were high-pitched with excitement as they chattered, and she was again thinking of voices, what they revealed. There was no need to hear any of the words the boys were using, the excitement in the tones was undeniable.

Something about Tony's voice, she thought then. Something not right. She had heard him when he was tired, and when he was hurting, amused, in easy conversation. What she had heard that day was something else.

"Look, there go Colleen and Stu," Marnie said as another car pulled onto Ridge Road a block or two ahead of them. Colleen and Stu were regulars at the potluck.

Something about his voice, Van thought again. Then she had it. Working in geriatrics, she had heard that tone, a tone of resignation, acceptance that belied any hopeful words the terminal patient used.

Resignation! she thought. Why? What was wrong? Something was. Something was very wrong. The car ahead had reached the highway, had stopped, waiting for a chance to merge into traffic, then it was gone.

She drove the last half block, stopped, and said, "Marnie, would you mind terribly if I don't go? I have a little headache, and I'd really rather not."

"Oh, dear. We'll just go back home," Marnie said. Josh and Petey both cried out.

"No, no," Van said hurriedly. "They'd be too disappointed. Can you manage them both? I'd really rather just go back home and have a quiet evening."

She undid her seat belt, and Marnie did the same. "I

think I can manage them," Marnie said drily. "Why don't I drive you back to the house?"

"No, I could use the walk and some air. Thanks, Marnie. I'm sorry to be a wet blanket like this." She and Marnie both got out of the car to change places, and soon Marnie was waiting for an opening in the traffic and Van was walking back up Ridge Road.

DALE'S FACE TURNED shades paler. He extended his hand slowly and set the sack on the trail. "Take two steps back," Tony said.

Dale stepped back and did not take his eyes off the gun. He kept his hands up. They were shaking. "Hey, man. I'm not fighting you. Just out for a hike up to the falls, have a bite to eat. You got the wrong guy."

"Shut up," Tony said. Looking at Dale, he saw that kid in New York, shaking and terrified, desperate for a way out. He blinked the image away. He should have disabled that kid. He should have let Dale make it to the house, break in, and then shot him with cause. If Dale hadn't drawn his own weapon yet, Tony could have finished preparing the scene. He hadn't wanted to kill him in Marnie's house, in Van's house. His finger was tight on the trigger and he relaxed it a little. There would still be a chance. Dale would do something stupid.

In that strange, remote voice Tony hardly recognized as his own, he said, "I told you there's one chance you'll come out of this alive. Believe that. You're under arrest for the murder of Stefany Markov. You make a break for it and I'll kill you. We're going to town and you'll be put in a cell and wait for the sheriff there. And you're going down in the creek. At the bottom, near the beach, you'll walk out or I'll haul you out."

252

The trail had twists and turns, Tony knew. And he knew that if Dale saw a chance to take off running while out of sight even a moment, he would not be able to catch him. His hip was throbbing, he could not run down a steep trail.

"In the water? Man, that's crazy! I'm not getting in that water! There's waterfalls."

"They aren't high. You can step down them. If you slip and your head goes under, hold your breath. Now get in the creek."

Although Dale was shaking his head vigorously, his gaze remained fixed on the gun. "I won't run. I swear—"

"You're going down there. In the water or strapped on a stretcher. Move!"

They were at one of the pools of quiet water, no higher than knee-deep. The water was clear, the rocky creek bed visible.

Dale looked at the water, then at the gun pointed un-waveringly at his chest. Gingerly he took a step into the pool.

"Out to the middle," Tony said. The pool was about twenty feet across here.

Moving cautiously, watching the rocky bottom, Dale took a few steps, hesitated, and moved again when Tony said, "I'll tell you when to head down."

After he took a few more steps, Tony said, "Now. Start downstream." He continued down the trail to the canvas sack and picked it up. It was quite heavy.

Muttering obscenities and protests, Oliver took cautious steps in the water toward the rapids a few feet ahead. He'd beat this, he thought grimly. He hadn't done anything and he knew enough to keep his mouth shut until a lawyer showed up. Out to take a hike, shoot off some rounds. It was the Fourth of July, for Christ's sake. No crime there.

And this nutcase threatened to kill him. He was the one that should be hauled off to jail.

Evidently the rocks were slippery. Dale began to slip now and again, catch himself, and carefully move ahead once more. He approached the rapids slowly, feeling his way on the rocks. The water was shallower, but it swirled around rocks, some sticking up out of the water, others submerged, covered with foaming water. It was swift, the creek narrower, and beyond the rapids was a shallow waterfall with a drop of no more than two feet.

Dale darted quick glances at the far side, as if weighing his chances. "Try it and I'll kill you before you make it," Tony said. "Keep moving." He cursed himself for warning him. He wished he hadn't, had let him clamber toward the other side and then shot. He rejected that instantly. Christ! Not in the back.

Dale came to the end of the rapids, to the drop, and looked over it to the pool below. Carefully he leaned over to hold on to a rock jutting out of the water, and he eased one leg over the edge, groped with his foot for a firm rock. His foot slipped and he cried out hoarsely, a short-lived, strangled cry as he went down with water pouring over his back.

"Jesus Christ!" he cried, regaining his feet, clutching a rock. "This is murder! I'm freezing!"

"Keep moving." Tony's voice was harsher, strained. Pain radiated from his hip, down his leg, into his back and groin. It occurred to him that he could fall, give Dale an opportunity to rush him, grab the Glock . . . He gritted his teeth and snapped, "Move!"

NEVER BEFORE HAD the eight blocks to the house seemed so long. She had walked it countless times after the school bus

254

stopped on 101. She reached the house, where her car was the only one in the driveway. She had expected to see Tony's Acura there. At the door she lifted a juniper branch in the planter, felt under it, and found the house key still in place. She let herself in, was greeted by a joyous Tipper, and walked into the living room with the dog at her side. The door stop was in place at the sliding door.

So much for intuition, for reading more into voices than was there, she told herself in disgust, but just to be thorough, she looked into the other downstairs rooms, then went up to her own room and Josh's. Empty. The house was empty. She walked through the studio, depressingly empty with a paint-stained floor and the long workbench, stained and bare.

Might as well do the rest, check out the front house, she told herself, and unlocked the door to the passage, stepped outside to look around.

Then she stopped. A forest fire up the road? Something glinted in the lowering sunlight. Not a fire, she realized, leaning forward against the rail, squinting. Sun on metal. Sun on chrome! Tony's car was up there, parked up there! She spun around and ran back inside the house, to her room, where she pulled on an old denim jacket that had deep pockets. She got her .22 from the drawer, put it in a pocket, and ran downstairs, through the house, out the sliding back door and to the path down to the trail by the creek.

DALE HAD FALLEN again, not flat out, but to his knees, and he was soaked front and back, and shaking hard. They had gone far past where Tony had joined Van and Josh. The trail had become much steeper.

"Please," Dale begged, sobbing, his voice shaking with cold, "for God's sake, stop this! I'm freezing. My feet are numb. I can't even feel them. I swear I won't run. I can't run. For God's sake have a little mercy!"

"Keep moving," Tony said. "Not much farther now. How much mercy did you have for Stef? Move!"

It really was not much farther, Tony knew, and was grateful for that. The sound of fireworks was louder, there were more rifle shots, and an occasional sky display that was still too pale. A faint sound of music was background for the other sounds.

Tony watched Dale struggling in the icy water, and he felt nothing but the same hatred for him that he had felt before. He had not shot that boy in New York because he had not wanted to hurt him. He had gotten him killed instead. And he had not shot and killed Dale Oliver, which he had come to do, because he had found that he was incapable of an unprovoked killing, murder. He didn't know the moment, when it came and went, that he might have shot him, but that moment had passed. Instead, he had done something stupid that would let Dale get away with murdering Stef. He was not even sure he could make it all the way down to the beach, to where he could call Will to come get Dale.

They were both moving more slowly. Tony had not realized that going downhill would be almost as bad as going up, but his hip felt afire, throbbing, with jabs of sharp pain radiating out to his groin, his back, down his leg. Every step was painful, forced. He was keeping close to the edge of the trail near the woods. Whenever he found something to hold on to, a tree, a bush, anything, he grasped it to steady himself, and even to lean against it for a second or two, then he forced another step. He was willing himself not to stumble and fall, to keep a grip on the Glock, to keep watching as Dale drew near the end of another pool, approached more rapids.

Dale moved sluggishly, sobbing, with his head lowered, trying to see into the swirling, hissing water. Tony was a dozen feet behind him on the trail. Then Dale stopped his forward motion, began jerking at his leg spasmodically. He reached down with both hands and pulled at his leg, reached into the water as if trying to feel his foot, or the rocks. He began to thrash about, jerking, pulling. Tony drew closer.

"Don't shoot!" Oliver screamed. "For God's sake, don't shoot! My foot's stuck! I can't move!" The words were hardly out of his mouth when his other foot slipped. He lost his balance and pitched forward and was unable to stop himself. His head hit a jutting rock hard, and for a moment it stopped as if in rest, then it slid sideways, down between rocks where water swirled and foamed before flashing forward over the edge of the waterfall. He didn't move. One arm, flung out before him, slid off a rock, over the edge of the waterfall, where the water lifted and released it again and again, making it look as if he were waving to whatever lived in the creek. Water swirled about his submerged head, the foam turned red, then pink, flowed onward.

Tony took a step toward the creek, another, stopped. He stood without moving for several minutes, and he watched Dale Oliver die. Finally he holstered his gun and stepped back into the middle of the trail again.

He looked inside the sack he still carried. A sweatshirt was wrapped around something. He shook the sweatshirt enough to uncover what was wrapped, a nine-millimeter semiautomatic pistol. He put the sack down, looked at the trail back to the house, and started up.

VAN TROTTED DOWN the path to the juncture with the trail where she paused briefly, listening. Cautiously she stepped out onto the trail. No one was in sight. No longer running, but moving fast, keeping her hand on the .22 in her pocket, she started down the trail, and at the first real turn where the continuation of the trail was not visible, she again paused, listening. She edged around the turn, then hurried to the next one. There he was. Tony was hunched over, holding a sapling at the side of the trail, not moving. Agonizingly slowly, he finally began to move his leg forward, without lifting his head.

She ran the rest of the way. At his side she took his arm and put it around her shoulders and held his hand firmly. She put her other arm around his waist and braced herself.

"Lean on me, Tony. Let go a little, lean on me."

He finally looked up. His face was almost gray, his lips almost colorless.

She nodded. "Lean on me. I can help."

His weight shifted, and she braced herself anew. "Good. Take a deep breath." When he did, she said, "Another, and we'll start."

Haltingly, with many stops for him to take deep breaths, for her to brace herself again, they made their way up the trail, to the path, and finally to the house.

Inside, she eased him to the couch. They were both sweating heavily. He was groping in his pocket, and she moved his hand aside and felt in the pocket. She pulled out a small pillbox, opened it, and recognized the two tablets inside as codeine.

"I'll get some water," she said.

She brought the water and held out both tablets. "It isn't too much for now," she said when he shook his head slightly.

He took the codeine and she helped him get his jacket off. He fumbled with his holster, and she helped remove that, then took off her own jacket.

"I could use a drink," he said in a faint voice.

"Later. I'll put on coffee." Half an hour, she thought, it would take half an hour for any relief. While the coffee was dripping, she hurried to the linen closet and brought out two pillows. Back at the couch, she told him to lie down and eased his legs up, took off his shoes. She slipped one pillow under his knees, raised his head, and placed the other one under his head and shoulders.

The pillow under his knees helped, Tony thought. Being off his feet, stretched out, helped. He drew in another deep breath. "Van, thanks." His voice was weak. "Not enough. Nothing would be enough. But thanks. I wasn't going to make it."

She nodded. "Don't try to talk now. Rest." She knew he would have fallen, crawled, dragged himself, then exhaustion, pain, would have made even that impossible. She knew.

"He's dead," Tony said in that low, faint voice. "It's over."

"Shh. You'll feel better in a few minutes. It can wait."

"I didn't shoot him. But he's dead." Tony closed his eyes.

Van poured coffee for them both and sat on the floor by him sipping hers, waiting for him to want his.

An hour later, propped up with two pillows behind him, sipping coffee, he told her about it, leaving out nothing. "How did you know? Why did you come?"

"You froze me out, Tony. You said you wouldn't do it

259

again, but you did. You sounded strange when I talked to you, you sounded resigned. I got suspicious and came home. To cover your back? Be backup? Something like that."

"You have a handgun in that pocket, don't you?" he said, motioning toward her jacket, which she had tossed over a chair. "What in God's name were you thinking?"

She had been thinking that this might be her chance to shoot Dale Oliver, to kill him. She said, "To cover your back if you needed help. Why didn't you tell me what you were up to?"

"I went down that trail to kill him. Shoot him dead. I didn't want you to see me kill anyone."

"But you didn't shoot."

"No."

Would she have shot him? She shook her head. She would never know. She hadn't been put to the test. Tony had.

She put her cup on the coffee table and looked directly at him. "That was a second thought, to help you. I was going to shoot him on sight, Tony. I saw that autopsy, and I know what it means. I was going to kill the man who did that to my mother. That's been my plan for a long time, to shoot him on sight."

Tony groaned. "Put the damn gun away. I want a drink now."

She shook her head. "No alcohol, not with that codeine in your system. Do you have any more of it in your apartment?" He would need it, she knew. In three or four hours, he would be hurting badly. It was going to be a long night for both of them.

"My suitcase." He winced as he reached into his pocket to bring out his keys.

"I'll put the gun away and then get that codeine," she

said. "I won't be long. Lie down now, try to relax until I get back."

They had not turned on a light, and it was getting dark as he lay on the couch and watched starbursts in the sky and even lapsed into a drug-induced stupor, only to wake with a jerk, not knowing where he was or why the sky was lighting up like that.

When Van heard Marnie's car in the driveway, she went to the door to meet her. They held a whispered conversation there, and afterward Marnie went to the couch. Tony opened his eyes at her approach. She leaned over and kissed his forehead. "Bless you, Tony. Bless you. We want you to move to my bed, where you will be more comfortable. I can use Josh's bed for the night."

He shook his head. "This is good. Fine. Better than moving, anyway."

The night passed. Tony dozed a little off and on or slipped into the stuporous state that wasn't really sleep, and Van gave him another codeine at intervals. They didn't talk.

22

TONY WOKE WITH a start, again forgetting where he was, why he was wherever he was. He had heard a siren. He was sure he had heard a siren. Slowly his head cleared. He really was awake, not in a drugged, crazy dream, he decided. In an easy chair near the couch, Van was sleeping. Her hair had come out from the ribbon and looked like a black river flowing over her shoulder. He wanted to touch it, to sink his hands in that black river. He watched her sleep, then slowly eased himself up and cautiously moved his legs off the couch. He stifled a groan. Van stirred but did not wake up. Moving with deliberate one-by-one decisions, he finally stood, keeping his weight off the bad hip, holding on to the arm of the couch.

Van came awake in time to see him holding on to a chair at the dining table. She started to go to him, to help, then made no further movement. He was making it. When he went into the small lavatory off the kitchen, she stood with every muscle in her body protesting. Her legs and back ached. Coffee, she thought. And another codeine for him. She went to the kitchen and put on coffee. It was fifteen minutes after eight. The last time she had looked it had been seven o'clock. She was grateful that they both had slept a little, after all.

He came out and again she watched as he made his way back to the couch alone, limping badly, holding any support within reach, but doing it.

"Do you need another codeine?"

"No. No more. I have mush between my ears."

"We'll try something else. Be right back." She forced herself to move more briskly than she wanted and went up the stairs to the bathroom on the second floor. The medicine cabinet held ibuprofen and Tylenol. She swallowed a Tylenol and slipped both containers into her pocket. She dashed cold water into her face, ran a brush through her hair and tied it back, and went down again.

"One Tylenol, two ibuprofen," she said, shaking out the tablets. "Not as powerful as an opiate, but it will take the edge off and won't mess up your head."

"I have to call Will," he said, after swallowing the tablets.

"After coffee." She went to pour the coffee. He accepted it with both hands, and she sat opposite him again. They were quiet as they sipped the coffee. She waited until his was almost gone, then asked, "What are you going to tell Will?"

He put his cup down and rubbed his eyes. He hadn't thought that far ahead and felt incapable of thinking ahead at all.

"Tony, I stayed home, skipped the fireworks to keep you

company, to let you rest a little. To take turns watching and resting. He never showed. He didn't come here."

"And I came home and just went to bed," Marnie said indignantly, entering the room as Van spoke. "Neither of you even hinted that you were watching for him." It was not true. She had sat with Van for hours, keeping watch on Tony's drugged sleep.

"Tony?" Van said. "Isn't that right? We waited and he never showed up."

He rubbed his eyes again and knew that was the way. She was doing his thinking for him. He nodded.

Van took his cup to refill, and slowly he began to feel as if he was coming out of a strange state of mind, not asleep, yet not awake. "I'll call him now," he said.

"Give it a few more minutes," Van said, handing him the cup.

"I'm going to start breakfast," Marnie said in the kitchen.

There were more sirens in the distance, and no one moved until the sound cut off abruptly. It had stopped in the village below.

"Sausage and scrambled eggs," Marnie said, "coming up. Unless you both are starving and don't want to wait, I'll make some biscuits."

Van said biscuits would be great, although she doubted that much of anything would be eaten that morning.

As long as he sat still, it wasn't too bad, Tony decided, and the coffee was helping clear the fuzz in his head. Tell Will no one had come, wait to see what was going on below. Simple enough even for a mush brain.

When he finally made the call, Will was so excited his voice was high-pitched and tremulous. "You still up at the house, partner? Stay there. Stay put and wait for me. All hell's broken out down here! I'll be up as soon as I can get away. You hear me, just wait."

"They found the body," Tony said after he disconnected.

WHEN THEY SAT down for breakfast, Tony chose the chair facing away from the bright windows. He had seen his face in the mirror over the sink in the lavatory and didn't want Will to see the ravaged look and the pallor.

The biscuits were steaming, sausage still sizzling, and Marnie served him and Van as if she fully expected them both to have appetites. They were still at the table, as was most of the breakfast food, when they heard a car in the driveway. Van got up to admit Will Comley.

"Tony, partner," he exclaimed, rushing past her, entering the dining area, "you were right on the mark! Right on the money! I know he didn't show up here. Forget that. Let me tell you!"

He pulled out a chair and sat opposite Tony, where Marnie had already set a place for him. She poured his coffee and he picked up a sausage link and took a bite, then said, "See, this morning early a bunch of kids decided to take a hike up to the waterfall. And they found a body in the creek. They hightailed it back down, called 911, and I got the call on the car radio just as the sheriff and the rescue team were coming in. I got Morgan to spell me and followed the sheriff. That body was him, Tony! It was Oliver! They hauled him out, had to cut his boot laces to do it. Leather swollen, like that. His boot was wedged in so tight they took a crowbar to move a rock and get it out of there. They found his ID and said it was what's his name, Olson, and I set them straight. It was Oliver, all right." Will was chewing the sausage, talking fast, all at once. His eyes were bright with excitement and his hands shook as he raced on.

"What we didn't think of, you and me, partner, was that he would come up here on foot, on that trail. City dude with his fancy clothes, I never gave it a thought that he might hike in. And no reason for you to even know about that trail. He had a sack, Tony. With a nine-millimeter semiautomatic in it!" His voice became hushed with the words, and he cast a significant look at Tony. To Marnie he added, "It's not what you use to pot crows. Gun like that's meant to kill people. That's what it's for, and that's what they figure he meant to do."

Marnie stood and went to the sink to put on another pot of coffee, and Will stopped talking for a moment, then said awkwardly, "God damn, Marnie, this is tough on you. But that's what he intended and you've got to know about it. You'll be hearing about it and might as well hear it straight up front. We figure he meant to break and enter up here, wait for you, Van, and the boy, and take you all out. He had latex gloves, probably meant to pick up a few things, some jewelry, silverware, whatever, and make it look like you walked in on a burglary."

"But he ended up in the creek?" Van said. "Have they figured that out? Why, how?"

"We think he waited too long to start up. It could of been getting dark already. He had a flashlight, but it was still in the sack. You know how ground fog forms sometimes, mist from the water? What did he know about things like that? Hurrying up, make a mistake, found himself in the water all at once, and he was stuck. He must have tossed his sack back to the trail, you know, to keep the gun dry, and then tried to get loose, and he slipped. Hit his head so hard it's really bashed in."

Marnie, still at the sink with her back turned, bowed her own head. Again Will seemed aware that his words were having an effect. "Marnie, I think your guardian angel was watching out for you. Or fate or karma. Maybe God Almighty stepped in and said, 'Enough.'" Will helped himself to more coffee and took another sausage. "Tony, that was damn fine detective work you put in. How'd you finger him for Stef's killing?"

In a distant voice Tony told him what he had told Van earlier. Will nodded several times as Tony repeated his reasons.

"And while everyone else was jumping off the deep end, you applied some brainpower and came up with the real goods. Mighty fine detective work. Gotta hand it to you, partner. Mighty fine work."

"Will," Van said then, "last night was really bad for Tony's hip. You know he has a problem with it, don't you? It's been very hard on him, sitting up all night like that. Do you think he can be spared questioning by the sheriff or anyone else, let him have a day to rest?"

For the first time Will really looked at Tony. "Damn, partner, you look beat. Me, too, but I'll get in a nap a little later on. Yeah, I can hold them off a day or two. I can tell them what they need, and they already are talking about searching his Portland apartment. We think there's a sister somewhere they'll want to get in touch with, just to confirm the identification by family."

"I have her name and telephone number," Van said with a swift glance at Tony. "I'll get it for you."

"Good," Will said. "Seems enough on their plates for now. I'll tell them you need to rest today, partner. Retired on disability, bum hip. You need to get some rest, some shut-eye.

You go on home and climb into bed. That's the thing, a little sleep."

There was nothing Tony wanted more than a long, soaking bath and a bed.

"I'll go on to my apartment now," Tony said as soon as Will bounced out again.

"I'll bring your car down," Van said. He handed her the keys. Minutes later she was back. "Come on, I'll drive you."

Tony started to protest, but held it. He didn't want to drive.

In his apartment he hobbled to the bathroom and turned on the water in the tub. His robe was hanging on the back of the door.

Van listened outside the door. The water stopped running. She imagined that he was bending over the tub, easing his good leg over, making not a sound as he pulled his other leg in. She waited another minute or two, then walked into his living room and surveyed it with disapproval. There was no good place for him to sit. The couch was a futon, uncomfortable in both roles as bed and couch. One chair might be barely possible. The padding was thin but it was the best the apartment had to offer. The chairs on the balcony were webbed, not meant for comfortable relaxation.

She looked over his pots and pans in the kitchen, checked his refrigerator, then sat down to wait for him to come out, to get into bed. It was a long wait. He ran more water, and she knew he would stay in it until it cooled. She intended to do the same thing as soon as she got home.

Finally he emerged, very pink, in his robe and was surprised to see her still there. "Go home, Van. I don't need tucking in," he said a bit sharply.

"I will. I'll be back later."

He nodded and slowly made his way to the bedroom. She went to the bathroom and picked up the clothes he had left where they fell, then waited another ten minutes and looked in on him. He was asleep. She left and started the walk home. She thought it might have been the longest walk she had ever taken by the time she arrived at the rear house.

"Van, you have to get some rest," Marnie said at the door. "You're exhausted."

"I'll be in bed before Josh is tonight," Van said. "Now a bath and get out of these stinky clothes. Marnie, we have to talk. After a bath, we have to talk."

"I know. Do you need anything, any help?"

Van shook her head. "This might take a while," she said, and went up the stairs.

TONY WOKE UP and lay still, trying to make sense of the last twenty-four hours. It was three-thirty. He'd had a good nap, and he felt refreshed, with a functioning brain, but his actions, the events of the previous day, still didn't make sense. Finally he gave it up, and moving slowly, testing every motion, he got out of bed, stood by it holding on to the nightstand. Marginally better, he decided, and was grateful for the slight improvement. It would clear up in another day or two with more soaking baths, more rest. More codeine. It would clear up.

He dressed, decided slippers were good enough, and went into the bathroom to shave. Keeping his weight on his good leg, bracing himself with one hand, he shaved, and that was an improvement. He went to his kitchen, found coffee in the thermos, and looked for a place to sit and drink it. Everything he did seemed to take an eternity, but he was doing them, he thought in satisfaction.

Sitting in the one possible chair, he sipped his coffee and returned to the thoughts he'd had on awakening. Yesterday just didn't make sense. He had gone to the trail to kill Dale Oliver. He had made the decision, was resigned to it, accepted it, and instead he had given him a way out, a free pass. The one thing he had determined to accomplish and he had failed. And he didn't know why. He no longer knew if he could ever shoot someone, kill someone who needed killing. He had failed the ultimate test, had made it almost guaranteed that another killer would get away with murder. Not a faulty system, not a failed witness, a phony alibi, but his own weakness, his lack of courage, or whatever it would have taken, had made it all but inevitable that Dale Oliver would have gotten away with the murder of Stefany Markov if he had made it down to the village.

With every step Tony had taken on that winding trail, he thought bitterly, the odds had gone up that he would have stumbled, fallen, and the body the kids found would have been his, shot to death with his own gun. Will would have testified that Dale Oliver never left the motel.

Except for that one misstep, he thought bleakly, Dale Oliver would have gotten away with murder.

If he had followed the plan outlined to Will, they would have nabbed Dale for breaking and entering with a deadly weapon, and that would have brought a conviction. But they would not have been able to connect it to a murder already judged an accident, based on nothing more than suspicion and conjecture. He would have gotten away with it.

And bringing in Will had not made sense either. Tony had not needed Will to watch a car that Tony knew would not leave the parking lot. He rubbed his eyes. But Will had made the identification. He had prevented a wild-goose chase off to New Jersey, possibly a dead end when that didn't pan out. Without Will they might never have connected Daniel Olson to Dale Oliver, unless Tony had stepped forward, and that would have resulted in a demand from the sheriff to know who Tony's contact had been, who had alerted him to the fake IDs. Illegal entrance, illegal search, his testimony would have been tossed out, and with it his credibility and his theory about the murder of Stefany Markov. Will had been a necessary part and one that he had not thought of, had not considered. He simply had decided to go to Will's office and bring him in. He rubbed his eyes again.

Back up, he told himself. He had decided and then, accepting his decision, had spent the day working in the shop and had not thought of it again. Had not thought of anything. That's what seemed to have happened, his brain went dead while he worked with his hands. He shook his head. Brains don't go dead, he told himself. That other part, the part forever out of reach and unknowable, must have been active. He had read about meditation, Transcendental Meditation, trance states, altered-consciousness states, but he had never applied any of that to himself and those hours without conscious memory of any thought. His unconscious? He shook his head again.

Something had said no to murder, that was the fact, and he had not made that decision consciously. He had not given a thought to making Dale Oliver go into the creek, wade down, until he had ordered him to do so. What he had planned would have been murder. He knew that, had accepted that it was his conscious intention to commit murder. Something had said no, and he had acted on that, not his conscious decision, like a robot, an automaton.

And he had not thought of any possible outcome if that had worked out, if he had hauled him out of the water down on the beach. Another murderer getting away with it? Likely, he thought. Even a charge of breaking and entering would have been tossed. Dale Oliver had not broken and entered.

He had not thought about it in any recognizable way, but he had not committed murder.

He had finished his coffee but continued to hold the cup, not willing to bend over to put it on the floor. The secret was not to move if he didn't have to, keep as still as possible. He held the empty cup and considered what had happened to him when Dale Oliver got stuck in the creek.

His first impulse, a reflex, had been to go in, to get him moving again. He had started in, then stopped. Again, no conscious decision. He had just stopped and watched Dale Oliver die.

He couldn't have saved him, he knew now. He might have been able to raise his head, but he could not have freed him, he couldn't have done anything about what probably had been a fatal wound, he wouldn't have been able to keep his head above water long. But he had started to try and stopped. He would have fallen, too, in all likelihood and, wet and cold, dragged himself out of the water, only to die of hypothermia on the trail somewhere. He knew that. But he had not thought of it while he watched Dale Oliver die. He had not thought of anything. He had stood and watched a man die in the water and thought of nothing, just like insane people who did exactly what voices in their heads directed them to do. Except without the voices.

He was rationalizing his actions, making excuses, unheard voices, directions from God knew where, and he knew that was not what he was doing. He was telling himself something important even if he didn't know why it was important.

Later, he said under his breath, he would think through it all later, after his hip stopped hurting like hell, after he was fully himself again.

He looked quickly at the door, which was opening. Van entered, carrying two big grocery bags.

"Oh, I hoped you'd still be sleeping," she said. "How are you feeling?"

"Better. What's all that?" He indicated the bags.

"Various things. A snack for now, a big pot from home to cook pasta, a chicken to roast, things to go with it. I'm going to make us dinner. I hope you like garlic. Garlic chicken, with rosemary. Things like that."

He scowled at her. "I know you're a hell of a doctor, a one-woman rescue team, and you can cook. Too much."

"Oh, that's just the beginning," she said airily, going into the kitchen to put her bags down on the counter and start unloading them. He could still see her as she busied herself.

"I can sew and change a tire, change the oil in a car, make jam and jelly. Marnie grew up on a farm and was driving a tractor by the time she was twelve, and her mother saw to it that she had housewifely skills, 'survival skills,' Marnie called them. Marnie took me in hand and did the same thing." Van paused, then said fervently, "Thank God we don't have a cow. She would have made me learn to milk it."

Tony laughed. He couldn't tell what she was doing, putting things in the refrigerator, doing something with a plate, a covered basket. After a minute or two, with her chatting all the time, she came to the chair where he was sitting, looked around, and saw an end table by the couch. She put a lamp on the floor and brought the table to within his reach and took the cup he was still holding.

"Will's been all over town extolling your genius," she said, as she moved about. "He's telling people how you figured it all out, that you were waiting for Dale at the house and an act of God finished him off. He's saying you make Sherlock Holmes look like an amateur. I'm afraid you have a big fan. It could be hero worship. Town people will want to touch you, just to look at you. And Freddi called, a lot of people were calling and Marnie turned off the ringer, let the answering machine handle it. Freddi is in a frenzy. This changes everything, she said. A prominent businessman committing murder to control artwork, planning on more murders. The price of everything just went up exponentially. Marnie told her it isn't about money and never has been. Freddi will come out here in a couple of days."

She didn't add that Marnie had also said that *Feathers and Ferns* was not for sale. She intended to give it to Tony. She had seen the way he looked at it, and it was to be his. That was hers to tell, Van thought, and came back to the end table with a plate.

"Cheese, ham, apple slices, and in the basket blueberry muffins. They're still warm. Marnie sent them. You need a little food to hold you over until dinner. I put on coffee, or do you want juice for now? If you haven't taken any more medicine since this morning, wine for dinner."

He said he would wait for the coffee and picked up a piece of the rolled ham and found suddenly that he was hungry, ravenous. He buttered a muffin, and it was delicious. As were the cheese and the apples. Van nodded with approval as he ate.

She took coffee to him and kept her own at the counter, where she started to peel garlic. When he pushed the plate back, she removed it and returned with a glass of water and a pharmacy medicine container.

"I talked to Dr. Cranshaw," she said. "He prescribed prednisone. You have a serious inflammation in that hip, we both agree, and the prednisone will control it and quiet it down. He sent a message to pass on to you. Anyone who needs a hip replacement and goes mountain hiking is a damn fool. Message delivered." She shook out a tablet and held it out. After a second or two he took it and the water.

"Good," she said when he swallowed the tablet. "Tony, you could have done serious damage to that hip. Only an MRI will determine that, a current one to compare to the last one you had in New York. As it is, it will take at least a week for the inflammation to quiet down, and another week or two to let the healing process proceed. We want to move you to the front house for that period, where we can help you with meals. You won't be in any shape to do much for a while."

He shook his head. She returned to the kitchen and started on the garlic again. "The house is empty, already a problem, and it's on one level. You're going to be besieged with media people. I'm surprised they haven't found you already, and they will make life miserable until you decide to talk to them. You won't be able to go out on the balcony, and besides, you don't even have a decent place to sit in this apartment. Anyway, that's the first thing. In two or three weeks, we'll go to Portland, to OHSU, the university hospital where I was for the past four years. They have a top-notch orthopedics department. I know, I trained with them. They are extremely good. They'll have had time to get your medical records, the pictures of that hip, and be ready to assess it. They will want to schedule the replacement procedure, probably not until September. Too many people take off in August. After that, it will be a facility they have nearby for people from out of town. They treat people from all over the Northwest. A couple of weeks there, and then back to the front house. Marnie will be happy to help you for the next few months during your recovery. Physical therapy can be done in Newport, so that's not a problem—"

Tony's voice was as cold as ice when he cut into her long

speech. "God damn it, Van, do you really think I'm going to let you and Marnie take over my life, make my decisions, run me? You're wrong. I'm more than ready to move on. After this little flare-up gets better, I'm out of here. So just forget it."

"Yes, that's what I believe," she said calmly, standing by the sink, looking at him. "We have to take over for now, temporarily, in this one area that you are so crappy about handling. If you don't get that hip replaced, you're going to end up in a wheelchair, and then probably assisted living or a home of some kind. That's your future if you keep doing nothing. I have no intention of letting that happen if it's possible in any way to prevent it. That procedure has a ninety-five percent approval rating from those who undergo it. They are able to walk, to run, to bend over without pain. They can hike a mountain if they choose to. We think that as soon as you take care of the hip, the stress on your knee will end and it will be okay."

He set his glass down hard and looked ready to haul himself to his feet, walk, or hobble out. She said, still keeping her voice calm and decisive, "Tony, you've been punishing yourself for these past years. You let others define you and accepted their self-serving definition. It's time to stop. You didn't kill that boy in New York, and you aren't responsible for those who did. If they had stopped for just a few seconds, they would have known that you had the situation under control, that he was going to hand that gun to you, and it would have been over. They didn't take those few seconds."

She drew in a breath. "It's time to stop the self-flagellation, Tony. You gave that boy a chance to save himself, and the others prevented it from happening. You know that's true. You did the same thing with Dale Oliver. You gave him a chance to save himself. That's who you are, how you are, what you are, and you have to stop the guilt trip now. Give yourself a chance to live."

He sat rigidly with his eyes closed, his fists clenched, and she went on, "Tony, one day I put my hand on your arm. I didn't intend it as a come-on, a pass. You recoiled, and I thought you were rejecting me. But you weren't. You were rejecting life. Since then, I've seen you looking at me. Marnie has seen it. You weren't rejecting me, Tony. That day, when I touched you, every cell in my body lunged toward you. I didn't know it could happen like that. But it did. I love you, Tony. I've loved you since that one touch, maybe before that, but that day I knew it. I love you. I don't want a commitment, nothing like that. Just tell me that when I come home from my internship, you'll be here. That's all I'm asking."

He finally looked at her and shook his head. "I can't do that. I'm not the man for you. I'm an old, broken-down guy who will be fifty-one when you come home."

"And I'll be thirty-one. My grandfather was nearly twenty years older than Marnie. Her years with him, she told me, was the happiest time of her life. She has no regrets."

"And she's been a widow for twenty-five years," he said raggedly.

"He caught pneumonia and let it go untreated too long. It killed him. We have better treatments now, and you'll have a very good doctor keeping an eye on you. It isn't going to happen."

He shook his head. "Think of Josh and his needs. He needs a father your age, one who will play ball with him, do—"

"Knock it off. I want him to have a father he can talk about when he's grown with the kind of respect and love you have for your father. A father who will teach him how to use tools so he will have the satisfaction of making things he can be proud of. A father strong enough not to have to shoot anyone. One with an unshakable innate integrity and sense of justice." She made a brushing-aside gesture. "That's all beside the point. I love you, everything else is secondary."

She did not move as he gathered himself, pulled himself from the chair, keeping his weight on his good leg. He started to move, hunched over, reaching for any support he could grasp. When he got to the kitchen table and held on to it, she crossed the few feet that separated them. Leaning against the table, he took her by the shoulders, examined her face, and in an agonized voice said, "God help us both." He pulled her closer and kissed her, a deep, almost brutal kiss. Her fingers dug into his back, and she met his kiss with a response equally strong.